Deep into that Darkness

A Yorkshire Murder Mystery

Tom Raven Book 4

M S MORRIS

Published by Landmark Media, a division of Landmark Internet Ltd.

Tom Raven® is a registered trademark of Landmark Internet Ltd.

msmorrisbooks.com

CHAPTER 1

The cold was as sharp as a knife between her ribs. Ava Jennings thrust her thin bare arms into the sleeves of her jacket, stashed her phone away in her jeans and headed out into the chill night air.

She'd had to work the late shift at the amusement arcade because Jade was off sick again. Or so she claimed.

Ava had her suspicions.

Jade was probably just skiving at home, or out on the town with her latest boyfriend. She made no secret about how much she hated working at the arcade. She was always going on about finding somewhere better. She said she wanted to be a dancer at one of those clubs where women danced for men. She liked to flaunt her bare midriff in skimpy crop tops, and had recently had her navel pierced. Well, good luck to her. As far as Ava could tell there wasn't a whole lot of difference between dancing at one of those clubs and being a stripper. You wouldn't catch Ava in that kind of place, even if the girls there did earn a fortune – according to Jade – in tips.

She zipped up her jacket against the wind blowing in off the North Sea, whipping thin strands of golden hair across her face. Ten o'clock on a Wednesday night in late February and the Foreshore was practically a ghost town. No point hanging around for a bus at this hour. It would be quicker to walk and would keep her warm. She set off at a brisk pace – she always wore her comfy trainers to work – and thought about what she'd do at the weekend. She was working all day Thursday and Friday but on Saturday she would go shopping and spend some of her hard-earned cash. She'd seen a dress in a shop in town she was desperate to try on. It was short, but not so short she'd freeze her arse off. You had to be realistic. This was Scarborough, not Tenerife.

And Ava wasn't a slut like Jade.

She skirted around the base of St Nicholas Cliff, glancing up at the huge edifice of the Grand Hotel towering above, and made a snap decision to avoid the subway under Valley Road. The subterranean passages were fine during the day when there were plenty of people about, but at night on her own, Ava didn't like descending underground. You never knew who might be lurking down there. It was the kind of place where weirdos hung out. You got a fair share of those in the arcade late at night – loners mostly. Ava supposed she should feel sorry for them, but some of them gave her the creeps. There'd been one guy this evening looking like he didn't have anywhere better to go. A sad case who didn't even seem to have money for playing the machines, but had simply hung about, watching others lose their cash. He'd tried chatting up Ava, but the manager had asked him to leave. Ava had braced herself for trouble, but in the end he'd sloped off without causing any fuss. She'd looked for him as she left, half-expecting to see him waiting outside the arcade, but there'd been no sign of him.

She passed under the Spa Bridge with its massive stone arches, darted across the wide expanse of Valley Road and started the long slog up Ramshill Road. Scarborough was nothing if not hilly. She'd moved here for work six months ago from a little village out on the moors. For the first few weeks, her legs had ached all the time from trudging up and down the steep hills. She'd thought Scarborough would be the death of her. But now she was fitter than she'd ever been. She'd even dropped a dress size, which was good enough reason to go shopping at the weekend.

Away from the seafront it wasn't so windy and she began to get hot walking up the long hill. She unzipped her jacket. It was the very first thing she'd bought with her first pay packet. A silver sequinned bomber jacket. She loved it to bits. It made her look like she was from a girl band. Or at least that's what Jade had told her.

The Ramshill Road was a long trudge, especially going uphill. To her left, a rising grassy bank studded with huge sprawling trees separated her from the big houses further up the slope. Those trees seemed to lean in towards her, spreading a canopy across the sky. Nice and cool on a hot summer's day, but gloomy in the dead of winter. To her right, on the other side of the road, the ground fell away sharply to the area known as Valley Park. The park lay deep in darkness and you'd have to be mad to venture in there at night. It was the kind of place where druggies might hang out.

Not that Ava had ever seen any, but you never knew.

Her destination was a house at the top of Ramshill Road, near the corner where it turned sharply into Belmont Road and doubled back on itself towards the seafront. She rented a room in a shared house with five others. Her bedroom was small and cramped and the kitchen was always in a right state, but what else could she afford on her wages? Perhaps one day she'd find a better job and get a place of her own, but for now she was happy enough. A shared house was a good way to meet people when you were new to a town.

She was suddenly aware of footsteps behind her. Still some way off, but unmistakeable over the moan of the breeze. Just one person. A soft tread on the pavement, not the clatter of heels. Could have been a man or a woman. Unconsciously she found her fingers reaching for the brass key to her front door. Not so far to her house now. Just another hundred yards or so.

She didn't turn her head, but increased her pace even though she was already walking fast. It was just one of those things you did if you were a woman out on your own at night. Jade had offered to get her some pepper spray to carry – she knew someone who had "stacks of the stuff" – but Ava had read about it online and found that it was illegal in the UK so she'd declined Jade's offer. 'Suit yourself,' Jade had said in that smug tone of voice that implied Ava was a silly fool.

Maybe she was. Right now she wished she had something more than a front door key at her disposal as self-defence. The footsteps were drawing closer.

Stay calm, she told herself. *Don't imagine things. It's just some harmless person on their way home like me.*

Still, she increased her pace a fraction more, as fast as she could walk without breaking into a run. She was sweating, breathing hard, her heart pumping away like a dynamo. She'd be down another dress size at this rate. If only this damn hill would come to an end.

The footsteps kept getting closer.

Her blood was pounding in her head. Her throat felt dry. She glanced to each side, but there was no one else about, no lights on in the houses. If she screamed, would anyone hear her? The street ahead was empty, the park silent and deserted. She could yell her head off here and still no one would come to her aid. She thought of the man in the arcade, the one who hadn't wanted to leave. Had he been waiting for her after all? Hiding somewhere so he could follow her home? She'd been an idiot not to wait ten minutes for a bus.

Hard breathing, heavy and ragged like a truck labouring up a steep incline. A cough, deep and throaty. Definitely a man. He was right behind her.

Her fingers closed around the short shaft of the key, her knuckles white.

She spun around, ready to shout at the man, to tell him

to get lost, but the words died in her throat.

It wasn't the guy from the arcade after all. It was someone much worse.

Her eyes widened as she took in his features. The face staring back at her wasn't even human. It was the face of a skull. One of those horrible latex Halloween masks you could buy from the joke shop near the arcade for a few quid.

'Got you.' His arm shot out and grabbed her, pinching her hard.

She screamed but the sound came out thin and strangled, even less effective than she'd feared. The wind snatched it away before there was any hope of raising the alarm.

A firm hand came up and covered her mouth. 'Shut your mouth, bitch!' He pulled her to him, drawing her closer until all she could see was the latex mask, two cold eyes staring at her through small holes. 'No one can hear you now.' He tugged at her arm, pulling her across the road in the direction of the park.

Ava didn't need much imagination to guess what lay in store for her there, in the thick of the trees at the hands of this monster.

She drove the point of the metal key into the arm that held her and was rewarded with a yelp. Shaking herself free, she broke into a run. Up ahead a streetlight beckoned warmly. It wasn't far to the main road now. There would be people there, or cars driving past. She could run into the road and flag down a driver. Anything to get away from this madman.

But she wasn't quite fast enough.

A long hand grasped her shoulder, spinning her around and making her stumble. The man loomed over her, skull face grinning, words pouring out breathlessly through a slit in the mask. 'I'll make you pay for that.' He reached out to cover her mouth again.

But Ava wasn't done yet. She grabbed his hand and bit down hard. The iron taste of blood flooded her mouth.

Her attacker screeched and flailed, his finger wriggling like a worm caught on a hook. Ava bit harder, sinking her teeth almost to the bone.

When she released him, he jerked his hand back, and in that moment she twisted away. Her bare arms slipped out of the silky lining of her jacket and she ran like the wind, leaving her favourite item of clothing behind.

In a few seconds she reached the safety of the main road. 'Help!' she shouted, her voice stronger now. 'I've been attacked! Somebody help me!' But when she turned her head to look back, the man had already gone.

CHAPTER 2

A squawking gull descended, landing on the bonnet of Detective Constable Jess Barraclough's ancient Land Rover as she parked by the fairground at the top of the outer harbour. It folded its wings away and regarded her with a beady eye, apparently in the expectation that she would have food to share.

'Dream on,' Jess told it.

If she'd had anything as tasty as a warm croissant she'd have eaten it herself by now, not shared it with a greedy bird. She hadn't even had time for a cup of coffee before being called out that morning. It was barely seven o'clock and far too early to be fending off sea birds.

No doubt the gull would leave a fine mess on her vehicle for her to clean off later. But right now Jess had more pressing matters on her mind. She jumped out and gave the driver's door a good slam. The gull didn't flinch, just glared at her disdainfully. Jess stared back but the bird seemed determined not to break eye contact first. With a shrug, she turned away and hurried down the east pier, the wind gusting salt spray in her face.

Across the sea, the rising sun tinged the thin clouds a

luminous orange. The days were slowly getting longer after the dark winter months, and today promised to be fine and bright. Good walking weather. Jess hoped it would last into the weekend. She and Scott, her boyfriend, were planning to walk the Cleveland Way to Robin Hood's Bay, a distance of about twelve miles along the coast. They would grab a bite to eat in a local pub and then catch the bus back to Scarborough. But before that, there were two full days of work to get through.

A call had come through to the station reporting a body in the outer harbour. Uniformed officers had been dispatched immediately to secure the scene. As the most junior member of CID, Jess had been asked to attend, probably because it was too early for more senior detectives to get out of bed, but possibly also because the deceased was most likely just a drunk who had toppled over the edge after closing time. Such things were not unheard of in a seaside town with a wide choice of seafront pubs. A sad accident, but there was no reason to suspect anything more sinister.

Halfway along the pier, a crime scene investigator in white coveralls was standing with a pair of police divers wearing black head-to-toe wetsuits. They were pointing at something in the water. Jess peered over the side of the breakwater but whatever they were looking at was hidden behind the hull of a boat. The tide was out, the harbour bottom caked in black mud. A rotten egg odour of algae, seaweed and decaying timber filled Jess's nostrils.

As she approached the group, she recognised the diminutive figure of Scott's boss, Holly Chang, the head of Scarborough's CSI. Scott might be around too, but Jess couldn't see him anywhere.

'Morning,' she called.

Holly eyed her up and down. 'DC Barraclough! Are you here on your own? What's happened to that boss of yours? He only lives across the road. Is he enjoying a lie in while we do all the work?'

'Um...' Jess's senior officer, DCI Raven, did indeed

live just next to the harbour, and it would have been very easy for him to attend the scene. Jess also knew that Holly held a low opinion of Raven, and that the two of them tended to rub each other up the wrong way. But she was also well aware that Holly had a dry sense of humour and was probably just teasing her. 'I'm sure he'll be here right away if it looks like we're dealing with an actual crime.'

'I should hope so,' said Holly. 'It would be nice for him to get out of bed for a change, instead of making me work all hours. Anyway, the person I was really hoping to see was Scott.' She peered over Jess's shoulder, checking that Jess had come alone. 'That lazy arse should be here by now. Is he still lying in bed too?'

Jess blushed to the roots of her hair. 'I don't know where he is,' she blurted. 'Scott and I don't live together.' She and Scott had been a couple for three months now, but so far there had been no talk of them moving in together. Scott was shy and didn't like to be rushed. Jess was pleased with how their relationship was developing, and was in no hurry to rush things either. She enjoyed her independence. Of course Scott spent the occasional night round at her place. But that was none of Holly Chang's business.

'Well, never mind. We can't stand around gossiping all day,' said Holly, leaving Jess with the clear impression that she would have enjoyed nothing more than that. 'What is it they say? *Time and tide wait for no man*, and in this case it's the tide we're up against.' She cast her gaze over the harbour where the ebbing water had left dozens of small boats marooned in the mud, still tethered to their orange buoys. 'In a few hours this will be full of water again and vital evidence will be washed out to sea, so we need to get cracking.' She turned to the police divers. 'Ready to do some work? Or are you two just going to hang about listening to me all morning?'

'Aye,' said the taller of the pair, cracking a wry smile. 'We'll get down there and see what's what.' The two men lowered themselves over the edge and began to climb down a metal ladder that descended fifteen feet or more to the bottom.

Jess stood by the edge for her first glimpse of the body. It was impossible to make out much, whether it was a man or a woman, young or old. The body was lying face down in the mud, caught in the mooring lines of a small pleasure boat called *Bluebell*. Jess made a note of the name. Had the dead person come from the boat or fallen off the pier? That was an obvious line of inquiry.

'A fisherman called it in at first light,' said Holly. 'It's usually a fisherman or a dogwalker, isn't it? What would we do without those nosy buggers?'

The police divers reached the bottom of the ladder and stepped cautiously into the squelchy bed of the harbour. Their feet sank into the wet mud up to their knees, but the tall one gave an okay sign with one hand.

Jess found herself holding her breath as they waded out into the harbour, each step obviously an effort as the mud sucked at their legs, dragging them back and slowing their progress. When they reached the body they bent down and carefully untangled it from the ropes that had prevented it being washed out to sea. They turned it over and with gloved hands wiped the worst of the mud off the face.

The face they uncovered was that of a young man. Even smeared with streaks of dark mud, his features were visible. Tanned skin, a light sandy beard, long wavy hair blackened by the mud.

Jess recognised the face instantly. 'Scott!' She let out a cry of anguish and dropped to her knees on the edge of the pier. 'No!' she cried. The sky began to spin as she leaned out over the edge. Her ears rang loud with the roar of the sea, like waves crashing against her, deafening her to all other sounds. She felt herself begin to fall.

Then strong arms were pulling her back from the brink, hugging her tight, holding her safe. Holly's voice was loud and steady in her ear. 'I've got you, Jess. I've got you.'

CHAPTER 3

It was sad when your builder was the nearest thing you had to a friend. But it spoke volumes about DCI Tom Raven's social life – or lack of one – that the person he had come to rely on most for local gossip, snippets of wisdom and general companionship was Barry Hardcastle, the man who was slowly renovating Raven's house.

Their relationship had got off to a shaky start, with Barry dropping off a load of building materials but then failing to do any actual work for about a month. It had hit an all-time low during the extended period of destruction during which Barry and his young assistant, Reg, had all but demolished Raven's three-storey Georgian terrace, pulling out rotten timbers, hacking off old plaster, knocking down walls, chucking out the old fittings from the kitchen and bathroom. The overflowing skip outside the house had been a constant bone of contention with the neighbours.

That phase of the work had coincided with a time when Raven's life had been stripped bare, just like his house. Back in December there had been a faint glimmer of reconciliation with his estranged wife, Lisa, only to be snuffed out when Raven had realised that all trust between them was gone forever. Raven had imagined that going through a divorce would be a harrowing experience, but he had actually found it rather liberating. And now he was a free man. He could start to rebuild his life.

The way Barry was rebuilding his house at last.

During the course of the last two months, Raven's opinion of his builder had shifted imperceptibly from someone who caused nothing but chaos and destruction to one who was gradually working a miracle on the ramshackle house in Quay Street that Raven called home.

The old boiler had been sold for scrap and a new energy-efficient one installed. The radiators had been replaced so the rooms weren't freezing all the time. New floorboards had been laid on joists that didn't squeak. Walls had been replastered and repainted in neutral tones. A bathroom fit for the twenty-first century with – Raven loved this – a power shower had been installed. There was now just the matter of the kitchen to sort out.

And not before time. A diet of fish and chips from the local takeaway was doing nothing for Raven's waistline.

In recent weeks a never-ending procession of plumbers, electricians, carpenters and other subcontractors had appeared in Raven's house. Now he was just waiting for the kitchen installers to work their magic.

'So,' said Raven, doing his best to pin down Barry to a firm timeframe before he left for work. 'How much longer before the kitchen units arrive?'

Barry puffed out his cheeks, seeming disappointed by the question, as if a tacit and unspoken bond of trust had been broken between the two men. 'Don't you worry about that, Raven, mate,' he said, laying a reassuring hand on Raven's shoulder. 'It'll be delivered in time, I promise.'

'Yes,' said Raven. 'But when?'

Barry cocked his head to one side. 'You're asking me for a date?'

'A date,' agreed Raven. 'That would be good.'

Barry broke into a wide grin and gave his skinny

apprentice a nudge in the ribs. 'A date. It doesn't always work that way, does it Reg?'

The look on Reg's face was vague. But then it often was.

Barry spread his hands wide as he prepared to elaborate on the subject. 'It's all about shipping times, you see? These kitchen units, they're coming all the way from China.' He waited for Raven to confirm with a nod that he knew where China was. 'By rights they ought to be in a shipping container by now, making their way across the South China Sea. Or wherever.' Barry paused to punctuate his explanation with a quick puzzled frown. 'But there's a backlog in Shanghai at the moment, so that means–'

'–more delays,' concluded Raven miserably. He sighed. In a fit of enthusiasm, he'd selected sleek black units from a glossy catalogue, unexpectedly excited by the prospect of designing a kitchen to suit his own requirements. Back in London, in his previous life, all interior design decisions had been made by Lisa, whose tastes had never quite gelled with his own. Flushed with new-found freedom, Raven had made his own choices about how his house should look. But perhaps he had over-reached. Grown too ambitious. Like Icarus, set his heart on a goal that no mortal should ever have yearned for.

'I just want a kitchen,' he moaned, annoyed by the whine in his own voice.

'No need to worry,' continued Barry in his ever-optimistic voice, 'there's plenty for me and Reg to be getting on with in the meantime. We've still got the painting to do, not to mention the rewiring to finish. You'll be wanting plenty of sockets in your new kitchen for all your fancy appliances.'

Raven nodded, although the only appliance he really craved was a state-of-the-art coffee machine. 'We couldn't just cancel these units and order some from a local firm, could we?'

Barry shook his head sadly. 'They're custom built, mate. Already paid for and on their way. No choice now but to be a little bit patient. Isn't that right, Reg?'

Raven looked to Reg, who nodded sagely.

It seemed that Raven had no choice in the matter. Already he could sense that by expressing his impatience he had dropped a notch lower in Barry's estimation. There was no point testing their *friendship* further.

'All right,' he agreed, 'but I'll definitely need the kitchen finished in time for Easter so that my daughter can come and visit.' He eyeballed Barry firmly, making it clear that this was a red line. He'd been disappointed that Hannah hadn't been able to come at Christmas because the house had been in such a state of disrepair. They'd had to make do with a Skype call instead. He was determined to have the place ready so that Hannah could come and stay with him during the university holidays. She was studying law at Exeter and if she didn't come at Easter it would be summer before she would be free again. By then Raven wouldn't have seen her for a year. He wanted them to have a better relationship than that.

'No probs,' said Barry, giving Raven a hearty slap on the arm. 'Easter's weeks away. Don't you worry, we'll be out of your hair long before then!'

Raven smiled weakly. Estimating how long a job would take was definitely not one of the builder's strong points. But it seemed that there was little more to be gained from prolonging the debate. It would be better to let Barry and Reg start work. Raven's phone rang and he reached for it with a sense of relief. 'Sorry, I need to take this.'

Barry held up a hand. 'You carry on, squire. Reggie and me, we'll get cracking.'

Raven stepped into the hallway for some privacy. It was the head of CSI calling, Holly Chang. He braced himself for some blunt words and a hefty dollop of sarcasm.

'Raven speaking.'

'Where are you?' The question was brusque even by Holly's standards. No 'good morning' or anything. Raven wondered what he'd done wrong this time. And what could possibly be so urgent at this time of the morning?

'At home. I'm just on my way into work. Can this wait until I get there?'

'No, it can't. And don't bother going to the station. You need to get down to the harbour, pronto.'

'Why? What's happened?' Raven was so taken aback that he didn't even think to remind Holly it wasn't her place to order him about.

'A dead body. One you'll recognise.' Her voice cracked with quite un-Holly-like emotion. She continued more softly. 'And one of your team is going to need looking after. She's had a nasty shock. We all have.'

CHAPTER 4

The mood at the station was sombre. That was only to be expected when the victim was "one of our own". To the people here, Scott Newhouse had been a friend and a colleague, and they felt his loss personally even if they hadn't known the young man all that well. At times like this, being a police officer was no longer just a job. An attack on one of them was an attack against them all. Raven had witnessed the same thing at the Met. He'd lost good colleagues on more than one occasion. He hadn't expected the same thing to happen in Scarborough.

Raven had never had much to do with Scott. Their paths had crossed briefly once or twice, but his interactions with the CSI team were usually with Holly. From what he'd observed, Scott had been a quiet, diligent guy who just got on with the job in hand. The kind who beavered away in the background, never seeking out the limelight. The kind of person Raven liked and respected.

After taking Holly's call, Raven had set off on foot to the harbour. The distance from Quay Street to the seafront was so short that for once he'd left his BMW M6 in the car park at the end of his road. One look at Jess, and he'd sent the distraught DC straight home in the company of a uniformed officer, leaving her Land Rover parked where it was at the top of the pier. She was in no fit state to drive. She was in no state to do anything. In the few months Raven had known her, Jess had always come across as a cheerful person, confident and strong. Now she was a wreck.

'Take as much time off as you need,' he'd told her. 'Do you have family you can stay with?' He knew she had come to Scarborough from Rosedale Abbey in the middle of the North York Moors.

Her reply had been a tearful nod.

Once she'd gone, Raven had assumed operational control of the crime scene and spent the next few hours with Holly and the police divers as they recovered the body from the harbour and began the search for evidence before the rising tide drowned everything.

Holly insisted on supervising the work despite her own personal connection to the victim. Raven could tell how much she had liked Scott. She referred to him as her "rising star" and was clearly very upset by his death, struggling to stay calm and professional in the face of such a devastating blow. Raven liked her more after getting a glimpse of her vulnerable side.

It was late morning now and Raven had gathered everyone together for a briefing. Present were Detective Sergeant Becca Shawcross and Detective Constable Tony Bairstow, both looking extremely upset. As an indication of how seriously the top brass were taking this incident, Detective Superintendent Gillian Ellis had also joined them, standing at the back of the room, her hands clasped behind her back, her expression grave. For once, Raven knew that he could count on her unequivocal support.

He felt he ought to say a few words before they got down to business to acknowledge what everyone was feeling. 'I just want to say that this is clearly a shocking and distressing situation for everyone, not least of all our colleague DC Jess Barraclough who was very close to Scott.'

'Poor Jess,' muttered Becca.

Tony nodded his agreement.

'So it goes without saying that we'll move Heaven and Earth to find out what happened to Scott and obtain justice for him.'

'Absolutely,' said Becca.

'Whatever's required,' said Tony.

From the back of the room, Gillian Ellis nodded her silent approval.

Raven was no good at speeches. Now that he had stated the obvious, he felt he was done pontificating. 'Right,' he continued, 'here's what we know so far.' He pinned up a photo of Scott that had been taken from his personnel file. While the body recovered from the harbour that morning had been pale and stiff, the young lad in the photograph looked so fit and healthy that Raven could hardly bear to look at it. He turned instead to face the room.

'Scott Newhouse was twenty-one and had been working as a crime scene investigator for two years. His boss, Holly Chang, told me it was what he'd always wanted to do. I asked her about next of kin. His mother is deceased and Holly doesn't know anything about his father. Scott had no brother, sisters or other relatives. The person closest to him was Jess, but she's in no fit state to answer questions. I told her to go home and take as much time off as she needs. She did manage to tell me that she'd last seen Scott the day before yesterday. Holly confirmed that he was at work yesterday until six, so we know he died sometime between then and six o'clock this morning when the body was spotted lying in the mud.'

'Low tide was at 6am so high tide would have been at midnight,' said Tony, who always had facts like that at his fingertips. He checked his watch. 'It'll be high tide again in another half hour.'

'I left the police divers still searching to recover evidence,' said Raven. 'They're in a race against time. At this stage, we can't be certain that Scott entered the water where he was found. He could have floated around before becoming entangled in the ropes of the boat.'

'Do we know how he died?' asked Becca.

'Not yet,' said Raven. 'The cause of death wasn't immediately apparent given the amount of mud on the body. The post-mortem will establish the cause, as well as confirming whether Scott was alive or dead when he entered the water. I've spoken to Dr Felicity Wainwright, and she's agreed to carry out the PM at the earliest opportunity.' Raven's previous encounters with the senior pathologist had not been pleasant. She was a prickly individual who had taken an intense dislike to him for no reason that he could discern. But once he'd explained the circumstances of the current case, she had proved to be quite obliging. He hoped it might mark a turning point in their relationship.

'Obviously we need to keep an open mind about whether we're dealing with a homicide,' he continued, 'especially at this stage of the investigation, but given what we know about Scott I would say it's unlikely that this was an accident or a case of suicide. He was a clean-living and fit young man, not given to excessive drinking, doing a job he enjoyed, and in a happy and steady relationship.'

Gillian Ellis accepted his assessment without question. 'In that case, Tom, I want you to pull out all the stops. Since it would obviously be inappropriate for DC Jess Barraclough to work on this case, I can offer you DI Derek Dinsdale as an extra pair of hands.'

Raven appreciated Gillian's offer of assistance, but at the mention of Dinsdale's name he balked. Dinsdale was the last person Raven wanted on his team. He'd had more than one run-in with the older detective inspector and regarded him as lazy and incompetent in equal measure. Raven suspected his antipathy towards the man was apparent on his face. He caught Becca's eye and could see that she had the same misgivings about letting Dinsdale onto the team. That settled matters.

'That's very good of you, ma'am, but I think I'd like to keep this tight-knit. Initially, at least. I'm sure that with the help of DS Shawcross and DC Bairstow I'll be able to make good progress.'

Gillian's eyes narrowed almost imperceptibly. 'As you wish, Tom, but my offer remains open. You can have whatever resources you need.' She left the room to return to her office.

Raven could see that Becca and Tony were anxious to get started. He clapped his hands together. 'Right, let's get to work. Tony, can I ask you to organise a team of uniforms to gather witness statements from people working around the harbour?'

'No problem, sir.'

'And Becca, you and I are going to try to piece together Scott's final movements. We'll need to get hold of his internet searches, bank statements, phone records, and any notes he may have left behind. Let's find out what he was doing down at the harbour and who he might have been with.'

Becca nodded eagerly. 'Where do we start?'

'In the most obvious place.' Raven picked his coat from the back of the nearest chair and shrugged it over his shoulders. 'Let's go and take a look around his flat.'

CHAPTER 5

'How are you feeling?' asked Raven once he and Becca were on their way to Scott's flat in the BMW.

'About Scott?'

'About things in general.' He was aware that she'd been a bit down ever since her long-term boyfriend, Sam, had left and gone to Australia. After what had happened to Sam's family, and indeed to Sam himself, Raven could understand the young man's desire for a fresh start somewhere far away. What he couldn't quite grasp was why Becca had chosen to stay here in Scarborough instead of opting for a new life somewhere hot and sunny. Then again, Becca had been born in Scarborough. Her family lived here. And maybe she didn't mind the cold winters too much.

'I'm fine,' said Becca in a tone that made it clear she didn't want to talk about herself. 'I just want to do my best for Scott and Jess.'

'Of course.' He didn't press her further.

Scott's flat was at the bottom end of Trafalgar Road, not far from the centre of town. Raven nudged his large car into the narrow street, missing the wing mirrors of the cars parked on the corner by mere millimetres. The houses here were tall terraces, once grand, now tending towards the shabby. Green wheelie bins crowded the pavements and there was, of course, nowhere to park.

'We should have walked,' said Becca.

Raven suspected she was right but didn't enjoy being told that he was wrong. He gritted his teeth and squeezed the car along the road until he found a lone parking space. It was just big enough to accommodate the M6.

'There you go,' he told her triumphantly once the car was slotted into position.

Scott's address was a redbrick terraced house that had been converted into five separate flats. The communal hallway was strewn with flyers for pizza delivery companies and Indian takeaways. Raven regarded the winding staircase that greeted him with trepidation.

Stairs didn't agree with him. Not since he'd taken a gunshot wound to the leg while serving with the Duke of Wellington's Regiment in Bosnia. He'd saved the lives of two members of his patrol, but it wasn't a time of his life he liked to dwell on. Being a hero hadn't really agreed with him either. The incident had ended his army days and left him with a medal for bravery, a new career in the police force, and a lasting limp that always seemed to get worse at the least opportune moments.

'Which floor is Scott's flat?' he asked Becca.

'The top one.'

'Of course it is.' Raven gripped the rickety wooden banister and braced himself for a long haul to the top.

On the upper landing he paused for a breather. They were up in the roof space of the original house, perhaps once an attic, now enlarged by the addition of a flat-roofed dormer with a low ceiling. A murky roof window let in green-tinged light from overhead. Raven unlocked the door to Scott's apartment, ducked his head and stepped inside.

The space beyond was dim, the curtains drawn closed.

The flat was small, just big enough to accommodate a single person, and bore the unmistakable characteristics of an orderly inhabitant. Raven recognised the hallmarks of the neat habits that he himself shared. The flat was sparsely furnished, the small sofa clear of objects, the table in the dining area bare. The open-plan kitchen was neat and ordered with no dirty pots and pans left in the sink or on the draining board. There were none of the empty drinks cans or abandoned food packaging you might expect to find littering a young man's personal space.

There were a few indications that the place was inhabited. Books on forensics and crime scene analysis as well as true crime were stacked against the wall. There was no television, but a pair of walking boots stood on the mat by the entrance. Hiking poles leaned in one corner and a waterproof coat hung from a hook on the front door.

Signs of a serious mind and a healthy, outdoor life.

'Jess and Scott liked to go on long walks together,' remarked Becca. 'It was one of their shared interests.'

She sounded wistful and Raven guessed she was missing Sam, thinking about the activities they had enjoyed together. Raven and Lisa had never really shared any interests. Perhaps if they had, their relationship wouldn't have ended in divorce. It was probably all Raven's fault. It usually was. What real interests did he have outside work? What did his life amount to, really? He pushed the unwelcome thoughts from his mind, dismissing them as he dismissed the ache in his leg.

He marched into the kitchen area and began opening drawers and cupboard doors. 'You look in the living area,' he told Becca.

'What are we looking for?'

'Anything that doesn't fit the pattern.'

He bent down, rummaging through kitchen cupboards, lifting pots and pans and peering inside, sliding his hands around the back and up into the hidden recesses. There was nothing there, scarcely even a layer of dust. It was the same with the drawers and worktops. All clean, revealing nothing but a need for order.

Becca was searching the living space but the job wasn't a big one. She shook her head. 'Nothing much here at all. I can't even find a laptop.'

Straight ahead was a tiny bathroom and to the left a bedroom, the door ajar. The corner of a bed neatly made was just visible through the opening. Raven always made his own bed too, tucking in the sheet and straightening the duvet before going downstairs to breakfast – a habit instilled in him by his mother and reinforced during his army days. He sensed that Scott was a man after his own heart – one who needed order as a bedrock in his life.

One who knew that chaos lay just a step away and could return at any time.

Becca pushed open the door to the bedroom and flicked on the light. 'Oh my God, come and look at this.'

Raven followed her in and immediately saw what had caught her attention. He stood next to her as they took in the scene before them.

The board fixed to the wall stood out like a sore thumb against the neatness of the rest of the flat. Here was where the chaos reigned. Contained within the four orderly sides of a rectangle but rampant nevertheless.

'It's like an evidence board,' murmured Becca.

Raven crossed the room in a few strides and touched his fingers to the wall. The board was covered with photographs, names, maps, newspaper clippings. It was clear that Scott had sought to impose order on the profusion of information, but even so the jumble of facts and figures threatened to spill out of its frame.

'It's not *like* an evidence board,' he said. 'It *is* one. Did Jess ever mention anything about this?'

'No, but perhaps she didn't see it. It's possible she never came to Scott's flat.'

Raven let his eyes wander over the mass of paper pinned to the board. A detailed street plan of Scarborough was fixed in the centre. Various locations on the map were marked with coloured drawing pins. A piece of string led from each marker to a cluster of photographs, newspaper cuttings and handwritten post-it notes. Coloured lines marked boundaries between the different groups of information. An attempt to bring order to the confusion. Handwritten annotations and dotted lines revealed Scott's thinking.

But had he succeeded in solving this riddle? The presence of the evidence board suggested otherwise. And what, precisely, was the mystery he was trying to solve?

★

By the time Tony reached the harbour the tide had been in and was already starting to turn. The eastern pier remained closed off and divers were still at work in the outer harbour, but in the old inner harbour, life went on. The smart motor cruisers and sailboats in the marina might all be resting for the winter months, but Scarborough still served a commercial fishing fleet, and the fish quay along the west pier was busy.

A trawler had just docked and men were unloading crates of gleaming cod and haddock onto the quayside. The gulls were going wild with excitement, wheeling and swooping, their ear-splitting cries carrying strong across the water and drowning out the noise of the road traffic.

Tony couldn't say he cared for gulls. Perhaps his dislike stemmed from a childhood incident involving a particularly aggressive bird and a peanut butter sandwich. In his mind, they always seemed much larger than they actually were, wings spread wide, sharp beaks ready to snatch at anything tasty.

He gave them a wide berth and approached a fisherman in an orange waterproof coat and rubber boots. 'Good catch you've got there,' he said, eyeing the silvery fish.

The man straightened his back and regarded Tony warily. 'Aye, not too bad for the time of year. What can I do for you?' Tony showed his warrant card and the fisherman glanced over his shoulder towards the activity in the eastern harbour. 'This about the drowned man?'

So the rumours had already started to spread. It was hardly surprising since it was a fisherman who had originally alerted the police to the presence of the body. Everyone around the harbour must already know, and that probably meant the whole town was aware. Tony slipped his warrant card back into his jacket pocket and opened up the file he was carrying. 'We haven't established the cause of death yet. Have you seen this man?' He handed the fisherman a photo of Scott.

'This the dead man?' The fisherman studied the photo before shaking his head sadly. A lifetime on the waves may have toughened him up, but a drowned body was always a tragedy. 'Let me ask the other lads.' He called the crew over and they studied the photograph in turn, each one giving it due consideration, but none had any information to impart.

Tony thanked them and walked back along the pier to Sandside. A flurry of activity was taking place at the side of the road. A large white van had pulled up by one of the ice cream kiosks, and a camera crew were disgorging, microphones and recording equipment in hand. A line of cars was already building up behind the vehicle, and drivers honked their horns in impatience.

Tony rapped on the side of the van. 'I'll have to ask you to move on,' he said as the window was wound down. 'You can't stop here.'

Before he knew what was happening, a microphone was thrust in his face. A young woman, dressed up and made up for the camera, fixed him with a smile that revealed two rows of well-spaced teeth. 'Can you tell us about the body that was discovered in the harbour this morning?'

'I'm sorry,' said Tony, 'but we have nothing to say at this stage of our inquiry.'

'Do you have an identity for the drowned man?' persisted the reporter.

'I'm going to have to ask you to move your vehicle. You're creating an obstruction.'

'Is foul play suspected?' pressed the woman.

Tony ignored her question and called one of the uniformed officers over to assist him. Before long the van had been moved along. But the reporter and her crew were making their way along the pier. They looked like they were here to stay.

Tony turned his back on them and studied the various buildings arrayed along the waterfront. Fish and chips, gift shops, cafés, not to mention the ubiquitous amusement arcades. The Golden Ball public house was taking a delivery of beer. Tony crossed the road and went inside.

A lad was busy polishing glasses behind the bar. Tony showed him the photo of Scott. 'Have you seen this man? Perhaps he was here last night?'

'I wasn't working last night,' said the lad. 'Maybe Julie can help you.' He called to a middle-aged woman in the back. She bustled over to the bar, giving Tony a querying look, tinged with suspicion. But her face softened as soon as he explained the reason for his visit.

'Let me see,' she said, retrieving a pair of reading glasses from the pocket on her apron. She studied the photo. 'Why yes, I never forget a face. And I certainly wouldn't forget a nice face like that. He was here in the bar last night.'

'Was he with anyone?' asked Tony, taking out his notebook.

'No, alone.' said Julie. 'He was sat right there at the bar with a pint. Made it last for an age. I thought maybe he was waiting for someone, a girlfriend or a mate, but no one showed up. I felt a bit sorry for him to be honest. He looked a bit of a lost soul. I tried chatting to him, but he seemed too distracted to talk. He kept checking his phone, as if he was waiting for a message or something. Then eventually he jumped right up and headed outside. Didn't even finish his drink.'

'What time was this?'

Julie screwed up her face in concentration. 'About a quarter to eleven, I'd say. We shut at eleven.'

'Did you see which direction he went?'

'Sorry, love. I was still inside. Didn't see owt. But I'll tell you one thing.'

'Yes?'

'After I finished my shift at eleven, I went outside. It was too cold to hang about, but as I was walking home I saw a couple of figures stood on the east pier.'

'Was one of them the man from the pub?'

'Could have been. It was too dark to be sure.'

'Were they both men?'

Julie shook her head. 'I couldn't say for certain. But one thing I can tell you. These two folk, whoever they were, they weren't strangers to each other. I could tell, even from a distance. Just from the way they were standing together. Yes, whoever they were, they definitely knew each other.'

*

Scott's evidence board would have to be taken back to the station and thoroughly examined. It was now evidence itself, this time in an official murder inquiry, not the off-the-record investigation that Scott had been engaged in. For already it was clear to Raven that Scott had been investigating a murder himself.

Or rather, a series of murders.

'Here's the first one,' said Becca, studying the board alongside Raven. 'Tanya Ayres, aged twenty-four, found dead in her flat in Gladstone Road.' Her finger traced the line of string connecting a pin on the map to a newspaper article describing the gruesome killing. 'The victim was discovered by a neighbour who had called in to feed her cat.' Becca grimaced as she summarised the article. 'Multiple stab wounds... vicious, senseless attack... blah blah... see our editorial on page twelve to find out why the police are failing to keep our streets safe.' She glanced up at Raven. 'I remember this. I was at university at the time.'

Raven turned back to the evidence board. His finger followed a second coloured string. 'This one took place the following year. A woman called Jenny Jones, found dead in a flat in Dean Road. A similar age to Tanya, same scenario, except her body wasn't discovered until a week after her death.'

'And here's a third,' said Becca. 'Caitlin Newhouse, aged thirty. Her body was discovered in an alleyway behind a town centre hotel. Another stabbing.'

Newhouse. That was Scott's surname. The newspaper article confirmed that Caitlin had a young son called Scott.

'It looks as if he was investigating his mother's murder,' said Raven. 'What do you recall about that? Was anyone ever charged?'

'I don't remember much about Caitlin's case, but a man was convicted for the other two. Here it is.' She read aloud from another newspaper article. 'Terry Baines was today found guilty of two counts of murder and sentenced to life imprisonment. He was convicted of killing Tanya Ayres and Jenny Jones. But there's no mention of Caitlin Newhouse here.'

'That would explain why Scott was carrying out his own investigation,' said Raven. 'He was searching for the truth.'

He turned his attention to Caitlin's photo. A pretty young blonde squinting into the camera on a sunny day. Raven recognised Peasholm Park in the background – the dragon paddle boats on the lake and the oriental pagoda on the island. It was a place he knew well. Who had taken the picture?

Becca was reading from yet another newspaper article. 'This one's a follow-up to Caitlin's murder. It says that the victim's son was taken into local authority care and sent to live in a children's home. There were no other relatives to look after him.'

Raven did a quick calculation. Scott must have been fourteen when his mother was killed. Raven knew first-hand what a tragedy like that could do to a young person – the grief and disorientation were unbearable. It was all credit to Scott's character that he'd turned out so well.

Raven's own mother had died when he was sixteen – killed by a hit-and-run driver when she was out one night looking for him. Raven would always blame himself for her death, but at least he didn't have the uncertainty of not knowing what had happened to her. Even though the driver responsible had never been caught, Raven had paid his own penance in many different ways, not least by leaving home and joining the army. It was hard to escape the notion that his injured leg had been given to him as a permanent reminder of how he had failed to protect the most important person in his life.

'We'll need to get Holly's team in to scour the flat,' he said. 'But we'll take the board with us now. We need to get up to speed with Scott's investigations as quickly as we can. It's quite possible that he found some new lead and got too close to whoever killed his mum.'

He swept his gaze around the small bedroom. A laptop was tucked away on a bedside locker, as well as a small object wrapped in brown paper. 'We'll take the laptop too,' he told Becca. 'And what's that?'

Becca picked up the parcel from the locker. It was about six inches by eight. She gave Raven a querying look. 'It's addressed to Jess.'

'Why don't you take it to her?' he suggested. 'Chat to her and see how she is.' Jess would no doubt respond better to Becca's sympathetic ministrations than to his own clumsy efforts. Raven knew his strengths – and he wasn't blind to his weaknesses. 'And while you're there, see if she knows anything about this.' He pointed to the evidence board. 'She surely must know something.'

Then again, if Scott had shared Raven's own tendency to keep his secrets close, Jess might be just as much in the dark as the rest of them.

CHAPTER 6

The drive from Scarborough took Becca inland along the arrow-straight route of the A170, the flat featureless landscape rolling out to either side of the road, the low fields barely visible now that the sun had set. It was a route she'd driven a hundred times, but she'd never felt quite so miserable as she did this time.

Raven had asked her to find out how Jess was getting on, and while Becca was keen to go and see the young detective, she was also dreading it. She and Jess had got to know each other quite well over the past few months, especially when Sam had been in hospital, and she liked to think of Jess as a friend not merely a colleague.

She'd liked Scott very much – he'd once run up a fire escape ladder and apprehended a suspect on her behalf – and she'd been happy for Jess. They'd seemed like a perfect couple, young and energetic, enjoying the great outdoors together. They'd had a bright future ahead of them and Scott's death was nothing short of a cruel twist of fate.

She wondered how Jess would cope. Becca knew that Jess was resilient and determined. But she also knew from personal experience how harrowing a personal loss like this could be.

This catastrophe had come at a time when Becca was struggling to move on with her own life. After a year sitting beside the hospital bed of her comatose boyfriend, clinging to hope against all the odds, she had been rewarded for her steadfastness when Sam had finally woken up. She had rejoiced in this change of fortune and had dared to hope for a bright future together. It would take time, but eventually they would get back to where they had been before. But then disaster had struck. A tragedy had decimated Sam's family and forced him to take an extreme, life-changing decision – he had emigrated to Australia. He'd asked Becca to go with him, but she'd refused, saying that she belonged here in Scarborough.

Now, as she turned off the main road and began the steady climb that would take her across the moors to Jess's family home, she questioned her decision to stay. And not for the first time.

Was she a fool not to have gone with Sam? A coward? She was only twenty-seven years old and had turned down the opportunity of a lifetime. Here she was, still doing the same old job. Still living in her childhood bedroom at the top of her parents' bed and breakfast on North Marine Road.

Single again.

All that could have changed if only she'd had the courage to pack her bags and get on that plane with Sam. And yet she didn't think it was cowardice that had held her back. It was something stronger that anchored her to the place she called home.

Their last parting had been emotional. She realised that Sam had been holding onto the hope she would change her mind at the last minute and go with him. She had disappointed him. If she was honest, she'd walked away from that final goodbye disappointed with herself. Had she given up her one chance of happiness?

At first he'd sent pictures every day. It was summer in

the southern hemisphere, the sky a startling blue. Clean, modern buildings gleamed in the bright sunshine. But gradually the photos had become less frequent. She found that she and Sam had less and less to talk about, less in common with each other. She hadn't heard from him in over a fortnight now. It was time to close a door on that part of her life.

She had made her choice. Now she had to live with it.

The road steepened and narrowed as Becca approached Rosedale Abbey and she had to concentrate harder. This was an unfamiliar journey to her, tricky in the dark, although she guessed that in daylight the views on either side would be spectacular. Jess had often talked about the beauty of the moors, and it was clear that she felt a bond with her home just as strong as the ties that had kept Becca in Scarborough while Sam went on his voyage of self-discovery.

She slowed down at a thirty-mile-an-hour sign on the edge of the village. After an hour's driving she had arrived. She immediately focussed her thoughts, pushing her own concerns to the back of her mind. She had a job to do. Scott was dead and Jess needed her. There was no time for self-indulgent moping.

She passed a stone-built inn with picnic tables in the garden, all empty at this time of year. Turning off the main road into the heart of the village she slowed to a crawl as she looked for Jess's parents' house. Old cottages with slate-grey roofs nestled around a village green; there was a local primary school, a church, a corner shop and an old-fashioned red telephone box. The village emanated a feeling of comfort and reassurance, as if by standing the test of time it was proof that life went on through all its ups and downs. She could understand why Jess liked it here so much and had returned to the bosom of her family for a period of respite after the dreadful shock of discovering Scott's body.

The Barraclough home was a rambling stone house set within a large walled garden. Jess's old Land Rover was parked on some gravel in front of a double garage. The trees were still bare, but a few early primroses were just starting to flower and daffodils were coming into bud. Delicate snowdrops bobbed their white heads along the edge of the path to the front door. It looked like an idyllic place to live.

Becca rang the bell. The door was opened by a woman in her mid-fifties who resembled an older, softer version of Jess. Her blonde hair was shorter, cut into a practical but flattering chin-length bob, but she had the same athletic figure as her daughter and the same inquisitive blue eyes. A Golden Retriever bounded down the hallway and gave Becca an enthusiastic greeting, sniffing eagerly at her coat and licking her hand. She patted its head.

'Sorry to bother you, Mrs Barraclough, but I was hoping to speak to Jess. I'm Becca Shawcross, a friend and colleague from Scarborough CID.' In her hand Becca held the parcel addressed to Jess that she and Raven had found in Scott's flat.

The blonde bob dipped and a welcoming smile spread over the woman's face. 'Of course, do come in. And please, call me Andrea.'

Becca followed her through into a wide, stone-tiled hallway. The hall felt cool, but in the lounge beyond, a log fire roared and crackled in a big open fireplace. Half a dozen pairs of well-worn walking boots were lined up on a rack. Waterproof coats and waxed jackets hung in a row on the wall, and hiking poles and umbrellas were stacked in a stand. This was a hardy family that got outside whatever the weather.

Andrea turned to her and dropped her voice. 'We're devastated by what's happened. Jess especially, obviously. But we're all upset. Scott was such a lovely person. He came to stay with us for Christmas and everyone liked him.'

Becca nodded her understanding. 'We're going to do everything we can to find out what happened to him.'

'Was it an accident or do you think he was...' Andrea's

voice trailed off, the word "murdered" left unspoken.

'We need to wait for the results of the post-mortem,' said Becca, slipping automatically into police mode. She hesitated before adding, 'But Scott wasn't the sort of person to fall into the harbour by accident.'

'My thoughts exactly.' Andrea passed a hand across her face. 'Oh dear, poor Jess. It will take her time to get over a shock like this. Come with me. She's upstairs in her room.'

She led the way up the creaking stairs and knocked on a door at the end of a long landing. Away from the warmth of the fire the landing felt chill. Becca ran her fingers along a wall-mounted radiator, but it was cool to the touch. The Barraclough family clearly didn't feel the cold.

'Becca Shawcross is here to see you, love.' Andrea didn't wait for an answer, but stepped aside for Becca and retreated down the stairs. 'I'll leave you to it.'

As soon as the door opened, Jess ran into Becca's arms. For a minute they held onto each other. There was no need to say anything. Both women had lost someone special, but while Sam might be on the other side of the world, in Jess's case the loss was final, never to be reversed.

They separated eventually and Becca followed Jess through into her room. She took a seat in a huge armchair while Jess sat on the edge of the bed. Becca could see that she'd been crying. Her eyes were red, edged with dark rings.

'I'm so sorry,' said Becca.

'Thanks. It's good to see you.'

'Everyone's thinking about you. They send their wishes – Raven, Tony, Gillian, Holly.'

Jess sighed. 'I feel as if I'm running away, coming back here. I ought to be in Scarborough helping to find what out happened to Scott. Not hiding away in my parents' house.'

'Not at all,' said Becca. 'This is exactly where you should be. You've had a terrible shock, and you need time to recover. Besides, Gillian wouldn't allow you to be involved. You were too close to the victim.'

At that, Jess burst into fresh tears and Becca reached

for a box of tissues on the dressing table.

'Sorry,' said Jess once she'd blown her nose and composed herself. 'I keep doing that.'

'No need to apologise,' said Becca. 'This is why you need to be here and not at work.'

There was a tap at the door and Andrea reappeared, bearing a tray with two mugs of freshly brewed tea and a plate of homemade biscuits. She cast an anxious look over her daughter. 'Make sure she eats something,' she said to Becca. 'She hasn't had a thing all day.'

Becca accepted the tray with thanks and put it down on the dressing table. She waited until they were alone again before continuing. 'Listen, I'm sorry about this but there are a few questions I need to ask you. Routine – you know what I'm going to ask.'

'Like had I noticed any change in Scott's behaviour recently?' suggested Jess. 'No. I've been thinking it over. He was always a bit secretive, that's just how he was. But I hadn't noticed any change.'

'Did he have any enemies?' prompted Becca. 'Someone who might have held a grudge against him? Someone he'd had an argument with?'

'No,' said Jess. 'Scott never argued with anyone. He was always so easy-going. He never so much as raised his voice.'

'Did he tell you anything about what he planned to do that evening? Did he mention going to meet someone, for example?'

'No, nothing. We'd planned to go walking at the weekend. But that evening, he just said he was busy. He didn't say what he was going to do. I said not to worry, we'd catch up later.'

It was much as Becca had thought. 'Raven and I went to Scott's flat this morning, and we found this.' She handed Jess the parcel. 'It's addressed to you.'

Jess looked at it in surprise. 'What is it?'

'I've no idea. It's not your birthday is it?'

'Not for months yet.'

'A Valentine's gift?'

'That was a couple of weeks ago.' Jess held the parcel in her hands, staring at it in puzzlement.

Becca was curious about the parcel's contents, but didn't press Jess to open it. No doubt she would want to look at it later, when she was on her own. 'You don't need to open it now,' she said.

Jess lingered over the parcel, seeming unsure what to do about it.

'Why don't you open it when I've gone?' suggested Becca.

But Jess's fingers were already moving, pulling at the knotted string that tied the brown paper. She undid the knot, removed the string and unwrapped the paper.

Inside was a book and a sealed envelope. Jess laid the envelope aside and showed the book to Becca. The collected poems of Edgar Allan Poe. It wasn't a new copy, but one well-thumbed. On the front cover was a line drawing of a raven.

'Have you seen it before?' asked Becca.

'No.' Jess opened the book and began to read. 'Oh, look. This book belonged to Scott's mother. Her name is inside the cover.'

Becca leaned in close to see. *Caitlin Newhouse* was written in a round script in purple ink with little circles over the letters "i" in the name. There was a date – 1996.

Jess turned the pages and a photograph slipped out and fell to the floor. She picked it up and studied it for a moment before passing it to Becca. 'This must be her.'

Becca held the photograph carefully between forefinger and thumb. The image showed an attractive blonde-haired woman giving a dazzling, carefree smile to the camera. A scooped-neck T-shirt revealed smooth, tanned skin, and around her neck a silver pendant on a leather cord glinted in bright sun. The design on the face of the circular pendant was an intricate carving of a raven looking over its shoulder. The creature bore a marked resemblance to the raven on the cover of the book. Becca turned the photo over but there was nothing written on the back. She returned it to Jess. 'Did Scott ever talk to you about his mother?'

Jess nodded, sliding the photo back into its place and closing the book. 'A little. He loved her very much. But she was murdered eight years ago when he was still a boy. After she died he was sent to live in a children's home.'

'I don't want to pry, but did you ever visit Scott's flat? On Trafalgar Road?'

Jess gave a noncommittal shrug of her shoulders. 'Not really. Well, I did go there once, but I didn't really look around, just waited in the living room. Scott was a very private person. He always said his flat was too small and not very nice, so we always went to my place instead.'

'You didn't ever go into his bedroom?'

Jess flushed a little at the question. 'No. Why?'

It was time for Becca to tell her what they'd found. Normally she would never reveal anything about the investigation to a relative, but Jess wasn't a member of the public. She deserved to know. And perhaps she could help. 'Raven and I visited Scott's flat this morning. We found a board fixed to the bedroom wall. It was an evidence board.'

Jess's lower lip began to tremble. 'Evidence of what?'

'His mother's murder. The murders of two other women as well.'

Jess's eyes opened wide. 'Three murders? Scott never said anything about that.'

'He didn't say that he was carrying out his own investigation into his mother's death?'

'No, but like I said, he could be very mysterious. Because of what happened to him he was always very private, but he was slowly opening up to me. I guessed there were things he was holding back about his past. But I knew he would tell me everything in his own time, when he was ready.' She burst into tears again. 'Now there won't ever be time, will there?'

'I'm sorry,' said Becca.

Jess paused, digesting the new information. 'You think

this is why he was killed? Because of something he'd found out about his mother's death?' Her eyes locked with Becca's.

Becca knew she couldn't conceal her thoughts from Jess. They were colleagues – police detectives as well as friends. There could be no secrets between them. 'I think it's a strong possibility. It's certainly a line that we'll be following up.'

A fresh tear appeared in the corner of Jess's eye. 'I should have asked more questions when I had the chance. I tried to give him space, to respect his privacy, but look what that brought.'

'You couldn't have done anything differently. It was Scott's choice not to open up to you.'

'I know.'

Becca decided it was time to leave Jess in peace. 'Before I go,' she said, 'is there anyone in Scott's life that you think we should talk to? Friends? Relatives?'

Jess thought for a moment. 'No relatives that I know of. But he did have a good friend from his days in the children's home. Cameron Blake. I'll text you his details.'

'That would be helpful,' said Becca. They embraced one more time. 'Don't worry, Jess, we're going to find out who did this. And when we get them, they'll pay for what they've done.'

CHAPTER 7

The cold, clinical interior of the mortuary was as icy as ever, but as Raven entered he wondered if he detected a slight thawing in the demeanour of its sole living occupant, Dr Felicity Wainwright.

In his previous encounters with Scarborough's senior pathologist, Raven had begun to think of her as a bridge to the dead – frosty, unfeeling and incapable of compassion. Certainly she always showed more interest in the cold corpses spread out on the slabs before her or stored in ranks of refrigerated drawers than in Raven's own feelings. Indeed she often seemed to take a perverse delight in making him ill at ease.

Yet today, a glimmer of concern played on Felicity's face, as if even she might realise the significance of Scott's death to everyone involved. Certainly the urgency with which she'd rescheduled her timetable to carry out the post-mortem pointed to a desire to move the investigation forward as smoothly as possible.

'DCI Raven.' She acknowledged his presence in her chilly domain with an incline of her sharp chin. 'You'll be here for the results of Mr Newhouse's forensic post-mortem?'

Mr Newhouse. Formality was the order of the day here. Procedures and regulations were the way things were done.

'If you have them.' Raven knew better than to presume anything in Felicity's presence. If she was ready and willing to reveal the cause of death, she would tell him. If not, no amount of persuasion would result in anything approximating cooperation on her part.

'I do.' Felicity made no move to pick up a report or refer to her computer screen. It was clear that she knew exactly what she wanted to say and required no prompting. 'Would you like to go and sit down somewhere more comfortable to discuss them?'

Raven shook his head, earning himself a grudging glimmer of respect.

'Good. That means I can show you my findings in the flesh, as it were.' She turned and stalked away in the direction of a stainless-steel bench, her soft shoes soundless against the white tiled floor.

Raven followed, his black coat sweeping behind him. He drew it closer against the chill, wondering how anyone could stand to spend their working day in such an environment. What drew someone to choose pathology as a profession? To spend their career surveying the folds and curves of decaying flesh, their hands wrist-deep in blood and entrails.

Time of death. Cause of death. Wounds, diseases and injuries; lacerations, tears and contusions.

Was it an affinity for the dead that wedded Dr Wainwright to her profession or a rejection of the living?

Or was there a beating heart in her narrow chest after all? Was she, at some level, rather like himself? Eager to discover the truth, and hungry for justice. There was no way of telling from the blank face she presented to the world.

She stopped at a bench where a white sheet rose and fell across the contours of a corpse laid out for examination. 'Ready?'

Raven swallowed. 'Go ahead.'

She drew back the sheet partway, revealing the torso of a man. White, naked, cold. Flat fluorescent lighting illuminated every nook and cranny in unforgiving detail. It was Scott, but not the fit young guy Raven had known in life. This cold corpse was merely the vestige of the man he had been. His vitality was gone, just like his hopes, his feelings, his future.

This thing on the slab was nothing more than a shell.

Dr Wainwright's long hands pointed out a slit near the centre of the abdomen. 'Clear evidence of a stab wound in the periumbilical region.' Her gloved fingers crawled across the skin like blind worms. They lingered at the side of the chest. 'Here too in the vicinity of the spleen. And here on the other side of the abdomen, close to the gallbladder. Three stab wounds in total. I'd say from a short blade with a serrated edge. But none of these were the cause of death.'

A slight burning of stomach acid hit the back of Raven's throat as he surveyed the injuries. 'No?'

Dr Wainwright's fingers retreated. 'No. The victim was still breathing when he entered the water. So technically, he drowned.'

'I see. Was there anything on the body to indicate the identity of his attacker? Hairs? Traces of DNA?'

'After fishing him out of the harbour?' scoffed the pathologist. 'I should say not.' She lifted the sheet by its corners and folded it back into position, covering Scott's face from view. 'I'll be sending you a full written report with my findings in the morning. Now, any more questions before I finish for the day?' Dr Wainwright folded her hands across her chest and Raven sensed that his window of opportunity to grow his short-lived sense of fellowship with his colleague had firmly closed.

'No, none,' he answered. 'Thank you for your help.'

★

'May I come in?' Raven poked his head around the open door of Holly Chang's office, half-expecting to be told that it was too late in the day for a meeting and that he should call back in the morning, but the head of CSI gestured wearily to a chair by the wall. She was hunched over her desk, typing at the computer. Raven dropped into the seat and waited for her to finish. It was the first moment of respite he'd had all day.

After a minute of bashing keys, Holly leaned back and said, 'What a bloody awful thing to happen.'

'It is.'

For once there was no discord between them. He and Holly may have got off to a bad start when Raven first arrived in Scarborough, but the loss of a close colleague swept all other matters aside and he knew that whatever happened now, past differences had been put behind them for good. She would probably always be a grumpy cow, but on this investigation there would be no gripes about working overtime or weekends. She would do whatever it took to find Scott's killer.

Raven had left her at the harbourside, eight hours earlier. Then, she had been covered from head to toe in her usual crime scene attire. Now she was wearing a white blouse and dark trousers, her jet black hair tied at the nape in a neat and practical bun. Her forehead was furrowed with worry, and she looked exhausted and windswept after a day supervising the work of the police divers. But there was a dogged tenaciousness to her expression, a determination to continue.

Raven stretched out his long legs, feeling far more at home here than in Dr Wainwright's mortuary. 'How did you get on?' he asked Holly.

She sighed. 'You wouldn't believe how much crap we pulled out of that harbour. Fishing lines, coins, bottles, sunglasses, a pair of old boots, even the wheel of a car. Most of it covered in mud, of course.'

'Of course.' Raven wondered if his own wedding ring was among the items the divers had retrieved from the mud. He'd tossed it into the harbour back in December after deciding to bring his marriage to an end. 'Anything interesting?'

'We recovered Scott's phone, but it'll be a bloody miracle if it ever works again. The forensics team are going to dry it off and see what they can do with it.'

'Excellent.'

'Plus,' said Holly, 'I think we may have found the murder weapon. In fact, I'd stake my reputation on it.'

Raven's eyes opened wide at the news. 'A knife?' His thoughts returned to the stab wounds that Dr Wainwright had shown him on Scott's body. Three in total, one near the stomach, one on each side of the chest, as if the attacker was making sure of the job. Made using a short blade with a serrated edge, according to Felicity, and Raven had never known her to be wrong.

'An automatic knife with a folding blade,' said Holly. 'The sort of weapon that could easily be concealed under clothing.'

Holly swivelled her screen so that Raven could see it and pulled up a photograph of a wicked-looking flick knife. A ruler by its side indicated its dimensions. The blade was curved and partly serrated, ending in a deadly point. A match for the type of weapon that had been used against Scott. 'Illegal to own in the UK,' Raven remarked, 'but easily available to import from Europe.'

Holly swung the screen back to its normal position. 'Don't expect to pull any prints or blood from it,' she cautioned. 'It's been washed clean by the sea.'

'Of course.' Still, it was more than Raven could have hoped for. First the post-mortem results, now the murder weapon itself. Excellent progress for the first day of an investigation.

'So,' said Holly, 'that's what I've spent my day doing. How about you?'

Raven leaned forwards in his chair. 'How much do you know about Scott's mother?'

Holly nodded in appreciation at the question. 'I

wondered how long it would take until you asked. Let me tell you what I know and then you can fill me in on what you've found out.' She picked up a mug of tea from her desk and cradled it in her hands, taking a single sip before continuing. 'Scott's mum is the reason Scott joined the CSI team in the first place. Or rather, her murder was the reason. It took me a while before I managed to ferret that piece of information out of him, but no one keeps a story that big from me for very long, not even someone as secretive as Scott.'

Raven smiled, not doubting it for an instant.

'You probably already know that Caitlin Newhouse was murdered eight years ago, her killer never caught. There was an almighty cock-up during the investigation – evidence went missing and the whole thing fell apart. And before you ask,' she added, sweeping Raven with a hard stare, 'it was before my time. Anyway, that's what drove Scott to train as a crime scene investigator, and I can tell you that he was the most meticulous person on my team. He was determined to ensure that no other victim missed out on justice because of an error on the part of CSI.' She finished her tea and plonked the mug back on the desk. 'Now you can tell me what you've managed to dig up.'

'Not much more than you've just told me about Caitlin's murder,' Raven conceded, 'but what I do know is that Scott never came to terms with his mother's death. I visited his flat today and found an evidence board on his wall. He was carrying out his own investigation into her murder.'

Holly nodded her understanding. 'That doesn't surprise me. He'd hinted as much to me. He was always asking questions, throwing out suggestions. Had he got anywhere?'

'I don't know yet. But my hunch is that he discovered something that brought him too close to the killer. Is there anyone else I can speak to about Caitlin's case? Someone with first-hand knowledge of the investigation?'

'Most of the police and CSI people involved are retired

now, I expect. But there is someone still around who worked on it.'

'Who?'

'DI Derek Dinsdale.'

Raven groaned. This was the second time Dinsdale's name had been mentioned that day. He couldn't continue to ignore it. If Dinsdale had been involved in Caitlin's murder inquiry, then it looked as if Raven was going to have to overcome his deep-seated antipathy to the man and at least hear what he had to say. Another experienced detective on the case would be useful too, even one as inept as Dinsdale. There was no point trying to pretend otherwise.

Raven reminded himself that he was doing it for Scott's sake. And for Jess too. In the search for truth he would have to lay his personal feelings aside.

'Yes,' said Holly, watching his doubts play out on his face. 'Dinsdale's a mixed blessing, but you never know, this might be the one time he turns out to be indispensable.'

'Maybe,' said Raven glumly. There had to be some use for Dinsdale. Didn't there?

*

'Get some of that down you, then tell me all about it.'

Becca took a grateful sip of the white wine that Ellie Earnshaw had placed in front of her. She'd asked for a small glass, but Ellie had ordered a large one nonetheless. The wine was chilled and refreshing and Becca quickly felt her spirits lifting. 'Thanks. I needed that.'

'I know. I'm psychic.' Ellie smiled, her face lighting up.

The first time Becca had met Ellie, she'd had a pixie haircut with purple highlights. Now she had grown her hair a touch longer and was trying out a striking scarlet. She was dressed in her usual eclectic style, with a green floral jumper over black jeans, Dr Martens boots, a chunky onyx necklace around her neck and an assortment of bracelets that looked like they'd come from a junk shop or perhaps a Moroccan bazaar. Somehow it all seemed to go together with effortless chic.

Ellie was Sam's cousin and had become best friends with Becca during the tragedy that had engulfed Sam's family. Although Becca had ended up losing Sam, she was grateful to have made such a good friend, someone who understood what she'd gone through and who always managed to stay positive and supportive. Still only in her late twenties, Ellie now ran the brewery that Sam's family had founded many years before. Yet despite holding such a responsible role at a young age, she always seemed to be relaxed and cheerful. Becca thought she was amazing.

They were seated at a window table in their favourite bar in the centre of Scarborough. Although she brewed beer for a living, Ellie would happily drink any tipple – beer, wine or cocktails. She had grown up with a restaurateur father and spent her teenage summers travelling around the vineyards of France and Italy picking grapes in return for board, lodging and free wine. She raised her own glass of Pinot Grigio and clinked it against Becca's. 'Cheers! Now tell me why you've got a face like a wet weekend. What could possibly have happened? I hope this isn't about Sam.'

Becca glanced around, but the people sitting nearby were engaged in their own conversations, and the music thumping away in the background was doing its best to drown out all other sounds. 'Did you hear about the body in the harbour?' Scarborough wasn't a large town and news of that sort tended to spread quickly.

'Sure,' said Ellie. 'It was on the news this evening, but the reporters didn't seem to know much. I think they were mostly making guesses, although they'd managed to track down some old fisherman who claimed to have discovered the body. Are you working on that case?'

Becca nodded glumly. Talking about the day's events felt like hauling a dead weight, but she knew it would do her good to share at least part of the story with Ellie. 'It was someone I knew. A colleague.'

'Oh no, I'm so sorry.' Ellie leaned in closer, her brows furrowing together in sympathy.

Her hand reached out and Becca held it tightly. There wasn't much more she could reveal without breaching confidentiality and she didn't really want to rake over all the details. But Ellie didn't pry, and Becca was grateful she respected that boundary. That was something that Becca's mum, Sue Shawcross, never quite seemed to grasp. She always wanted to know whatever Becca knew, so that she could trade gossip with her friends and acquaintances. 'Everyone's devastated. We just want to track down the killer.'

'Of course you do,' said Ellie. 'And you'll find them. You always do.' She turned her head to look out of the window, perhaps recalling the events of the previous year resulting in the manhunt that had ended on the cliffs at Flamborough Head.

That was something else Becca didn't want to think about.

'Anyway,' she said, quickly changing the subject. 'There's something else I've been meaning to tell you.'

'Go on. What is it?'

Becca took a deep breath then let the words come out. She'd been bottling them up for too long and needed to tell someone. 'I think it's time I moved out of my parents' place. I want to get a flat of my own.'

There, she'd said it. Now it was a fact.

In truth, she'd been considering the idea for a while. She and Sam had planned to get a place of their own once. But that was before the hit and run incident that had put him into a coma for a year and had changed everything. Although it was convenient living at home – having her laundry done for her and her meals cooked – she couldn't stay there forever. During the difficult period when Sam had been hospitalised, home had been a refuge, but now it was starting to feel like a chain around her neck. A leash holding her back, preventing her from becoming a fully-fledged adult. 'I need to move on and put the past behind me.'

'I think it's a brilliant idea,' said Ellie, her voice full of enthusiasm, just as Becca had known it would be. 'Have you found anywhere you like?'

'Not yet,' admitted Becca. 'Not anywhere really nice, I mean.'

In reality, she hadn't even begun to search, other than taking a casual glance at a couple of property websites and standing in front of the window of one of the local estate agents. The idea seemed daunting, the choice too wide. Leaving home sounded easy in theory, but where would she go? Did she want somewhere close to the B&B, handy for popping back when she wanted to see her family, or should she move as far away as possible in order to make a clean break? Now that felt truly daunting.

'Are you thinking of buying or renting?' asked Ellie.

'I don't know.' Now Becca felt foolish. Buying a flat was a serious undertaking. She would need to arrange a mortgage, get a survey done, take responsibility for all kinds of things she currently took for granted. She didn't even know how much she would need to borrow, or how much a lender would allow her on a detective sergeant's salary.

'Well whatever you decide, don't leave it too late,' warned Ellie. 'The property market really heats up in the spring. You want to get in there before demand starts to rise and all the best places get snapped up.'

Becca nodded. That was surely good advice. She wished she'd mentioned the idea to Ellie earlier so that she could have started researching the market already. She hadn't even realised how little she knew.

The only other person who would be willing to offer advice, asked-for or not, was her brother, Liam, who worked in the "property business", a vague term that included everything from holiday apartments to buy-to-let flats and who knew what else. But Liam's wheeling and dealing always sounded dodgy to Becca's ears, and she didn't want to enquire more closely about what he was up to. Besides, it was Liam who had recommended a builder friend of his to work on Raven's house, and as far as Becca could tell, that job still wasn't finished after nearly four months.

'What does your mum think?' asked Ellie.

Becca swallowed another large mouthful of wine. *Oh God, what will Mum say? She'll freak out!* So far, Ellie was the only person Becca had dared to speak to about her idea of leaving home.

'You haven't told her yet, have you?' said Ellie, bursting into a peal of laughter.

'I'll get round to it,' said Becca miserably. 'One day. Soon.'

CHAPTER 8

Even before his alarm clock was due to go off, Raven had been lying awake for nearly an hour, feeling the weight of expectation pressing down on him like a physical burden. If ever a murder investigation counted, it was this one. All eyes would be turned on him like spotlights. And with Jess on indefinite leave, he was missing one of his best detectives. He turned once more under his duvet, seeking comfort in oblivion, but the raucous cries of the gulls kept him from returning to the relief of sleep.

Keen to get started and not wanting to get waylaid by Barry, he turned off his alarm, showered and dressed quickly, then set off, picking up a coffee and Danish pastry en-route. He could eat his breakfast at his desk just as well as in a café, and he wanted to get his thoughts in order before the rest of the team showed up. There was a lot of information to work through. Not just the usual witness statements and physical evidence of a normal investigation, but also the material that Scott had assembled relating to his mother's death and the murder of the two other women. Though whether that would prove to be a productive line of inquiry was anyone's guess.

As he strode along the corridor, pastry in one hand, coffee in the other, alternating bites and sips as he went, he almost ran straight into Detective Superintendent Gillian Ellis. He stopped short, his thoughts interrupted, his feeling of overwhelm suddenly heightened in her presence.

'Tom,' she said, her well-padded figure blocking his path, 'just the person I was hoping to bump into. I'm glad to see you're making an early start.'

'There's a lot to get through,' said Raven, hoping she would take the hint.

Her eyes bored into his. 'Yes, and I don't want to take up any of your valuable time. You'll have a busy day ahead.' Yet still she made no move to get out of his way.

Raven felt helpless with his hands full of food and drink. He gestured at her with his Danish. 'You have a question for me?'

She pursed her lips. 'I just want to make certain that you're fully aware of what's at stake. This is no routine murder investigation. When something like this happens, it threatens the morale of the whole workforce. It's your job to restore that morale.'

Great. So he wasn't just charged with finding Scott's killer. He also had the welfare of Scarborough Police on his plate. Gillian was right though. Despite Scott being shy and a relatively new addition to the CSI team, those who had known him regarded him with respect. And in Jess's case, far more than that. They weren't just saddened by his unexplained death. They were angered by it. They wanted answers and they wanted them quickly. And it was Raven's job to get them.

He tried to inject as much reassurance as he could muster into his reply. 'I do understand that, Gillian. I have experience dealing with similar cases in the Met.' That was an exaggeration perhaps, but he'd certainly handled one situation when an officer had been killed during an investigation. He knew what he was supposed to do. And he knew how to do it.

Gillian, however, seemed unimpressed by this not-so-subtle reminder of his years of experience. 'Don't imagine that we're all in awe because you worked in London, Tom. North Yorkshire isn't some rural backwater, as I'm sure you're aware.'

Her comment stung and Raven drew himself a little straighter in an effort to reclaim some dignity. He wished he wasn't so encumbered by the food and drink in his hands. It must make him look ridiculous. 'Of course, ma'am.'

'So I hope you'll handle this with the proficiency I'd expect from a DCI.'

'Absolutely, ma'am. I'll do my utmost to ensure a swift and satisfactory outcome to the case.' Even as the words fell off his tongue, he knew he was parroting the kind of empty-headed management speak he detested.

Gillian made an exaggerated sigh at his performance. 'Don't give me that bullshit, Tom. You sound exactly like my boss. Just make sure you get the job done.' She didn't wait for a reply, but turned on her heels and stalked away down the corridor like a sumo wrestler. A junior bobby ducked to get out of her way.

Raven breathed a sigh of relief to see her go. As if his job wasn't hard enough already, now he had Gillian on his back when he could have used her support. If her intention had been to ensure he performed to the best of his ability, she had badly misjudged the effect of her little pep talk.

He crammed the last of his breakfast into his mouth and headed off before anything else could go wrong.

★

Raven eyed the wall of the incident room with displeasure. Often at the start of a new investigation there was little to go on: an initial crime scene report, a tentative sketch of the victim's life, perhaps an eyewitness account if you were lucky.

That wasn't the problem here. It wasn't that he didn't have enough material to work with.

He had too much.

The evidence board from Scott's flat had been transferred to the police station and fixed to the wall of the incident room, next to the board that dealt with Scott's own murder. Raven hardly knew which one to examine first.

The crime he was charged with investigating or the ones that begged for his attention. In the case of two of the women whose deaths Scott had documented, a man had already been found guilty and convicted. But Caitlin's murder had gone unsolved.

So how many killers were there in total? One, two, three?

'Morning, Raven.' The door of the incident room swung open and Becca made her way inside, shrugging off her coat and dumping her bag on a desk. 'I guessed you'd want to make an early start. I'll go and put the kettle on, shall I?'

'Right,' he managed. A coffee to follow the one he'd only just finished. Well, he'd need all the help he could get to bring him up to speed.

He moved away from the evidence boards and began sifting through the mounds of files and boxes that had been recovered from Scott's flat. It seemed that the board Scott had created was just a handy summary of all the information he'd accumulated. Here was the material that supported his findings. Along with newspaper articles, Scott had somehow managed to obtain copies of all the official documents relating to the three historic murder enquiries. Court judgements. Transcripts of police interviews. Forensic evidence and post-mortem reports. It was probably best not to probe too deeply into how he'd managed to get hold of some of these documents.

But where to begin?

On top of Scott's own death, Raven now had three further murders to examine. He would have preferred to come at the case with no prior evidence. It could take longer to unpick the twisted, tangled thoughts of another than it did to start with a blank slate, and there was always the risk that Scott had been barking up the wrong tree entirely. This could all be simply the delusions of a young man still struggling to come to terms with his mother's senseless killing, refusing to accept that it would forever go unsolved. Yet Raven's instincts told him that this was the place to start. It was simply too much of a coincidence to ignore the fact that both Scott and his mother had been stabbed to death.

By the time Becca returned with teas and coffees all round, Tony had arrived and they were ready to get started.

Becca leaned against her desk, studying the two evidence boards. She had already seen the one dealing with the murder of Caitlin Newhouse and the two other women. The board devoted to Scott's death was largely new to her. Raven had pinned a photo of Scott at the top of the board, together with a location map and the details that Tony had uncovered of his last sighting – late at night, in the company of an unidentified person, who surely had to be the prime suspect. The cause of death – drowning following multiple stab wounds – was written beside the map, together with a photo of the flick knife recovered from the harbour.

Raven's eyes darted between the two boards. The first had too much information on it, the second too little. He decided to find out if anyone had anything fresh to add. 'Becca, did you manage to catch up with Jess yesterday evening?'

'Yes, I went to visit her. She's staying with her parents at Rosedale Abbey.'

Raven was glad to hear that Jess had taken his advice. Putting some distance between herself and the crime, and staying with people who loved her was the best way to begin healing. 'Good. How is she?'

'Devastated. She didn't know why Scott would have

gone to the harbour that night. He'd told her he had something to do, nothing more. And she had no idea that he'd been carrying out an investigation into Caitlin's death.'

'What about the parcel that Scott left for her?'

'She opened it while I was there. It was a book of poems by Edgar Allan Poe that had belonged to Caitlin. There was a photo of her inside the book.'

Raven furrowed his brow in puzzlement. 'A book of poems? So there was nothing Jess could tell us that might help?'

'She did give me the name of a close friend, someone Scott knew from the children's home. Cameron Blake.'

Raven wrote the name on the board below Scott's photo. 'We should definitely speak to him. If he knew Scott from the home, he may have some insight into Scott's thinking about Caitlin's death.' He tapped his pen against the other board. 'And then there's this.' He glared at Scott's evidence board as if he could somehow force it to reveal its secrets.

'Would you like me to start sorting through Scott's notes, sir?' asked Tony. 'I can see there's a lot of information there.'

'Yes, I would,' said Raven. Tony was by far the best person for a painstaking job like that. He hesitated, hating what he was about to say, but knowing he had no choice. Only one person could provide them with the insight they needed to make rapid progress in the inquiry. 'What I think we need first is an overview from someone with inside knowledge of the historic murders. And that person is DI Derek Dinsdale.'

Raven's bruising confrontation with Gillian had reinforced the conclusion that Raven had already arrived at the previous evening – that he couldn't continue to exclude Dinsdale from the team. If he refused to allow Dinsdale on board, Gillian would be down on him like a ton of bricks. Besides, it would be churlish to let old animosities get in the way of progress. Raven was bigger than that. He would just have to swallow his pride and ask Dinsdale for his help.

He registered the look of surprise on Becca's and Tony's faces. Understandable, given Dinsdale's well-deserved reputation for laziness and incompetence. Not to mention the way he had resolutely failed to cooperate with Raven on one of their previous cases.

Yet they must know that Raven had no choice in the matter.

'Let's just hope I don't regret it,' he told them.

CHAPTER 9

'Take your time, Derek,' said Raven.

Against his better judgement he had let Dinsdale have the floor. The older DI stood with his back to the room, giving everyone a clear view of his dandruff-flecked shoulders as he pored over the evidence board recovered from Scott's house. 'Yes,' he muttered to himself. 'I remember that.'

Not for the first time, Raven wondered if he had made a colossal mistake allowing Dinsdale onto the team. If they were relying on the older man's expert knowledge of the case, then God help them. They didn't have time for a leisurely trip down memory lane.

Becca glanced at her watch and even Tony began flicking through some of Scott's files, impatient to get started.

But if the DI sensed the growing restlessness in the room or noticed the sarcasm in Raven's remark he wasn't letting on. Perhaps he was enjoying the attention. He scratched himself as he peered at the photos and newspaper articles, seeming determined to read every one of them to the end.

Eventually he turned round.

'It's all coming back to me now. This was a high-profile case at the time. No stone left unturned. We put some long hours in, I can tell you.'

In Dinsdale's case, that was hard to believe.

'What can you tell us about the first two women on the board, Tanya and Jenny?' prompted Raven.

'I was just coming to that.' Dinsdale pointed to the photographs of two blonde women. At first glance they looked remarkably similar – flawless faces framed by long, silky hair; startlingly blue eyes; brows plucked to a thin line; long black eyelashes; ruby red lips. 'Tanya Ayres and Jenny Jones. Both aged twenty-four. They worked at what, in polite society, you might call a gentlemen's club.'

'And what would you call it?' asked Raven.

'A strip joint.'

'Familiar with the place?' Raven was unable to resist the jibe.

'Only in the line of duty,' Dinsdale countered peevishly. 'As I was saying, they were dancers at a club called the *Mayfair.*'

'Pole dancers?' asked Becca.

'I believe that's the term.' Dinsdale's distaste was plain for all to see.

Raven wondered if attitudes to what the women did for a living had prejudiced the investigation in any way. 'Tell us what happened to them,' he said.

'Tanya was the first to be killed. She was found in her flat by a neighbour who popped in to feed the cat. Multiple stab wounds to the chest. What you might call a "frenzied attack".'

'And Jenny Jones?'

'She was killed a year later. Her body was also discovered in her flat, but in her case she wasn't found until two weeks after she went missing.'

'Did no one look for her?' Becca sounded indignant, and rightly so. 'Surely, after Tanya's death, a missing woman who worked at the same club should have been a high priority.'

Dinsdale dismissed the idea with a wave of his hand. 'Jenny had always been a bit flaky, apparently. When she didn't show up for work, everyone assumed she'd buggered off. Women in that line of work aren't always the most conscientious. They come and go, it's how they are.'

Becca shook her head, her anger plain to read.

'But someone was convicted of their murders,' said Raven. 'Tell us about him.'

'Terry Baines. The owner of the club. A sleazy character, just the kind of lowlife you'd expect to find running a place like that. The DCI in charge of the investigation liked him for Tanya's murder right from the start, but there was the tricky matter of evidence, or rather the lack of it. He was arrested and brought in for questioning but he managed to cover his tracks too well. It wasn't until after the second murder that we had enough to charge him. He got what he deserved too. Life imprisonment.'

'What was his motive for the killings?' asked Raven.

'Sexual assault.'

'So what happened to the club after Terry was convicted? Did it close down?'

'Oh, no, it's still going strong,' said Dinsdale. 'Terry's missus runs the place now. A Swedish woman. They go in for that kind of thing, don't they, those Scandinavians?'

'Do they?' Raven waited to see if Dinsdale had any further prejudices to get off his chest, but he seemed to be content for the moment with what he'd said. 'How does Caitlin fit into all this?'

'She worked at the club too, but not as a dancer. She was behind the bar.'

'And why was no one convicted for her murder? Surely this Terry Baines must have been a strong suspect?'

'Aye, he was arrested and charged. The SIO was convinced he'd done it. He would have nailed the bastard for it too, but proceedings against Baines were dropped in Caitlin's case because of insufficient evidence.'

'Sounds like they didn't look hard enough,' said Raven.

'I can assure you that we looked damn hard,' said Dinsdale, his eyes narrowing to slits, 'but the Crown Prosecution Service decided otherwise.'

'Which is why,' concluded Raven, 'eight years later, Scott Newhouse was carrying out his own investigation into Caitlin's death.'

'So what are you thinking?' asked Dinsdale. 'That his murder is somehow connected to his mother's?'

'We have to keep an open mind.'

Dinsdale's mouth turned down at the corners, his scepticism plain to see. 'Terry Baines is safely behind bars. Or do you want me to phone the prison governor to check he's still banged up? Since we're keeping an open mind?'

Raven regarded him with hostility. He was already thoroughly regretting his decision to get Dinsdale involved. 'Let's try not to jump to conclusions. Someone killed Scott, and the fact that he was stabbed suggests a possible link with the three other murders. Now let's begin from first principles. Tony, once you've finished working through Scott's files, could I ask you to get hold of his mobile phone records?'

'I'll get onto it, sir.'

'And what about CCTV down at the harbour?'

'There isn't any, I already checked. Maybe the killer knew that and arranged to meet Scott there because of it.'

'There's one more thing you could do for me, Tony. Find an address for Scott's friend, this Cameron Blake.'

'I'm onto it, sir.'

'Derek, could I ask you to dig out the original files for the deaths of Tanya, Jenny and Caitlin? I'd like you to prepare a summary of the evidence against Terry Baines in each case.'

'If you insist,' muttered Dinsdale.

'And what about me?' Becca asked.

'I want us to get up to speed on these historic murders, and go and speak to Terry's wife.'

'You want to pay a visit to the pole dancing club?' said

Becca, one eyebrow raised inquisitively.

'If you don't mind.'

'Not if it's in the line of duty.' Becca treated him to a quick smile. Or was that possibly a smirk?

CHAPTER 10

The heart-stopping sight of a young woman hanging upside down from a vertical pole with gravity-defying weightlessness was enough to stop Raven in his tracks. Wearing little more than black underwear complete with stockings, suspenders and high heels, her long hair cascaded to the floor like a golden waterfall.

'I'd probably end up in the emergency department if I tried that,' remarked Becca.

Raven was reminded of the assault courses he'd been put through while training to be a soldier. Fine as a sixteen-year-old lad with energy to spare and a ton of self-loathing to work out of his system. Nowadays he struggled to walk up and down Scarborough's many hills without the twinge in his leg refusing to let him forget his army days. The pole dancer's lithe body made him feel ancient. He watched mesmerised for a few moments longer before dragging his eyes away from the performance.

The *Mayfair* may not have been open for business at eleven o'clock in the morning, but there was still plenty going on. Cleaners were hard at work vacuuming the carpet, polishing the mahogany tables and shining the chrome fittings. The smell of leather and polish masked a pervasive undertone of stale whisky and beer.

The place was more upmarket in appearance than Raven had expected, and appeared to be aiming for the feel of a country house library crossed with a Parisian café. Chesterfield sofas and chairs upholstered in brown leather huddled in groups around bistro tables. Mirrors and bookcases covered the exposed brick walls. The lighting was expensive, managing to appear bright and decadent while still swathing the corners in an inviting darkness. Music blared out from hidden speakers. The building had no windows, but Raven imagined that the club's patrons came here to feast their eyes on a very different kind of view.

He approached the dancefloor, where the dancer on the pole appeared to be practising her moves or maybe auditioning for a job. Up close, Raven could see that the young woman was perspiring as she contorted herself around the pole, her body glistening with sweat. She grunted with each move, the illusion of effortless grace broken at close quarters. A second, older woman was shouting instructions to her, giving her quite a workout.

'Relax your neck and facial muscles, Jade. Don't grit your teeth. Try to look like you're enjoying it. That's better. Now slide slowly... I said *slowly*. Okay, next I want you to show me a firefly spin. Can you do that?'

Jade returned her feet to the floor and stood gasping for breath. 'I'll try.' To her credit she seemed undaunted by the relentless demands of her instructor. She tossed her blonde hair over her shoulder and grasped the pole with one hand, preparing for her next manoeuvre.

'Excuse me,' said Raven before she had a chance to launch herself into the air once more.

The older woman turned round sharply and her eyes took him in at a glance. 'I'm sorry, you'll have to come back. We're not open to patrons until this evening.' Dark-haired and slim, Raven guessed she was in her late thirties. Her sleeveless sports top showed off muscled upper arms patterned with a tattoo of interlocking chains.

'We're not patrons.' Raven produced his warrant card. 'We'd like to speak to the manager.'

'Frida?' The woman lifted her plucked eyebrows. 'I'll take you through to the office. Keep practising,' she called to Jade before leading Raven and Becca to the back of the club. A studded red leather door marked "private" led into a narrow, windowless corridor. She knocked on another door, opened it a fraction and stuck her head through the gap.

'What is it, Dani?' The voice from behind the door was sophisticated and clearly articulated, with a melodic intonation.

'Cops here to see you.'

'All right. Thanks. Send them in.'

If the main part of the club was determinedly masculine in feel, the sight that greeted Raven now was an oasis of graceful femininity. He and Becca entered a stylish room of the sort that could have featured in the pages of a glossy magazine. Two sofas covered in pastel-coloured scatter cushions faced each other across a glass-topped coffee table on which stood a vase of lilies filling the office with their heavy scent. Fitted shelves in light wood displayed artfully arranged books, ornaments and framed photographs. A stylised oil painting of a female nude, her back to the viewer, hung on the wall behind the desk. And the opposite wall held what seemed to be the building's only window, allowing natural light to flood the room.

The woman who rose to greet them was tall and slim with long blonde hair that fell over her shoulders. Prominent cheekbones gave her face a sculpted look as if she were made from marble and might shatter if struck. She wore a black trouser suit with high heels, simultaneously feminine and business-like. She approached Raven with an enquiring look and extended a perfectly manicured hand. 'Frida Baines. How may I help you?' The owner of the *Mayfair* had a natural self-assurance and didn't appear remotely disconcerted by the arrival of the police in her club.

Raven took her hand and introduced himself and Becca. Frida was a match for him in height and he found himself looking directly into her clear, sapphire eyes, something he rarely experienced with women. He wouldn't have liked to guess her age. With her classical beauty she could have been anywhere in her forties or fifties. Younger or older than himself? He couldn't say. There was an agelessness about her, a combination of good genes and meticulous grooming. 'What do you want to see me about, Chief Inspector?'

'A man's body was discovered yesterday morning in Scarborough harbour.'

Raven watched closely for a reaction to his abrupt statement. She remained calm, just tilting her head to one side as she considered the matter. 'I saw it on the news,' she acknowledged. 'Very unfortunate, I'm sure. But what has that got to do with me?'

Raven noted that she hadn't asked whose body had been found. 'We believe there may be a link to the murders of Tanya Ayres, Jenny Jones and Caitlin Newhouse.'

Frida's eyes flicked from Raven to Becca then back again. She appeared puzzled. 'Those murders took place seven years ago – no, eight – how could they possibly be connected?'

'I was hoping you might be able to help us determine that by answering a few questions,' said Raven.

'Very well, but if we're going to get into that, I think we should have coffee first.' She gestured towards the sofas. 'Why don't you take a seat while I make some?' Her voice had a siren-like quality that Raven found hard to resist. He took a seat on the nearest sofa as she crossed the room to where an espresso machine was tucked into a corner behind the desk. 'How do you take it?'

'Black for me.'

Frida operated the machine with smooth, practised movements and Raven waited patiently as black liquid hissed and steamed into a small white cup.

'Does your fancy machine brew tea?' asked Becca.

A smile twitched the corners of Frida's lips. 'I'm sure it can be persuaded to.' She selected another pod from a rack and inserted it into the machine. She returned with three cups and placed them on the glass table. Taking a seat opposite, she crossed one long leg over the other.

Raven suspected that the ritual of preparing drinks had been a tactic to give her time to sift her memories and gather her thoughts. She didn't seem to be the kind of person who enjoyed being caught off-guard. 'I'd like to start with Tanya and Jenny, if you don't mind,' he said. 'What can you tell us about them?'

Frida assumed a pose of studied casualness. 'What do you want to hear? They were dancers at the club. Tanya had been with us for three years, Jenny only six months when she died. They were both extremely good at what they did. Contrary to public perception, pole dancing takes hours of daily practice and skill to perform well. Good dancers have the stamina and flexibility of top-flight athletes. There are calls for pole dancing to be included at the Olympics.'

The statement had the ring of a prepared speech, as if she was used to hearing criticism and had decided to get her own defence in first. Her voice was clear, with an over-precise intonation, perhaps compensating too hard for not being a native speaker. Or maybe that was how all Swedish people spoke English.

It was a very pleasant voice to listen to.

'Their deaths must have come as a tragic shock,' said Raven sympathetically.

'It was dreadful.' Her voice betrayed raw emotion for the first time and Raven sensed a heart of fire beating beneath that composed exterior. He was beginning to suspect that her cool outward appearance might merely be an armour to protect herself against the ravages of a cruel world.

As Becca stirred milk and sugar into her tea, Raven reached for his coffee and took a sip. It was good. Black, bitter and strong, good for sharpening his mind. 'Tell me about that time,' he said.

Frida stirred her coffee with a silver spoon and set it down on her saucer. 'Tanya and Jenny were two of our first dancers. They were both extremely popular with the patrons. Dani – the girl who brought you in to see me just now – was also a dancer back then. She was very close to the other girls, like family. Now she auditions and trains young hopefuls. So many girls have ambitions of becoming dancers, but the bar to entry is high. We only take the best.'

'How long has the club been running?'

'Almost twelve years. We've grown in popularity over that time. Now we have more than a dozen dancers working here. We cater for tourists, stag nights, lads' nights out. And we have our loyal, regular clientèle too. We stay busy all year round.'

'You started the club with your husband, Terry,' prompted Becca.

'I did,' Frida acknowledged. 'And now I run it alone.' She regarded Becca with an unflinching stare, as if challenging her to offer some criticism of her choice of career. 'I divorced Terry seven years ago after he was convicted of Tanya and Jenny's murders. But surely you already knew that, Sergeant?'

She spoke directly, with no attempt whatsoever to defend her ex-husband. But why should she? He had killed two of her dancers after sleeping with them. She was a victim here too.

'How did you and Terry meet?' Raven was more than a little curious about how a Swedish woman could have ended up in Scarborough, married to a Yorkshireman and running a pole dancing club.

Frida sipped her coffee, licking her lips to remove a speckle of froth. 'I came to this country at the age of eighteen to improve my English. I come from Sweden, perhaps you already knew?' Her tone was playful.

'And why Scarborough?'

'Why not? I liked the beaches, the countryside, the

quaint little houses by the harbour. And, you know, the Vikings came here a long time ago. Perhaps I felt at home.'

Raven was descended from Viking stock himself, or at least that was the legend that had been handed down to him. *Raven* was certainly a Viking name, derived from the Old Norse. But he had never visited Sweden, or any Scandinavian country for that matter. He pictured long dark winters and bright white summers. Forests and lakes. Clean cities and wholesome people. Abba.

There was probably more to it than that.

'And you chose to stay here?'

'I was waitressing, working in bars and hotels. I met Terry and fell in love.' Frida gave a self-deprecating smile in mockery of her younger self. 'Terry was a charming man, handsome in a roguish way. He had a gift for telling women exactly what they wanted to hear. He was very passionate. Passion drove him in everything he did. From setting up in business to… to the events that landed him in prison. He was a few years older than me and already a successful businessman when we first met. He owned a large share in the bar where I was working. With the profit from selling that, we founded the *Mayfair* together. We married and became business partners. What more is there to say?'

Quite a lot, Raven guessed.

'What did Terry see in you?' asked Becca. 'I mean, what business skills did you bring to the partnership?'

Frida regarded her with a wry smile. 'I knew what men wanted. I still do.' Her smile became sultry and she turned it in Raven's direction.

He drained the last of his coffee and set his cup and saucer down with a clatter. 'How would you describe Terry's relationship with Tanya and Jenny?'

Frida's composure didn't change. 'You're asking if he was in the habit of having affairs? As I said, Terry was a passionate man. He adored women and liked to spend time in their company.'

'He was sleeping with the two murdered women?'

'They weren't his first, and they wouldn't have been his last. But Terry would never have left me.'

Raven wasn't sure why someone as independent as Frida had chosen to stay with an unfaithful partner. Especially one like Terry, who had clearly been a serial adulterer. A sleazy lowlife, according to Dinsdale. But love was a powerful force. It could make you do anything.

'You kept your husband's surname after your divorce,' pointed out Becca. 'Why was that?'

'It just seemed easier that way,' said Frida. 'My maiden name isn't easy for English people to pronounce correctly.'

'Why do you think he killed them?' asked Raven. 'Tanya and Jenny.'

Frida inclined her head towards him and bit her lip. It was the first time he'd seen her hesitate. Perhaps his question had been too direct. 'Terry's passion wasn't always' – she sought for the right word – 'tender.'

'You mean he was violent?'

'When he'd had too much to drink he found it hard to control himself.' She touched her cheek with one hand, flinching as if recalling some act of brutality.

Raven fell silent. Frida's words had touched a raw nerve. His own father had been free with his fists when he'd had one too many. Which was every night of the week. A vision of his mother cowering in a corner, her hands raised to shield herself, pushed its way unbidden into his mind's eye and he felt an anger grow within him.

The same anger that had turned his father into an unthinking brute.

Raven's greatest fear was of becoming like his father, a man he despised even beyond the grave. He often wished he'd stood up to Alan Raven and done more to defend his mother. It was too late for Jean Raven now, but not too late for him to protect other women in her position. If Terry had killed those women and laid a finger on Frida, Raven hoped he would rot in prison.

'Caitlin Newhouse also worked here, didn't she?' said Becca.

'Yes, but not as a dancer.' A sad expression shaped Frida's features. 'Poor Caitlin, she came from a difficult background. She was Dani's friend and started working here as a cleaner during the daytime when her little boy was at school. In the school holidays she would bring him along and he would sit at one of the tables with his colouring books while she cleaned. Such a sweet little thing. When Scott was old enough to be left at home she moved on to bar work in the evenings because it paid better. I was so sorry for him when Caitlin died. I wished I could have done more for him, but he disappeared into the care system.'

Raven steeled himself to break the news to her. 'I'm afraid it was Scott Newhouse's body that was found in the harbour yesterday. We're treating his death as murder.'

'Oh, no!' Frida's hand flew to her mouth. 'I had no idea.'

Raven studied the blue eyes now moistened by tears. 'That's why we're investigating the possibility of a connection to Caitlin's death.'

Frida seemed dumbfounded. She sat bolt upright, staring at the far wall. 'You think the person who killed Caitlin also killed Scott?'

'It's one avenue of our investigation.'

'But...' a frown creased Frida's smooth forehead as she turned over the implications, 'then what about Terry? I always assumed that he killed her.'

'Your husband wasn't convicted for Caitlin's murder,' said Raven carefully.

'But the police told me that Terry killed her too. That's what I've believed all these years.' She turned back to look at Raven, her eyes still filled with tears. 'I find it very hard to think otherwise.'

CHAPTER 11

It wasn't easy for Becca to understand why a woman would be running a place like this – a club that catered exclusively to a male clientèle. A venue that indulged their fantasies, exploiting the young women who danced for their pleasure. It would take a certain kind of woman to choose to run a pole dancing club. But Frida Baines was certainly a strong and determined individual, the sort who could handle the sort of girls who worked at such a club, and the patrons they attracted.

Becca wondered how old she really was.

Fifty plus, she guessed, but resolutely determined not to show it. Beneath the layers of carefully-applied makeup and the Botox treatments, time had wrought its damage the way it did to all mortal flesh. Yet even at her age she was a striking woman, the sort who would turn heads whenever she walked down the street. It hadn't escaped Becca's notice how she had captivated Raven from the start of the interview, how he had lingered on her every word, how he had hardly been able to drag his eyes away from her.

It was like she had cast a kind of spell on him.

What was it she'd said? *I know what men want.* Well, she had clearly demonstrated that particular skill already.

As Frida escorted Becca and Raven back into the main body of the club, the dance session was just wrapping up. 'You did well, Jade,' Dani was telling her protégée. 'We can definitely use a dancer like you.'

The younger woman's eyes lit up. 'So can I hand in my notice at the arcade?'

'Sure. You can start work tonight, if you like. Now go and get some rest. You'll need it.'

Jade went off to get changed, and Frida approached Dani. 'How did she get on?'

'Not too bad. Let's give her a chance to see how quickly she can learn. Find out what the punters make of her.'

The punters. Becca tried to imagine what it must be like to have all those male eyes observing and judging your near-naked body. She had been impressed by Jade's athleticism and agility, but she knew that wasn't what drew the men here. She couldn't resist asking a question that had been bothering her since arriving at the club.

'These dancers, do they just perform on the poles, or are they expected to' – how best to phrase it? – 'come into more intimate contact with the patrons?'

Frida caught her meaning immediately and was quick to rebuff her suggestion. 'This is not a lap dancing club. There's strictly no physical contact between the dancers and the patrons. We have a public entertainment licence, not a sex establishment licence.'

'And they don't strip naked?'

'Definitely not. We have rules about what our dancers are allowed to wear.'

From what Becca had seen so far, the rules didn't seem to be terribly strict – Jade had been wearing little more than bra and panties, plus an outrageously tall pair of heels – but she felt better knowing that the dancers weren't expected to remove all their clothes. Dinsdale might have described the club as a strip joint, but Becca put that down to his general ignorance and prejudice.

The cleaners had finished their work and preparations were being made for the evening ahead. Thankfully the music had been turned off, the only sound now the gentle clink of glasses and bottles as the bar was restocked.

Frida took Raven's hand once more and bade farewell. 'I hope your visit proved to be useful, Chief Inspector.'

'Thank you. You've been very helpful.'

Becca watched his gaze linger on her as she returned to her office. Reluctantly his eyes peeled away from the leather door as it closed. He seemed ready to leave, but Becca hadn't yet satisfied her curiosity. 'Have you got a moment, Dani?' she asked the – for want of a better term – *dancing instructor*. 'I wonder if we could have a quick word with you before we go.'

Dani looked surprised, but led the way over to one of the booths, a semi-circular banquette arranged around a circular table with a good view of the raised dais and pole. VIP seating, Becca guessed, the kind that would be reserved for a high-spending and presumably high-tipping group of punters. Dani took a seat and motioned for Becca and Raven to join her.

Of slim build and average height, Dani was in her late thirties, but with the kind of suppleness and grace that could only be maintained by a rigorous regime of daily exercise. Unlike Frida's pale complexion, she was olive-skinned with dark hair. Her upper arms were decorated in ink with a stylised knot design.

'I like your tattoos,' said Becca.

'Thanks. They're Celtic knots.' When Becca said nothing Dani added, 'Symbols of love, loyalty and friendship.' She held out her hands, showing matching designs on the back of each.

'Nice.' Becca had once thought of getting a tattoo done. Nothing showy – police officers weren't allowed to have visible tattoos or facial piercings – but a small, hidden mark that would forever remind her of Sam. Now she was glad she'd had second thoughts.

'What do you want to talk to me about?' asked Dani.

'Frida said you were a friend of Caitlin Newhouse.'

'Yeah, that's right. We were at school together.' Dani looked from Becca to Raven. 'What's this about?'

Becca waited to see if Raven would volunteer any information, but it looked like it was going to be down to her to break the news. Well, she was used to that. Police officers rarely came bearing good tidings. 'I'm afraid we have some bad news regarding Caitlin's son.'

'Scott? Why? What's happened to him?'

'His body was recovered from the harbour yesterday morning.'

'His body? Scott?' Dani covered her nose and mouth with her hands and shrank back against the leather upholstery, her eyes filling with tears. 'You can't be serious. Please, tell me this is some kind of cruel joke!'

'I'm very sorry.' Becca fished in her pocket for a packet of tissues, pulled one out and passed it to Dani. Really, all officers should carry tissues as part of their standard kit. She glanced at Raven who sat helplessly at the other end of the banquette. Becca had never seen him pass anyone a tissue. She gave Dani a moment or two to compose herself then asked, 'How well did you know Scott?'

'I've known him all his life,' said Dani. 'Caitlin was only sixteen when she had him. She was so young. Well, we both were back then. But we thought we knew it all. You do at that age, don't you?'

Becca acknowledged the remark with a nod, even though her own teenage years had been somewhat different to how she pictured Caitlin and Dani's. She'd worked hard at school and had helped her mum and dad with the guest house, not to mention having a Saturday job on top. At sixteen, the idea of having a baby had been unimaginable.

'What was Caitlin's family background?'

Dani gave her a shrewd look, as if guessing that Becca's own childhood had been rather different to her friend's. 'Caitlin's parents split up when she was small. When Caitlin got pregnant, her mum didn't want to know. She turfed her out, said she wasn't having a baby in the house and Caitlin needed to find a place of her own. The old cow died a couple of years back. Good riddance to her!'

'What about Scott's father?' asked Becca.

Dani scoffed. 'Don't get me started on that waste of space! He was useless even when he was around, and he vanished for good when Scott was still a toddler.' Mention of Scott's name set her off again. Becca handed her a fresh tissue.

'Frida told us that you helped Caitlin get the job at the club.'

Dani nodded. 'Yeah, I started dancing here when I was eighteen. It's what I'd always wanted to do. Obviously Caitlin couldn't do anything like that, not after she'd had a kid. You need a washboard stomach to perform those routines. It's all about core strength.' She patted her own flat stomach. 'No one wants to look at a woman's stretch marks.'

Becca glanced down at her own stomach, which was anything but flat and was growing steadily rounder. Too many of her mum's cooked breakfasts. Too many unhealthy meals and snacks while at work. Not enough exercise.

Might as well face facts – no exercise at all.

She turned to Raven to see if he had anything to ask, but he merely nodded encouragingly at Becca to keep talking. 'So Caitlin worked as a cleaner?' she prompted.

'At first,' said Dani. 'Then, as soon as Scott was old enough to be left at home on his own she started doing bar work in the evenings.'

'How old would Scott have been then?'

'About ten.'

'Ten.' In Becca's opinion, ten was a bit young for a child to be left at home, but there was no law in the UK that said you couldn't leave a child of that age alone if they were mature enough, whatever that meant. Anyway, it was a bit late to worry about Caitlin's parenting style. No doubt she'd done the best she could under difficult circumstances. And Scott had made it to adulthood unscathed.

Until now.

'Did Caitlin enjoy working here?'

'Enjoy it? She needed the money, didn't she?' Dani shot Becca a look that said she had no idea what it was like to be a single mum surviving on benefits. 'But yes, Caitlin liked working behind the bar, and she was popular with the punters. Very pretty, she was, with all that lovely blonde hair.'

'How well did you know Tanya Ayres and Jenny Jones?'

Dani's eyes clouded over again. 'Really well. There were just a few of us dancers back then. We were like sisters.'

'Were you aware at the time that Terry Baines was having a relationship with them?'

A sneer passed over Dani's face. 'Oh, everyone knew that. Terry wasn't exactly subtle about hitting on women.'

'And what about Caitlin?'

Dani scowled. 'You couldn't put Terry in a room with an attractive girl without him trying it on.'

'Yet Frida stuck with him despite his affairs,' said Becca.

'Terry had a kind of magnetism about him. It was hard for her to stay angry with him for long. Plus, Swedish people are more open-minded about that sort of thing, aren't they?'

Raven leaned in and asked a question at last. 'Do you have any doubts about whether Terry killed Tanya and Jenny?'

Dani looked surprised. 'Of course not.'

'And what about Caitlin?'

'Who else might have done it?' Dani wiped her eyes clear and turned them defiantly in Raven's direction. 'If the police had done their job properly, he would have been convicted of her murder too.'

Dani's attitude had turned markedly hostile, which wasn't surprising given the way the police had messed up the case against her best friend's killer. The interview seemed to be over, and Becca stood up, thanking Dani for her time.

'Any thoughts?' Raven asked her on the way out.

'I think we're wasting our time here,' said Becca. 'All the evidence points to Terry Baines having killed all three women.'

'Maybe,' said Raven. His phone pinged with an incoming message and he turned the screen so that she could see the address that Tony had just sent. 'Let's try a different angle then. Ready for another interview?'

CHAPTER 12

Raven glanced up at the house on Filey Road, his forehead creasing into a puzzled frown. It wasn't at all what he'd been expecting.

Clearly Becca was thinking the same. 'Are you sure this is the right place?' she asked.

'It's the address Tony sent me.'

The large redbrick house – either Edwardian or nineteen-twenties, Raven was never sure of these things – occupied a substantial plot screened from the road by a high hedge. It was in stark contrast to the cramped flat on Trafalgar Road that Scott had called home. Yet according to Tony's intel, Cameron Blake, Scott's best friend from the children's home, had never held a full-time job since leaving the home at the age of eighteen. It seemed highly unlikely that he could afford to live in a place this grand.

'Well, we'd better go and check it out,' said Becca, pushing the car door open and stepping out.

Raven joined her and they crunched their way together up the garden path. On closer inspection the house was a little ramshackle and not as smart as first impressions had suggested. Paint was peeling from the front door. The wood of the window frames was beginning to rot. The garden, however, was well cared for in a chaotic kind of way, with a throng of spring bulbs poking their heads above ground in cautious preparation for a big show if the weather proved not too dispiriting in the weeks ahead.

A wind chime jangled in the breeze and was quickly joined by another in discordant clanging. Raven strode up to the front porch before any more could join in, and leaned his thumb on the doorbell.

After a short wait, creaking floorboards heralded the approach of the house's occupant. But it wasn't a young man who appeared in the doorway. Instead the door was opened by a woman for whom the term "ageing hippie" might have been specially coined. In her late sixties with flowing grey hair, she wore a long dress of purple velvet embroidered with flowers, a multi-strand necklace of turquoise beads looping her neck. A heady scent of patchouli and other pungent aromas followed her out from the dark interior of the house. Raven wondered if he detected a hint of weed.

The woman scrutinised Raven and Becca through large tortoiseshell-framed glasses. 'Yes?' Her tone was cool. Not exactly unfriendly, but not welcoming. Well spoken. Not a local.

Raven politely introduced himself and Becca. But at the sight of his warrant card the woman's apprehensive expression turned unmistakeably hostile. 'Police? What do you want with me?' She gripped the edge of her door protectively, as if expecting them to make a sudden baton charge inside. Raven wondered if she had encountered the police before, perhaps on a peace march or an anti-nuclear protest during her more youthful days.

'We're looking for Cameron Blake,' he explained. 'Does he live here?'

Her expression turned frostier still. 'I don't have to answer your questions. I know my rights.'

'I'm sure you do, Mrs ...?' Raven waited politely, allowing an expectant silence to stretch out.

The woman frowned in annoyance but was unable to stop herself from finishing his sentence. 'Gibson. Veronica Gibson. And it's Miss.'

'Thank you, Miss Gibson. I can assure you that Cameron isn't in any kind of trouble. But we do have some news for him.'

'Well if you tell me what it is, I'll be sure to pass it on.'

'It's a personal matter, I'm afraid,' said Raven. 'We need to speak to him ourselves.'

A ginger cat appeared in the hallway and padded forwards, wrapping its tail around Veronica's ankle. She reached down to give it a stroke. 'There, there, Thumbelina, there's no need to be afraid. It's the police, come to see Cameron. I'm not sure we should let them in. What do you think?'

The cat said nothing, of course, just blinked slowly.

'Cameron does live here, doesn't he?' prompted Becca.

Veronica's resolve to be unhelpful was beginning to waver. 'Yes,' she conceded. 'I'm his landlady.'

'May we come inside?' asked Becca.

Veronica gripped the door tighter and the cat slinked away into the depths of the house. 'I don't have to let you in unless you have a search warrant. Do you have one?'

'No,' said Raven growing tired of the woman's hindrance. 'But we do need to speak to Cameron ourselves.' He flashed her what he hoped was a persuasive smile. 'If you don't mind.'

A second cat emerged from a side room and came to the threshold, giving the air a delicate sniff. Veronica scooped it up in her arms protectively, as if afraid Raven might take it hostage.

'What's her name?' asked Becca, reaching out to touch the cat. She ran her hand along its spine and it began to purr in contentment.

'Cornelius,' said Veronica. 'It's a he.' She allowed Becca to stroke the cat but remained suspicious, especially of Raven to whom she gave a particularly dark look. 'Cameron doesn't actually live in the house. He rents an annexe at the bottom of the garden.' She subjected Raven to a final scrutinising gaze before acquiescing. 'Come on, I'll show you.'

Still cradling the cat, she led the way around the side of the house, where rambling roses and other climbers valiantly scaled the brickwork, covering the upper windows and competing with each other to reach to the rooftop. The rear garden was even bigger than Raven had expected and was crammed with so many varieties of plants that Veronica must be single-handedly doing more for Scarborough's biodiversity than all its other residents combined. A lawn may have grown here once, but now there was only a narrow labyrinth of bark-covered pathways winding their way between dense knots of shrubs and flowers. If there was a pattern to the planting, Raven couldn't spot it.

'What exactly do you want to speak to Cameron about?' asked Veronica as she picked her way along the paths.

'I'm afraid I can't tell you that,' said Raven.

'It's just that he's a very sensitive individual. He had a traumatic upbringing. His parents died and then he was sent to live in a children's home.'

'We're aware of his background,' said Raven. 'Can you tell me how you came to know him?'

Veronica stopped beneath a holly tree, setting the cat down. Her nails were turquoise, the fingers heavily decorated with silver rings. 'I discovered him at a craft fair,' she said, making him sound like a piece of artwork himself. 'He was virtually homeless when I met him, drifting from one place to another, sleeping on other people's sofas. He needed a safe environment where he could get on with his work. I was happy to provide that space for him.'

'What kind of work does he do?' asked Becca.

It was the right question to ask. Veronica clapped her hands together in enthusiasm, making her necklace clatter. 'Oh, Cameron's the most wonderfully creative person. He makes sculptures and jewellery out of driftwood he collects from the beach.' She drew back the sleeve of her dress to reveal a set of bracelets made from wooden beads decorated with tiny stars and moons. 'Aren't they exquisite?' She didn't wait for an answer, but continued, 'He's been with me for a couple of years now, and I've been able to give him the security he needs to create and to find healing.'

They had come to the end of the garden. Almost hidden from view beneath the tangle of greenery was a flat-roofed outbuilding with white rendered walls. It might once have been a store or a workshop. A thin curl of smoke emerged from a metal chimney.

'This is where Cameron lives.' Veronica stood in front of the door as if still hoping to find a way to keep the police at bay. She wrung her hands together. 'I do hope you're not going to tell him anything too distressing.'

Raven gave her a reassuring smile. 'We'll do our best to break our news gently, Miss Gibson. But now, if you don't mind, we'll take it from here.'

★

Raven knocked at the door of the annexe but no answer came. After a moment's wait he pushed at the door and found it unlocked. The door swung open and he stepped inside, finding himself in what appeared to be an open-plan studio and bedsit. At one end was living space: a single bed, an old sofa, a tiny kitchen area with a table and two unmatched chairs. At the other end stood a series of large wooden workbenches. A log stove was belting out heat in one corner, but still the room felt cold. Hardly surprising since the windows rattled in their frames as the door swung shut behind him.

The division between workspace and accommodation appeared fluid, with pieces of driftwood and the tools of Cameron's trade – chisels, hand saws, sanders, files, a hammer – spread out all around. A health and safety nightmare, not that Raven cared about such things. He was happy to leave all that to the box-tickers of the world. Stepping around an ancient wooden ladder propped against the wall he approached the nearest workbench.

A thin young man wearing safety goggles leaned over the bench, a piece of blackened wood spinning on a lathe. The whine of the machine tool as it cut into the wood was enough to drown out all conversation and explained why Raven's knocking had gone unanswered.

'Cameron Blake?'

The man looked up, a startled look spreading across his face, like a rabbit caught in the glare of car headlamps. He was little more than a boy. Twenty-one, but still with the slight build and uncertain bearing of a teenager. He flipped a switch and the hiss of the lathe died quickly to a whisper. 'Who are you? What do you want?' The lad grabbed a chisel and held it up in a protective gesture. 'Don't come any closer.'

Raven lifted his hands in a genial manner. 'We're the police, Cameron. No need to be afraid. Your landlady, Miss Gibson, showed us here.'

Cameron lifted his goggles to reveal sad, dark eyes that viewed Raven and Becca with something akin to fear. If the boy's body seemed too young for his age, then his eyes carried the cares and worries of someone far older. Too old. 'Veronica? What have you done with her? Have you arrested her?'

Raven spoke soothingly. 'Of course not, Cameron. She's just gone back to the house with her cats. She said we'd find you here, doing your woodwork.'

At mention of his work, Cameron visibly relaxed. He placed the chisel on the bench and removed the piece of wood he'd been turning on the lathe. 'I'm making a chess set.'

Raven took the piece from him and admired it. 'Nice.'

More pieces were arranged on the bench and dozens of wooden carvings and sculptures stood on shelves against the back wall. Animals, trees, flowers and abstract forms. Items of jewellery hung from hooks or were spread over the worktops and tables, even in the kitchen area. Some were still in their natural finish, others were painted or varnished. Still more had been merged with recycled or reclaimed objects to create unique works of art. The variety was bewildering.

'Perhaps you'd like to sit down,' said Becca. 'We have some news for you.'

'For me?' Cameron moved to the living end of the annexe and took a seat on what looked like an old bar stool. 'What is it?'

'It's about your friend, Scott Newhouse.'

Cameron removed the goggles from his head and laid them in his lap. 'Is he dead?'

'Why would you ask that?' asked Raven.

Cameron shrugged. 'Why else would you be here?' The lad sounded like he was no stranger to tragic news. That it was only to be expected.

'You're right,' said Raven softly. 'I'm sorry to tell you, but yes, Scott's dead.' He sat down on one of the hard wooden chairs at the table and waited to see what Cameron would say.

But the lad continued to show little surprise at the revelation. He asked no questions, but simply said, 'Life's crap, isn't it? Just when you think it might be okay for a while, something else comes along to give you a good kicking. People like me and Scott, we never did anyone any harm, but shit just happens to us all the time.'

'You knew Scott from the children's home, didn't you?' asked Raven.

'Yeah. I lived in care for most of my life, from the age of six. Scott arrived later, when he was fourteen. We became good friends. He's the only real friend I've ever had.'

'I'm sorry,' said Raven.

'If you don't mind me asking, what happened to your parents?' said Becca.

Cameron sighed and looked away as if the answer was obvious. 'Dead.'

'When was the last time you saw Scott?' asked Raven

Cameron considered the question for a moment, staring at the flames that flickered behind the glass of the log burner. 'About a week ago. I didn't see him so much in recent months, not since he found himself a girlfriend. But he still used to call round sometimes after work.'

'Did you go anywhere together?'

He looked up. 'Like where?'

'I don't know. Anywhere.'

'We just stayed here,' said Cameron, his gaze returning to the fire.

'What did you talk about?'

'Just what we were up to. He was always interested in what I was making. He couldn't talk much about his own work. It was confidential.'

'Did you mind that he didn't come and see you so often in recent times?' asked Becca.

Cameron shook his head. 'No. I was glad he'd found someone. Jess was good for him. He was happy with her.'

'Did you ever meet her?'

'Just once.' A hesitant smile broke out across Cameron's face, lighting up his eyes. 'She was nice.'

Raven nodded at Becca to continue. 'Did Scott ever talk to you about his mum?' she asked.

'Sure. All the time.'

'What did he tell you?'

'That he would find out who killed her. That he would get justice for her.' Cameron turned his gaze to Raven, the smile fading from his lips. 'Is that what got him killed?'

'It's one possible line of inquiry.'

Cameron nodded as if that was exactly the sort of answer he'd expected – an evasive one.

Raven wished he could tell the lad more. But he scarcely knew any more himself. 'Did Scott have any enemies?'

The look of surprise on Cameron's face gave Raven his answer, but he said, 'Scott? No. Scott never did anything to make anyone hate him.'

'What about during his time at the children's home? Perhaps someone took a dislike to him there?'

Cameron's expression turned grim. 'I don't talk about that place.'

'Why not, Cameron?'

The lad's voice took on a harder edge. 'It's in the past. Leave it.'

Raven decided not to push it. Veronica had warned him to treat Cameron with care. 'Can you think of any reason why someone would want to hurt Scott?'

'Apart from the person who killed his mum, you mean? No.'

Raven hesitated. It seemed that once again he was being pushed in that direction, though whether he could attach much significance to Cameron's views remained to be seen. 'Did Scott have any theories about who might have killed her?'

Cameron ran a hand through his hair. 'He had lots of ideas. He put them on a board in his flat. If you go there you'll find it.'

'We've already seen Scott's evidence board.'

'Then you'll know what he thought, won't you?'

Raven wished that he did know what Scott thought. So far all he'd been able to fathom of Scott's investigation was the suggestion of a link with the murders of Tanya Ayres and Jenny Jones. But those two murders had been solved. Hadn't they?

He would have to wait for Tony to finish working through Scott's files to discover if he'd identified any fresh leads on Caitlin's death. For now, it seemed that he wasn't going to get any more out of Cameron. He stood and tried to give the lad a reassuring smile. 'Don't worry. We'll do our best to find your friend's killer. We'll leave no stone unturned.'

Cameron looked up, but his eyes were blank, empty of all hope. 'That's what the police told Scott when his mum was stabbed. They promised him they'd catch whoever did it, but they never did. Some people just get away with murder.'

CHAPTER 13

The knocking on the door sounded like nails being driven into the lid of a coffin. Jess started awake, not even aware that she had drifted off to sleep.

Her bedroom door creaked open and her mum popped her head around. 'Jess, love, were you sleeping?'

Jess looked at the time on her phone. Just after six in the evening. Somehow she had managed to fall asleep lying fully clothed on her bed. At night, by stark contrast, she was unable to grab even a moment's respite. She hadn't slept properly since the day Scott's body had been found. All she could see when she closed her eyes was his corpse half-submerged in mud at the bottom of the harbour.

'It's time for dinner,' said her mum. 'Are you hungry?'

Jess nodded dumbly. She ought to be hungry, she supposed. She'd had nothing to eat since... she didn't know when. Time had ceased to have meaning. It had slowed to a crawl, the seconds dragging out like minutes, the hours stretching to fill an entire lifetime of aching void. How many days was it since Scott had died? She really had no idea.

'You need to eat,' her mum said, bustling into the room

decisively. 'Jacob and Nicola are here again, and Dad's home too.'

Jacob and Nicola were Jess's brother and sister. They both lived locally so it was "no bother" for them to pop in for dinner, as they had assured her the previous day. Her dad worked as a vet at a practice in Kirkbymoorside and spent most of his time out on the road visiting local farms. What he didn't know about livestock wasn't worth knowing. Lambing season had begun, which meant long hours, so he had obviously made a big effort to be home in time for the evening meal.

A gathering of the family, everyone rallying around to be at Jess's side. She knew she ought to be grateful.

'Come on, Jess,' said her mum. 'It'll be on the table in five minutes.'

The door closed again and Jess lay staring at the ceiling. Oak beams, providing sturdy support. White plaster between them. An unchanging backdrop that had been there since long before she'd been born. If only human life could be so solid, so unyielding.

'Scott,' she whispered, but there was no answer to her plea.

She turned to the side, propping herself up on one elbow. She was still fully dressed. 'Got to get up,' she told herself. She didn't feel hungry, but she knew she had to drag her heavy limbs off the bed and somehow get downstairs. If she didn't, she might never move again.

The book that Scott had left her lay untouched on her bedside table, along with the sealed envelope with her name on it. She'd not yet found the strength to open it. She had cried enough tears already. Opening the letter might be more than she could bear.

She heaved her legs over the edge of the bed, feeling for the floor with her feet. With an effort she forced herself into a standing position and stumbled out onto the landing. The bathroom door beckoned to her, but the prospect of seeing her own tear-stained face in the mirror was too dreadful. Instead she gripped the banister and made her way downstairs.

The family was gathered together in the big farmhouse kitchen. The Aga had been at work, cooking venison steak and slow-roasting red cabbage. Jess knew that it would be served with fluffy mashed potato and thick homemade gravy. Most likely it would be followed by bread-and-butter pudding with custard. Her mum had made the same meal a hundred times when the children were growing up. It was as if nothing had changed.

And yet everything had changed.

'Jess!' Nicola crossed the kitchen and swept her into a huge hug. 'How are you feeling today? Any better?' Jess's older sister had always been a robust and hearty girl. She believed in "getting on with things" and tragedy had sensibly steered a wide berth around her. Jess had never seen her cry.

She eyed Nicola blankly, not knowing what to say. How did she feel? She had no idea. 'Yeah, good.' It was easier not to think. It was safer not to feel anything.

Her brother showed more empathy. He patted her lightly on the shoulder and gave her a kiss on the cheek. 'Come and sit down. I'm just opening a bottle of wine.'

She joined them at the table, sitting in her usual place, just as if she'd never been away. Those years in Scarborough, joining the police force, forging her own way in life, meeting Scott – had they ever happened? Or was it all a dream?

She thought back to Christmas – only a couple of months back, but feeling like another life entirely – when she'd brought Scott here for the first time to meet her relations. Not just her immediate family, but aunts, uncles, cousins and goodness knows who. She'd been so proud to introduce him to them, yet mindful of the fact that he had no family himself. They had welcomed him into their hearts, giving him a taste of what he'd missed growing up, showing him what might lie ahead if he and Jess settled down together. Got married. Started a family of their own. Now his absence felt like a black hole, swallowing all joy.

'More wine, Jess?'

She looked up and realised that she had swallowed a whole glass of red. Her plate lay before her, the food half-eaten. Had she eaten it? She couldn't remember. There was no recollection of taste on her tongue, no feeling of fullness in her belly.

No feeling anywhere.

She tried to tune into her surroundings, allowing Jacob to refill her glass, to listen to the constant stream of chatter about goings-on in the village. Her father told an anecdote about a flock of sheep escaping from a nearby farm. Her mother was full of the Easter celebrations being planned in the local church. Nicola had plenty to say about the new head at the primary school where she taught the reception class. Her brother had big ideas for the caravan site he managed.

Jess knew what they were doing.

By talking about Rosedale Abbey as if it were the centre of the universe they were reminding her that this was home. She may have moved all the way to Scarborough – some thirty miles or so – but this was where she truly belonged. And she could stay here, if she wanted.

Rosedale Abbey, where life went on much as it had always done. Where crime was virtually non-existent. And where people you loved didn't get brutally murdered.

But what did Jess want? The only thing she truly wanted was Scott, and if she couldn't have him, then she wanted nothing more than oblivion.

Her brother poured more wine.

Her dad rose to his feet and began collecting the dishes, politely saying nothing about the leftovers on Jess's plate.

Her sister looked on critically, as if Jess had somehow brought this on herself.

Her mum gave a smile. 'Bread-and-butter pudding anyone?'

★

The incident room was silent, save for the soft whirring of Raven's laptop. The room lay in shadow, with only the light from the lamp on his desk slicing a swathe through the darkness.

He had sent Becca and Tony home at eight o'clock. Dinsdale had needed no such prompting, having downed tools on the dot at five. Still, he'd done what Raven had asked him and had retrieved all the old case notes relating to the murder of Caitlin Newhouse and the two other women who had worked at the club. Now Raven was perusing them in peace.

The notes painted a sorry tale of police incompetence.

The body of the first victim, Tanya Ayres, had been found soon after her death by her neighbour. Raven studied the photographs that had been taken, showing vicious stab wounds all over the victim's torso. A post-mortem examination had found evidence of recent sexual activity, and Terry Baines, the owner of the club had been arrested the following day. Under questioning, Terry had admitted having sex with the murdered woman, but denied any involvement in her death. With no evidence to charge him, he had been released soon after. The case had grown cold.

Astonishingly, the body of the second victim, Jenny Jones, had lain undiscovered in her flat for two whole weeks after her death. It wasn't until Caitlin was stabbed to death and her body left in an alleyway that police had gone to Jenny's flat. Terry had been arrested again and this time a search of his home had led to the discovery of the murder weapon used to kill Jenny.

Terry's fingerprints and DNA were subsequently found at the scene of the crime, and an eye witness had placed him outside Jenny's flat on the day she had gone missing. With three murders under his belt, Terry had been charged and taken into custody to await trial.

Yet the story hadn't ended there. Evidence recovered from the scene of Caitlin's murder – her phone, the knife used to kill her, fingerprints, DNA and blood samples –

had all gone missing while in police custody. A subsequent investigation had found nothing – neither the actual evidence nor the reason for its disappearance. But the upshot was that the CPS had been obliged to drop charges against Terry for Caitlin's murder.

Intriguingly, while Terry was on remand awaiting trial, his cellmate had gone to the prison authorities claiming that Terry had made a full confession to the murder of Tanya Ayres and Jenny Jones. Terry later denied it, but it was just one more damning piece in the mounting pile of evidence against him.

The jury had unanimously found Terry guilty of two counts of murder. Meanwhile, Caitlin's case had gone unsolved for all these years. With no evidence to go on, it had grown completely cold. Until Scott had begun his own private investigation.

Raven noted down the name of the senior investigating officer at the time – a DCI Gareth Peel, now retired. It looked, from the date of his retirement, as if this had been his last big case.

Had the man cut corners in his eagerness to secure a conviction and go out in a blaze of glory? Raven had seen it happen during his years with the Met and Scarborough would be no different. The desire for adulation was the same wherever you went, and the higher someone climbed up the ladder the more they came to believe in their own greatness.

Or had Peel been quietly shunted into early retirement amid the fiasco of the missing evidence?

Dinsdale had talked about insufficient evidence in Caitlin's case, but that wasn't the whole truth by a long shot. The evidence hadn't been insufficient – it had vanished under mysterious circumstances while in police custody. Was Dinsdale's memory playing tricks on him, or had he purposely misrepresented the reason charges over Caitlin's death against Terry Baines had been dropped? Raven wondered what else Dinsdale might have misremembered.

The deeper he delved into the case, the more his sympathy for Scott grew. All these unanswered questions from the botched police investigation must have been a torment to him. No wonder the lad had been unwilling to let the matter drop. Let down by the authorities, he'd smelled the same rat as Raven, and had gone searching for it tirelessly. Had that trail led him ultimately to his own death?

It was up to Raven to find out.

CHAPTER 14

It might have been a Saturday, but everyone involved in the investigation was determined that work should continue regardless. Tony and Becca were both at their desks by half past eight in the morning, and by nine o'clock even Dinsdale had put in a reluctant appearance. Gillian, Raven knew, had already been in her office when he'd arrived first thing. She had said nothing to the team, not even a word of encouragement. But her presence was felt by everyone.

After their morning ritual of tea and coffee, they gathered in the incident room for a briefing. Raven was keen to find out what Tony had been up to and whether he had managed to make sense of Scott's own investigation. He really needed to get some insight into Scott's thinking. More to the point, he needed a lead. And quickly.

He kicked off the meeting by inviting the DC to fill them in on what he'd found.

It was unusual for Tony to find himself the centre of attention. He was more often the backroom boy. He took up position next to Scott's evidence board, pushed his glasses up the bridge of his nose and cleared his throat before beginning. 'So, I've worked through Scott's files and pieced together all the leads he was following. The files are mostly full of reference material. It seems that Scott was determined to gather together every piece of documentation he could find relating to the murders of the three women.'

'No doubt he wanted to make sure he didn't lose anything the way the official inquiry did.' Raven shot an admonishing glance in Dinsdale's direction and was rewarded to see the DI turning his head away. Whether in remorse or embarrassment remained to be seen.

'Scott's evidence board served as a high-level summary of his theories,' continued Tony, 'and he used his laptop to document his detailed thinking on each possible line of inquiry. There's a lot of material there, and firm evidence to justify every angle.'

'What was his favourite theory?' queried Raven.

'Scott didn't seem to work like that. He wasn't quick to jump to conclusions, but considered all possible explanations without prejudice.'

'Just as you might expect from a crime scene investigator,' remarked Becca. 'An evidence-led investigation.'

'Textbook,' said Raven in approval. It was already clear in his mind that the original police investigation had been run along quite different lines. Dinsdale had said that the SIO, DCI Gareth Peel, had "liked" Terry as the killer right from the start. Raven wondered whether that bias had led to other possible suspects being side-lined. 'So, I guess the question is, did Scott find anything that the police failed to uncover?'

'Unlikely,' chipped in Dinsdale, seeming unable to keep quiet for too long. 'That was a high-profile case. Three dead women. You can imagine the kind of press interest there was at the time, not to mention the pressure from on high. We followed every possible avenue of inquiry.'

'And still didn't obtain justice for Caitlin,' said Raven. In his experience, pressure from "on high" often resulted in the polar opposite of its desired effect, pushing officers to take shortcuts in the rush to make a collar. 'Tony?'

'Well, sir, Scott did identify one suspect who didn't appear on the police's radar. A man called Dennis Dewhurst. He was a regular at the club where Caitlin and the other women worked.'

Raven turned back to Dinsdale. 'Dennis Dewhurst – did he come up in the original investigation?'

'The name doesn't ring a bell.'

'Then why was Scott so interested in him?' asked Raven.

'I'm not quite sure yet, sir,' admitted Tony. 'I'll need to work back through the files and see what Scott had on him.'

'Make that a high priority.' Raven wasn't too surprised to learn that at least one suspect had slipped through the police net entirely. The thought of that lost opportunity was galling. The chance to interview the man, to check his fingerprints, to trace his movements and follow up with witnesses and alibis – all lost. 'Anything else?'

'Well, sir, I've also been sorting through the various photos Scott kept on his laptop. They're mostly of him as a child, presumably taken by his mother. But there are a few with other people in them, like this one that I printed.'

He handed Raven a photo showing Scott aged about twelve standing amid a group of women. Raven recognised the backdrop of the nightclub immediately. Apart from Caitlin and Frida, the rest of the women were dancers, kitted out in their skimpy lingerie. They gathered around Scott as if he were a mascot, while he looked embarrassed and did his best to appear invisible – the typical reaction of a young boy surrounded by glamorous members of the opposite sex. Raven pinned the photo to the board.

'Have we had any luck with Scott's phone?'

'Sorry, sir,' said Tony. 'Forensics say it's completely busted. But the phone company has provided us with his call logs. I've worked through them and eliminated his work calls and calls to Jess.'

Mention of Jess's name served as a reminder of why they were all so determined to find Scott's killer, and Raven felt his own resolve harden. He would spare no effort in his quest for answers. 'Okay, and what does that leave?'

'Apart from one-off calls or texts, I identified two numbers that he called or texted on a regular basis.' Tony produced two sheets of paper from his notes, one the original transcript from the phone company, all known numbers duly crossed out. The other listed the two remaining numbers.

Raven pinned the second sheet of paper to the board beneath Scott's photo. 'And these numbers belong to?'

'Unregistered subscribers, sir.'

'Burner phones?' The bane of every police investigation. In an age when privacy was almost impossible, the ability of criminal gangs to make untraceable calls irritated Raven beyond measure.

'Or simply phones with a prepaid SIM card,' said Tony.

'Let's put in a request to see if we can track them.'

Next, Raven filled them in on what he and Becca had uncovered at the club and from talking to Scott's friend, Cameron. It wasn't much, now that he put it into words. 'Terry's ex-wife, Frida, told us that Terry could be violent, especially when drunk.'

'I could have told you that,' interjected Dinsdale. 'Did his wife tell you that he was always chasing other women?'

'She did,' said Raven. 'As for Cameron, he didn't have much to offer us, other than endorsing the theory that Scott was killed by the person who killed his mother.'

'Who is currently locked up in a prison cell,' said Dinsdale, refusing to keep silent.

Raven gritted his teeth and pressed on, ignoring the comment. 'Also, Cameron refused to discuss the time he'd spent at the children's home. He gave the impression that he may have suffered abuse there, and we can't ignore the possibility that the same thing happened to Scott, or that Scott may have made an enemy while at the home.'

'Do you want me to check it out?' queried Becca.

'I think that would be useful. Why don't you pay the place a visit and see what you can find.'

'I'll go there straight away.'

'And I'll finish going through Scott's notes,' said Tony, 'and see what I can find out about Dennis Dewhurst.'

Dinsdale checked his watch and did his best to stifle a yawn. 'Is there anything you want me to do, or shall I go home?'

Raven treated him to a wicked grin. 'Don't worry, Derek. I've got a job lined up for you. It's one that I think you're going to enjoy.'

CHAPTER 15

Hiddenbeck Hall was a squat, Georgian house located on the very edge of Scarborough and backing onto open countryside. Built from dark stone and overshadowed by trees, its appearance was forbidding rather than welcoming. The sort of place where a nineteenth-century governess with a nervous disposition might encounter precocious children, a matronly housekeeper, and a sinister manservant.

Or had Becca been watching too many period TV dramas since Sam had gone to Australia?

She told herself not to be fanciful. This was a twenty-first century children's home run by the local authority, not a Victorian-era asylum. There were inspections and safeguards to protect children and vulnerable adults. Still, she found it hard to shake the feeling of being watched from one of the many blank-faced windows as she stepped out of her car, as if a madwoman in a nightgown might be peeping out at her from behind a curtain.

She pressed the buzzer at the porticoed entrance and was admitted, after introducing herself through an intercom system, into a hallway where the hall's grand features – high ceiling, elaborate staircase, moulded coving – were brought down to earth by the scuff marks, linoleum flooring, and walls painted a dingy shade of institutional green. The smell of fried breakfasts hung in the air. Through an open door she heard the unmistakable sounds of an action movie – screeching tyres, shouts, gunshots – and saw teenagers lounging on beanbags and hurling empty drinks cans at each other.

Close supervision, then.

She was met by a young woman who was nothing like the matronly housekeeper of her imaginings. 'Hiya, I'm Cheryl, can I help you?' The receptionist was dressed in lilac-coloured dungarees with fair hair tied back in a ponytail and looked to be barely out of her teens herself. Becca wondered if she was a former inmate.

'I'd like to speak to the person in charge.'

'That's Colin,' said the girl. 'He's in his office. Do you have an appointment?'

'No.' Becca showed her warrant card and Cheryl grinned.

'Guess that will do instead.' She led Becca down a short corridor and knocked on a door with a brass plaque that read *Colin West: Manager.*

'Come.' The broad Yorkshire accent from within the office sounded gruff and unwelcoming.

Undaunted, Cheryl opened the door and poked her head inside. 'Copper here to see you, Colin.'

'What's it about?'

'Dunno.'

'All right, send 'em in.'

The room that overlooked the open fields at the back of the house was overfilled with filing cabinets. Between them, in front of the tall window, nestled a desk piled high with paperwork. Becca had imagined that all the admin of a place like this was done on computers these days, but there was scarcely room on the manager's desk for him to reach his keyboard and screen.

Colin West was a portly man about Dinsdale's age,

close to retirement but not quite over the finishing line. Thinning grey hair cut in a side parting met a pair of Elvis-style sideburns. His eyebrows were thick and untamed and more hair protruded from his nostrils. He wore a suit that, like the hall itself, had seen better days, and a narrow tie with his top button undone.

'Thank you for seeing me, Mr West,' said Becca.

'Chuffed.' The manager stayed in his seat but reached across the desk to shake her hand, treating her to a lukewarm smile that stopped firmly at his lips. 'Police, eh? What's so important that you had to come t'see me on a weekend?' He gestured at the sprawl of paper that covered his desk. 'Saturday's my admin day. Oh no – my mistake – every day's my admin day.' He chuckled heartily at his own joke.

'Do you mind if I sit down?' said Becca.

'Oh, yeah, go ahead. Treat yourself.'

She took a chair from the edge of the room, brushed dust off its seat and dragged it up to the desk. 'I wanted to speak to you about a former resident, Scott Newhouse. He would have left here three years ago.'

West nodded in satisfaction. 'In that case, he's nowt to do wi' me. Once they leave 'ere, that's the last I see of 'em.'

Becca wasn't surprised to learn that former residents weren't queueing up to return for a catch-up over tea and biscuits with the manager.

'Got himself into trouble, has he?' asked West.

'His body was found in the harbour on Thursday morning,' said Becca coldly.

The manager barely batted an eyelid at the news. 'I'm sorry to hear that, but some of these kids, they get into drink and drugs. Always ends badly.'

Becca was tempted to point out that if any of the kids in the children's home took drugs, then it was the manager himself who was responsible. 'Scott Newhouse didn't take drugs. He was murdered.'

The man's unruly eyebrows huddled together in surprise. 'Murdered? Well, like I say, he must have got in wi' the wrong sort o' folk.'

Becca felt her temper rising at the man's quickness to assign blame. 'Scott was a CSI professional working with Yorkshire Police,' she said indignantly.

In response, West folded his arms across his broad chest. 'Well, good for 'im. I like to see folk do well for themselves when they leave my care. But what's his death got to do wi' me? You said he left here three year ago.'

'How long have you been the manager at this home, Mr West?'

He puffed out his chest in pride. 'It's going on ten year now, and I worked as a care assistant for another twenty year before that, so I think I know what's what.'

'So you must remember Scott? He was sent here at the age of fourteen after his mother died. He had no other family.'

West gave her a vague look. 'You 'ave a photo of 'im?'

Becca reached into her notebook and retrieved a photo of Scott. It had been taken when he first joined the CSI team. Just eighteen years old, his whole life ahead of him, he looked impossibly fresh-faced. She passed it across the desk.

The manager took the photo and studied it for a moment, his brow furrowing in concentration. 'Newhouse,' he said at last. 'Now you show me his picture, I do remember 'im. A good lad, not like some of the tearaways that are sent here. He were quiet, kept 'imself to 'imself.'

'Do you recall if Scott had any particular friends?'

'There was one. Another loner. Cameron Blake. Them two didn't mix a lot with the other kids.'

So the manager's recollection of his charges wasn't quite as sketchy as he'd led Becca to believe. 'Did Scott make any enemies during his time at the home?' she asked. 'Was there anyone he didn't get on with, who might have held a grudge against him?'

West dismissed the idea with a wave of his hand. 'Kids – they're always falling out wi' each other. Usually blows over in a day or two. Not worth worrying about every little thing.'

So there was something. 'Did Scott experience bullying at the home?'

'I wouldn't call it that. Rough and tumble. Nowt to be concerned about.'

'And what about his carers?'

The manager's expression darkened. 'What about them?'

'Were there any issues with staff during the time Scott was here at the home?'

West leaned towards her on heavy forearms, dislodging a box file and spilling a pile of papers across his desk. 'I don't follow your way of thinking. What kind of "issues" might you be alluding to?'

'Anything that might have involved a disciplinary matter.' Becca let the words hang between them. It was no secret that carers at children's homes had sometimes been found abusing the youngsters in their care. It was rare these days, more the kind of thing you expected to hear about back in the seventies, but it still hadn't been completely eradicated from the system.

'You'll find none of that sort o' thing here,' West told her, his voice stern. 'We run strict background checks on all staff and have rigid procedures in place. Why d'you think I have so much paperwork to deal with?' He spread his arms expansively to encompass the full extent of his workload.

'So, no staff dismissed or otherwise disciplined during the years Scott was at the home?'

'No. Never.'

'And no records of bullying by other residents?'

'That's not the sort o' thing we keep a written record of.'

'Still, Mr West, I'd be grateful if you could supply us with a copy of Scott's personal file from his time at the home.'

He met her request with an obstinate frown. 'Haven't

you heard of data protection rules? I can't just give out personal information willy-nilly.'

Becca summoned up one of her sweetest smiles, the kind she reserved for the most obnoxious people she encountered. 'I can apply to the county council if that makes it easier for you. Or return with a search warrant. Whatever works best for you.'

The manager gave a weary gesture, as if Becca had just made his job ten times harder. 'All right, all right, I'll do it,' he said, conceding defeat. 'Where d'you want it sending?'

'I'll just take it with me, if you don't mind, Mr West. Perhaps your receptionist could fetch me a mug of tea while I wait?'

*

Jess awoke to a searing pain that split her skull from side to side.

Too much wine the evening before.

Several glasses over dinner. More afterwards. Far too many. But at least she had slept, for the first time in days.

And a hangover could be fixed.

In a matter of hours it would be gone, speeded on its way by a couple of aspirins and a strong black coffee. The real pain was in her heart, not her head. And she had no idea how it might begin to heal.

Pale sunlight was poking its fingers through a gap in the curtains, but Jess had no desire to face the day. To fetch a drink she would have to go downstairs, and she wasn't yet ready for company. No doubt her mum would be all too happy to make her whatever she fancied, but Jess was already drowning in cups of tea and sympathy. She needed to be alone.

She reached across the bed and picked up the collection of Edgar Allan Poe's poems that Scott had left for her. She had dipped into the book briefly the previous day, but couldn't say she'd taken much of a liking to Poe's work.

The poems seemed morbid, focusing on death and mourning. But then there had always been more than a hint of melancholy following Scott like a shadow. The tragic death of his mother, the miserable years spent in the children's home that had robbed him of his confidence, the loneliness, the inability to trust. Jess had hoped she might be able to dispel that blackness over time, but now it was too late.

The darkness had swallowed him.

On the cover of the book lay Scott's unopened letter. Her name, *Jess Barraclough*, written in his careful handwriting. The envelope was slim but felt heavy in her hands. A sense of foreboding gripped her as she lifted it, but she had put off opening it for too long, not feeling brave enough to hear Scott's final words to her. She had told herself she was saving them for a special moment, but really she had just lacked the courage. What if the letter contained some clue to his death?

Now the fear and foreboding gave way to a sense of urgency to read the words he had left behind. She had been a fool to put it off for so long.

She broke open the envelope and removed the single folded sheet of parchment paper it contained. It was old-fashioned stationery of the sort that was no longer used in the days of email and instant messaging. Had this writing paper, like the book itself, also belonged to Caitlin? She rubbed the corner between thumb and forefinger, feeling its crispness, then pressed her nose to it, hoping to catch some final trace of his scent before starting to read.

Dearest Jess,

I want you to know that you're the best thing that's ever happened to me. Seriously. The best. I don't think I've ever told you that, and I really wish now that I had.

It's not always easy for me to open up, because when you've experienced everything I have, you realise that sometimes the people we trust are the ones who hurt us most. And when you've been starved of love for so long, it's hard to remember how it feels to be loved. But you've given me back that feeling.

You've brought me so much joy in such a short time. And you've enabled me to really love another person again. Because I do love you, Jess, I hope you know that.

Until I met you, the only thing that mattered was finding out who killed my mum. I never told you what I was doing, about all the evidence I'd collected, and I didn't show you around my flat, because I was afraid you would think I was crazy. Maybe I was. Maybe I am.

For the longest time it felt like I was getting nowhere, that it was just an obsession that would lead me to a brick wall.

But now, finally, I think I'm close to the truth. There's just one final piece of the jigsaw I need to confirm. Then I'll have all I need to go to the police. When I do that, I'd like DCI Raven to lead the investigation. I know he'll do whatever it takes to get justice for Mum. The Raven *by Edgar Allan Poe was always her favourite poem, so it seems appropriate.*

I'd like you to have her copy of Poe's poems. They were special to her and mean a lot to me too.

I can't help feeling nervous about what I'm about to do. So I'm writing this to you now in case anything happens to me. But even as I write these words I know I'm being ridiculous. I'll tear this letter up and give you the book in person next time I see you. And I hope I'll have the courage to say to you face to face what I've written here.

But now I have to go and meet someone. I feel as if my whole life has led to this point. I've been so confused, but you are my rock. I know we will be happy together.

All my love,
Scott.

Oh, Scott, thought Jess as the tears started to fall, soaking into the paper and running with the ink. What did you find out? And who did this to you?

CHAPTER 16

'**Y**ou can't be serious,' groaned Dinsdale when Raven explained where they were going.

'I thought you'd be happy to catch up with an old friend.'

'That evil bastard is no friend of mine. He murdered those women, Raven. All three of them. Don't let anyone convince you otherwise.'

'Let's try to keep an open mind, shall we?'

Raven had visited Full Sutton, the prison where Terry Baines was now serving a life sentence on two counts of murder, once before. He and Becca had gone there to conduct an interview with a man convicted of shooting a local drugs dealer. It had been Raven's first case in Scarborough after an absence of over thirty years. Now, almost six months later, it was beginning to feel as if he'd never left the town. On a trip back to London to collect the rest of his belongings and return the key of his rented flat, the capital had felt alien, a place where he no longer belonged.

Perhaps he had always felt like a stranger there. Perhaps he had been a stranger to himself for most of his life. If so, he was slowly rediscovering who he truly was.

'They're all evil bastards in that place, Raven.'

Raven wished that Dinsdale would shut up. But he wanted the older detective where he could keep an eye on him. And if that meant enduring his company during the prison visit, then so be it.

Besides, in this case Dinsdale was probably right. Full Sutton was a category A prison, a maximum-security establishment holding male prisoners exclusively. Murderers, rapists, high-risk offenders and those posing a threat to national security. Some of the most notorious inmates included Jeremy Bamber, the mass murderer convicted of the White House Farm killings, in which he had gunned down his parents, his adoptive sister and her six-year-old twins in cold blood. Another contender for the prison's chart of most notorious criminals was Freddie Foreman, otherwise known as "Brown Bread Fred", a gangster and associate of the Kray twins. Foreman was now a free man, but for many of those doing time at Full Sutton, "life" meant life and they would never be released.

'This is a waste of time,' moaned Dinsdale. 'You won't get anything out of Terry Baines apart from self-pity and lies. He's where he belongs, behind bars.'

'Humour me,' said Raven. He pushed his foot to the floor, the M6 dropping a couple of gears in response, and pulled out to overtake a slower vehicle, leaving Dinsdale looking like he was about to disgorge his half-digested breakfast all over the dashboard.

'Do you have to drive like a maniac?' complained the DI.

'No,' said Raven. 'But I do enjoy it. Especially with you in the passenger seat.'

'Well, try not to kill us both before we get there.'

On arriving at the prison and enduring the multiple security procedures that were needed to gain entry, Raven found himself sitting beside Dinsdale in a windowless interview room much like the one he had been to on his previous visit. The chairs and the metal table in front of them were bolted to the floor, as were the two empty chairs opposite.

'He'll try to play you,' warned Dinsdale. 'Don't believe a word he says.'

'I think I know to handle men like him,' said Raven. Although he wasn't yet certain what kind of man Terry Baines would turn out to be.

Charming, Frida had said. *Passionate*. But what else had she said? That he could be a man of violence who sometimes hurt the women he loved.

Raven hardened his resolve. If Terry Baines tried any charm on him, he would receive short shrift.

The door on the other side of the room opened and a man shuffled in, followed by a prison guard. The guard escorted the prisoner to a seat and took up position by the door.

Baines wasn't quite what Raven had been expecting. He'd anticipated someone with a rougher look – maybe sporting a boxer's nose and a crew cut. With a few tattoos to his name, at least. Instead, the man sitting opposite him had a full head of dark, wavy hair, only lightly sprinkled with grey, giving him a rakish look, like a middle-aged film star. He was one of those men for whom a little wear and tear merely added to his appeal, the grey strands like silver threads lending him an air of distinction. In a suit and tie instead of a prison tracksuit, he would easily have passed for a businessman with a dash of entrepreneurial flair, and it was easy for Raven to picture him in that role.

Raven and Dinsdale showed the prisoner their warrant cards. Terry studied them both carefully. Then, after dismissing Dinsdale with little more than a passing glance, he focussed all of his attention on Raven.

'Thank you for agreeing to speak to us, Mr Baines.' Raven was still trying to get the measure of the man and was keen to hear his voice.

Terry gave him an appraising look, as if assessing Raven's competence. When he spoke he sounded educated and articulate, again not what Raven had been expecting.

'Thank you for coming to see me, DCI Raven.' The way he talked it was as if he had summoned the detectives to visit him. 'I never pass up an opportunity to put my case to someone in authority. As I've said many times, I shouldn't be here. My conviction was a miscarriage of justice. I was set up.'

Raven knew that Terry had consistently protested his innocence, but he was intrigued to hear what he had to say for himself. 'Who set you up, Mr Baines?'

'Why, DCI Gareth Peel, of course. The SIO in charge of the case. He fancied an easy win to carry him to his retirement.'

'Bullshit,' muttered Dinsdale.

Terry carried on as if Dinsdale had said nothing, addressing himself solely to Raven. 'Peel never liked me. I could tell that from the start. I think he was jealous when he saw how much money could be made in my line of work. Or perhaps he just fancied the girls I hung out with. Envy can be a very toxic emotion, you know.'

'What utter nonsense,' interrupted Dinsdale again.

'The fact is,' continued Terry, 'I didn't kill anyone. I didn't kill Tanya Ayres or Jenny Jones. Or Caitlin Newhouse for that matter. Is that why you're here? You're investigating Caitlin's death?'

Raven ignored the question, unwilling to share any information about the current investigation with Terry. 'You had sex with Tanya and Jenny immediately before they were murdered,' he accused. 'Semen residue recovered from the bodies of both women matched your DNA.'

Terry wrinkled his nose in distaste. 'Please, there's no need to be so base, Chief Inspector. If I'd known my wild oats were going to become a matter of public record, I'd have taken more care where I sowed them.'

Dinsdale thumped the desk with his fist, the veins in his neck bulging. 'You raped those women!'

Terry recoiled at the sight of Dinsdale's loss of control. 'Chief Inspector, I think you need to keep your gorilla on a tighter leash. As for Tanya and Jenny, I did no such thing. The sex was consensual.' He leaned forwards again and lowered his voice as if about to impart a great secret. 'They were pretty girls, Chief Inspector. Very pretty. At the club we always employed the best lookers. I love women – always have done. Frida knew that when she married me. She understood perfectly well what she was getting into. All the women I slept with knew the score. I never tried to deceive anyone.'

'They were young women in your employment,' said Raven. 'You took advantage of them.'

Terry smirked. 'They seemed happy enough to find themselves in my bed. I don't think I left them disappointed.'

Raven regarded the man sitting opposite him with a growing distaste. His vanity seemed to be matched only by his own sense of self-pity, and it was hard to picture him as the victim here. It was easy to see why Dinsdale held such a low opinion of the man. 'At your trial, Frida said you could be violent.'

Terry's face drooped, clearly disappointed by Raven's response. 'She was lying. I never laid a finger on Frida, not once. I never hurt any woman.'

'Why would your wife lie to the court?'

'I don't know. Perhaps it suited her purposes, to play the victim in this affair. She always had a keen eye for business. With me out of the way, the club became hers to run as she saw fit. Frida's a good liar, she's had a lot of practice.'

Raven's dislike for Terry Baines was steadily growing. Was there no depth the man was prepared to sink to in order to try and save his skin? 'What are you suggesting? That your wife killed those women and lied in order to pin it on you?'

Terry sighed in frustration. 'No, of course I'm not suggesting that. I have no idea who killed Tanya and Jenny. I'm just trying to make sense of what happened.'

'And what about Caitlin, did you have sex with her

too?'

Terry spread his arms wide. 'Don't misunderstand me, Caitlin was a beautiful woman, just my type. But I never slept with her.'

'Liar!' growled Dinsdale at Raven's side.

Although Terry seemed calm and reasonable, the gaps in his story were becoming more obvious as the interview progressed. Dinsdale had warned Raven that Terry would try to play him. The man was a charmer, a deceiver, a narcissist. He couldn't be trusted.

'What about the murder weapon that was used to kill Jenny? It was found in your possession.'

Terry raised his palms in a gesture of innocence. 'It may have been found in my possession, but I swear I never laid eyes on it before Peel clapped his greasy fingers all over it.'

'If you're innocent,' said Raven, 'then I wonder how you make sense of the inconvenient matter of your confession.'

Terry groaned, as if the very mention of it pained him. 'I've said a million times that I never confessed. That was all a lie. A complete fabrication.'

'Someone else had it in for you?' said Raven. 'Along with your own wife and a senior police officer?'

Terry turned his face away, as if he had expected better from Raven. As if Raven was just as incompetent as all the other police officers he'd ever dealt with. In profile, the man's features were less refined. The nose hooked, the hair receding, the jawline weak. He looked like what he was – a shameless philanderer, a violent husband, and a convicted murderer, grasping desperately at any chance to save himself.

'Anyway,' said Raven, 'it's Caitlin Newhouse's death I want to talk about.'

Terry's head snapped back and he met Raven's eyes. 'You can't pin that on me. I wasn't even tried for her murder. Not even Peel tried to stitch me up for that.'

'Then who do you think did it?'

'I would have thought that would be obvious. The same

man who killed the others.'

'And who might that be?'

Terry's shoulders slumped. 'I don't know. Isn't that supposed to be your job?' He turned to address Dinsdale for the first time. 'If you and your boss had done your job properly at the time, I wouldn't be here. Instead, the real killer's still out there, my liar of a wife is living it big without me, and I'm rotting here in this hellhole!'

Raven was an inch away from grabbing Baines by his sweatshirt and giving him an earful. Now that the charming mask had been pulled from his face and the snakelike wretch it hid revealed, it was a mystery to Raven what Frida had seen in him. The thought of Terry's drunken hands pawing her and slapping her about made his blood boil.

Only the presence of the prison guard prevented him from giving Terry Baines a taste of his own medicine.

'I think our job here is done.' If Raven had entertained any doubts about whether Terry had killed the three women, those doubts had now been thoroughly dispelled. Tanya Ayres, Jenny Jones, and Caitlin Newhouse. Even though the crime scene evidence from Caitlin's case had unfortunately gone AWOL, the mass of evidence in the two other murders had been enough to convince a jury, and it was enough to sway Raven. No doubt those twelve men and women had looked into the eyes of the man sitting across the table and seen exactly what Raven had seen – a liar, a cheat, a self-centred egoist who would say whatever he could to try and get himself off the hook.

Raven rose to his feet.

'Wait,' said Terry desperately. 'You can't just leave me.'

'Why not?' sneered Raven. 'What were you expecting? For us to take you home with us?'

'But no...' Terry looked around wildly, as if in fear that the guard would seize him and drag him back to his cell before he could speak. 'There's been a desperate miscarriage of justice. Surely you can see that?'

'All I see,' said Raven, 'is a man who took advantage of vulnerable women, who seized every opportunity to use and abuse them, who cared only about his own gratification, and who's getting exactly what he deserves for snuffing out three young lives.'

'But I couldn't have killed Caitlin!' Terry wailed as the guard came to take him away. 'I had a cast-iron alibi for the time of her death.'

The claim was news to Raven and he paused. There had been no mention in the case notes about any alibi.

'Don't listen to him,' urged Dinsdale. 'He's making it up.'

'No!' cried Terry. 'It's all true. I met Caitlin at a hotel in town. We'd agreed to meet there, and I'd booked a room. We had a drink in the bar together before going upstairs. That was the plan, at least. But as we sat there, Caitlin had second thoughts. She said she had her son to think about. She left, but I stayed behind for another drink and a chat with the manager of the hotel. He was a mate of mine. By the time I left, she was already dead. God knows who killed her, but it certainly wasn't me.'

CHAPTER 17

'Why the hell didn't you tell me that Terry Baines had an alibi for Caitlin's murder?'

Raven had waited until they were back at the car before turning his fury on Dinsdale. Away from the prisoner. Away from the prison guard. This was between him and his DI. A continuation of the war that had been raging ever since the two men had first been introduced to each other.

Raven planted both of his palms against the car, deliberately positioning the vehicle as a barrier to prevent him lunging out at Dinsdale or wringing his neck in frustration.

Despite almost two tons of metal separating them, Dinsdale shrank back before replying. When he spoke it was with his usual bluster. 'You didn't believe a word of what Baines told us, did you? You saw for yourself that he's a liar. This so-called alibi is simply that: another lie.'

'Was it ever checked?' demanded Raven.

'Checked?'

'The alibi!' shouted Raven. 'Did someone take a witness statement from the manager of the hotel?'

Dinsdale stared at the ground. 'This was eight years ago, Raven. How do you expect me to remember that kind of detail?'

'It was vital evidence in a murder inquiry. If Terry Baines's alibi checked out, then he couldn't have killed Caitlin Newhouse, and that probably means that he didn't murder the other women either. And that means that the killer is still at large.'

Dinsdale lifted his eyes to meet Raven's, but his shoulders remained bunched in a protective huddle around his ears. 'He *did* murder them,' he insisted. 'The evidence was overwhelming. The DNA, the eye witness accounts, the confession... God damnit, Raven, we even found the blood-stained knife in his possession! The case was as solid as any I've ever worked on.'

Raven fixed him with his stare for a few seconds longer before clicking the car doors open. 'Then who murdered Scott?'

Dinsdale had no answer for him, of course. He climbed into the passenger seat, clicking his seat belt into place.

Raven had no answer either. Yet.

But the number of unanswered questions was growing by the day.

*

Comfort food. A ham and cheese pie lovingly baked in the Aga and brought upstairs to Jess's room on a tray, along with a slice of fruit cake and a cup of tea. Her mum was going to so much trouble to make her feel better but it was having the opposite effect. Jess had no appetite. Not for food, anyway.

Maybe it had been a mistake to come home. To run away.

Her family, who she loved dearly, were smothering her with love and kindness. But she was unable to respond with the gratitude she knew they deserved. The pie lay untouched on its tray as she lay on her bed, staring at the walls of her childhood bedroom. The stencilled stars and moons that she'd painted as a girl. The bookcases packed with books she had loved during her teen years. The teddy bears lined up in a cheerful row along the top shelf. It all felt oppressive to her. The room was no longer the sanctuary it had once been. It was more like a prison cell.

She was starting to suffocate.

She had to get out of the house. She scooped up a rucksack, slid the volume of Poe's poetry inside and made her way stealthily downstairs. The hallway was empty, her mum occupied in the kitchen, her dad out doing his rounds, her brother and sister off living their own lives.

She pulled on her walking boots, donned an all-weather jacket, and headed outside before her mum could ask her where she was going. She needed to be alone with her thoughts.

She set off on a well-trodden route that would take her through her beloved valley of Rosedale. A route she knew by heart, that she had walked a thousand times.

The last time she had gone this way, Scott had been by her side.

Cutting through the churchyard by the ruin of the old priory she followed the footpath out of the village. The way led across fields where new-born lambs were tottering on spindly legs. She walked through gates and strode through sleepy hamlets. In summer, these paths would be bordered by jewelled carpets of wildflowers, but now the only colours were the grey of dry-stone walls and the green of fresh pasture. The ground rose steadily, requiring her to put more effort into walking. But she didn't slow her pace, trying instead to fight the grief through physical exertion.

She paused by the ruined kilns of the old ironstone mine – a row of brick arches with the hillside rising steeply behind them. For seventy years, from the mid-nineteenth century until the 1920s, this place had been the heart of the iron ore mining industry that had brought wealth and prosperity to the region. Now the kilns lay crumbling, gradually turning to dust. Rubble filled most of the arches, and a sign warned of "Danger – Falling Masonry".

Maybe Poe had been right with his laments and sorrows. Perhaps everything in this world was doomed to fall into ruin and decay.

But the thought of the new-born lambs restored her hope.

She sat down on a tuft of grass and allowed her gaze to drift across the dale. The views from up here were spectacular. It was awe-inspiring to be so immersed in nature, knowing that this landscape had been here for thousands of years and would outlive both her and the kilns. A black-faced sheep approached, regarding her with idle curiosity before trotting off down the hill to join its flock. A red kite circled overhead, scouring the ground for carrion.

The natural world, in all its beauty, in all its cruel indifference to her beating heart.

She slipped her arms through the loops of the rucksack and drew out the book. Turning the pages, she came to Caitlin's photograph. A striking woman, the picture taken when she wasn't much older than Jess was now. Caitlin had been only thirty when she died, having had Scott at a frighteningly young age – sixteen. Just a child herself. Jess traced the line of her cheek, noting the slender nose, the keen blue eyes, the full mouth and soft golden hair that fell in waves. It was a beautiful face. A kind face. Whatever mistakes Caitlin had made during her short life, Jess felt sure that she had always done her best for Scott.

She wondered what had happened to the necklace Caitlin was wearing in the photo. It was a striking piece of jewellery – a black leather cord threaded through a silver pendant of a bird. *A raven*. Scott had written in his letter that *The Raven* was Caitlin's favourite poem. Had it been one of his favourites too? Now she would never know.

The book fell open naturally at the page marked by the photograph and Jess found herself staring at the opening verse of the poem. She started to read.

Once upon a midnight dreary, while I pondered, weak and weary,

Jess knew what it was to feel weak and weary. Her limbs were worn out with fatigue, but it wasn't the walk up here that had almost finished her off. It was the hours spent languidly sprawling on her bed. Who knew that grief could be so exhausting? She took a breath of the refreshing air and read on.

While I nodded, nearly napping, suddenly there came a tapping,
As of some one gently rapping, rapping at my chamber door.

She shivered, remembering the night many years ago when an overgrown tree had scratched its wooden fingers against her window during a storm. She'd been reading *Wuthering Heights* at the time and had been frightened almost to death. Her dad had cut the branches back the following day.

Deep into that darkness peering, long I stood there wondering, fearing,
Doubting, dreaming dreams no mortal ever dared to dream before;

Bad dreams. She'd had plenty of those since losing Scott. The poet seemed to be describing her current situation exactly. His longing for his dead Lenore matched Jess' own yearning for Scott, although she would never be able to express it quite so eloquently.

She read on, hopeful that Poe might help her come to terms with her loss, but the poem was ultimately tragic. To all the poet's pleas, the raven who had come to visit him responded:

Quoth the Raven "Nevermore."

Never more would the poet see Lenore. Never more would Jess see Scott. Never more would the raven – a symbol, she understood now, of pain and sorrow – go away.

She closed the book and returned it to her bag.

Then she screamed her pain across the valley where no one could hear her.

CHAPTER 18

Raven took the journey back to Scarborough as fast as he had ever driven that road, impatient to return to the station, eager to remove himself from Dinsdale's company, and troubled by his encounter with Terry Baines.

Frida's ex-husband wasn't the man he had been expecting. Not a thug, nor a brute. That would have been easier to handle. Instead, the worst Raven could say about him was that he was an arrogant, self-regarding and self-pitying individual. That, plus a faithless husband, a perpetrator of domestic violence and a murderer.

Or was he? Raven had hoped that by going to speak to Baines in person, he would be able to put aside any residual doubts he harboured about the man's guilt. Instead, those doubts had multiplied.

He channelled his frustration into his driving, urging the M6 onwards, up hills and down dales, shooting out to overtake slower road users. In other words, every vehicle he encountered.

Beside him, Dinsdale cowered in the passenger seat, his seatbelt firmly locked in place, his knuckles white on the handle of the door.

Neither man spoke a word, unless you could count Dinsdale's faint whimperings, thankfully mostly drowned by the sound from the engine. It was distressing to hear a grown man bleating so much, but Raven felt not a drop of sympathy. It was Dinsdale who had sabotaged his interview with Terry Baines, failing to brief him on a vital piece of evidence. And Dinsdale who had worked on the original investigation, during which critical evidence had disappeared without trace and in which a vital alibi had apparently gone unchecked.

If Terry's statement could be believed, which was anything but certain. Raven felt as if he was trying to kick his way out of a paper bag, frustrated at every turn, blind to the truth.

Arriving back at the station, he turned his back on the other detective and went in search of genial human contact. Tony was still busy with Scott's laptop and Becca wasn't yet back from the children's home, so instead he sought out Holly Chang, knowing that even though it was the weekend and Holly's kids would no doubt be expecting her to take them to swimming lessons or go and watch their football matches, she would be at her desk, doing her bit to find Scott's killer.

He wasn't wrong. She looked up as he entered her office, a glimmer of hopeful anticipation on her face, but that hope was visibly dashed as she registered the frustration he was feeling.

'What's wrong?' she asked. 'Has something happened?'

He slumped into a seat, the weight of the investigation feeling like a lead weight around his neck. He rubbed his eyes, resting his elbows on his knees. 'How can evidence simply go missing from a police investigation?'

Holly had no need to ask what he was referring to. 'In the case of Caitlin's murder, the inquiry into the missing evidence failed to come up with an answer to that question. Neither did Scott's own investigation. But in general, there are two possible explanations.'

Rubbing Raven's eyes was only making them worse. Instead he sat up and paid attention. 'And they are?'

'The usual. Cock-up or conspiracy. In this case, there's simply no way of knowing what happened. But cock-ups are more common than people think.'

Raven nodded glumly. He had personal experience of cases collapsing because of forensic evidence being lost, contaminated or incorrectly processed. All that painstaking police work – months of evidence gathering, witness interviews, expert statements and so on – all ruined because of a moment's carelessness. A shocking, but regrettable fact of life in law enforcement.

Is that what had happened in Caitlin's case? The wholesale disappearance of every piece of physical evidence: blood, DNA, fingerprints, Caitlin's phone, even the murder weapon itself. 'But how could it all simply vanish into thin air while in police custody?' he wondered aloud. 'Where did it go?'

Holly gestured wearily, indicating the futility of this line of questioning. 'Who knows? Filed incorrectly? Mistakenly sent for destruction? Sitting at the bottom of someone's filing cabinet?'

'You really think that's possible?'

'Cock-up would be by far the most likely explanation,' said Holly, 'unless you have good reason to suspect conspiracy.'

Reason. Did Raven have a reason, or was it simply a hunch? A bad taste in his mouth, the stink of corruption. Was Dinsdale's involvement in the matter prejudicing his opinion? Or had he taken an irrational dislike to the senior investigating officer, DCI Gareth Peel, a man he had never even met?

Peel never liked me, Terry Baines had bleated. But was that really a good enough reason to put an innocent man behind bars?

'In cases of conspiracy,' Holly continued, not waiting for Raven to put his thoughts into words, 'it's far more common for evidence to be planted or contaminated. Why would evidence be removed from an inquiry?'

Raven lifted his palms in a gesture of ignorance. His leg was playing up again. That dull ache that never truly went away. The ghost of a wound inflicted so long ago that he could hardly remember the details of the event itself. He no longer suffered the flashbacks and nightmares that were the main legacy from his army days, but that nagging leg would follow him to his grave. 'I don't know, Holly. I don't know who did what or why. But something isn't right.'

*

'Sir, do you have a minute?'

After leaving Holly's office, Raven had returned to the incident room, keen to get back on the case. He had wasted time today, driving all the way to Full Sutton to conduct an interview that had left him less certain than ever about the soundness of Terry's conviction for the murders of Tanya Ayres and Jenny Jones.

Not to mention coming *that* close to losing it with Dinsdale.

'Always, Tony, what have you got for me?' Raven crossed the room to Tony's desk. As always it was neat and uncluttered, just the way Raven strove to keep his own space. In Raven's case, there were good reasons for wanting to stamp order on his world. *To keep the forces of chaos at bay.* He wondered what made Tony so neat and tidy. Perhaps it was just a meticulous nature and a desire for an efficient workplace.

'I've been looking into this Dennis Dewhurst chap, the one Scott identified as a possible lead in his mother's murder.'

Raven could tell by the hint of excitement in Tony's voice that he had found something significant. 'Yes?'

Tony checked his notes. 'Dewhurst was living in Scarborough at the time of Caitlin's death. Council tax records put him at an address on the Esplanade. He'd been living there for several years.'

Raven raised an eyebrow. 'The posh end of town.' That wasn't quite what he'd been expecting to hear. Tony had described him as a man who frequented the *Mayfair*. But perhaps the place attracted a more upmarket clientele than Raven had imagined. The club's fancy décor certainly signalled grand aspirations. 'What did he do for a living?'

'He had interests in several different business ventures – small hotels, a chain of fitness centres, a restaurant. Companies House shows him as a director in three separate companies. But he sold all his shares, resigned his directorships and left the country some six years ago.'

'Shortly after Terry Baines was convicted,' mused Raven. 'Do you know where he went?'

'Spain. Alicante.'

Raven wrinkled his nose. If he remembered rightly, Dinsdale had taken a short winter break in the Spanish coastal resort just recently. Why did everything have to remind him of that infuriating man? 'Did Dewhurst decide to retire to a sunnier climate?'

'I don't think so, sir. He was arrested in Spain on suspicion of fraud – something to do with a property development that went bust – but the charges wouldn't stick. He returned to Scarborough at the end of last year.'

Like the proverbial bad penny. 'So he's been back in town for about three months. Where does he live now?'

'Close to his old haunt. Montpellier Terrace.'

Montpellier Terrace, just off the Esplanade. No sea view, but just as grand. 'Do we know what he's up to?'

Nothing good, Raven was willing to bet.

'I checked with Companies House, and he's a director and majority shareholder in a brand-new company. The company's so new it hasn't yet filed any accounts, so I don't know much about it.'

'Good work, Tony,' said Raven. 'Let's keep our ears to the ground, see if we can find out any more about him.' He turned to leave, then stopped. 'I don't suppose you've seen Becca?'

'She was here earlier, but she's gone again. I think she

may have finished for the day.'

'Already?' Raven checked the time on his watch. *Late.* He'd probably been talking to Holly at the time Becca came back and was annoyed with himself for missing her. 'Did she say how she got on at the children's home?'

'Nothing concrete but she did mention she was following up a lead.'

'Good. That's something.'

But it didn't sound like a lot. All they had was a name here, a snippet of info there. No strong leads, no clear suspects. Was it worth going to speak to Dennis Dewhurst? Raven would like to find out more about the man before paying him a visit.

He rubbed his eyes, doing his best to push away the fatigue. Three days into the case and he was feeling the pressure. It was only a matter of time before Gillian summoned him to her office, wanting to know why he had so little to show for himself. Whatever she might say to him, he had already thought worse himself.

But he knew that didn't give him permission to make unreasonable demands of his team. The burden of responsibility was his to bear, and his alone. 'Why don't you head home, Tony?' he said kindly. 'I'm sure you've done as much as you can for one day. Get some rest and come back refreshed in the morning.'

Tony hesitated for a moment before bowing his head in agreement. 'You too, sir. If you don't mind me saying, you're looking dog-tired.'

*

'As you can see, the kitchen has all new appliances, a built-in fridge-freezer, a dishwasher, an induction hob which is very easy to clean, and plenty of storage space.' The estate agent opened a cupboard door to demonstrate and gave Becca a winning smile. He was young and keen – he'd agreed to show her around the apartment at short notice after work – and Becca was already feeling bad because she knew she was going to have to disappoint him. She nodded and tried to match his smile, but her jaw was starting to ache from the effort.

It was hard to focus on sleek worktops and gleaming appliances when her mind was on the case. She had taken an instant dislike to the manager of the children's home, Colin West. It wasn't just his indifference to Scott's death that was bothering her, it was his arrogant attitude, the way he clearly believed he knew best.

That way of thinking led to negligence – or worse.

Talking to Cameron Blake it was hard not to arrive at the conclusion that he had suffered some sort of abuse during his time at the children's home. You didn't have to be a detective to work that out. All the clues were there – the way his landlady had spoken about his traumatic upbringing and his need to heal, his own refusal to discuss the home. Cameron had said that it was all in the past, but the past had a nasty way of reaching out to the present.

The way Scott's delving into his mother's death had come back to claim his own life.

And yet there was nothing in Scott's file to indicate that he had suffered any kind of mistreatment at the home, nor made any enemies who might have exacted revenge. Another dead end in a case that seemed to be heading nowhere.

The estate agent cleared his throat. 'The surname was Shawcross, wasn't it?'

Becca emerged from her introspection with a start. 'Becca Shawcross, that's right.'

'Any relation to Liam?'

Becca stifled a groan. 'He's my brother.' She wanted to say her good-for-nothing brother, yet she was the one casting about in a fruitless search for a place to live while Liam already owned his own flat.

The agent's smile broadened even further. 'I've done business with Liam a couple of times. He's a great guy, isn't he?'

'Is he?' Becca wondered what Liam was like to do

business with. A shark, she guessed. He certainly liked to boast about how much his hard-nosed negotiating tactics had managed to slash the cost of adding properties to his ever-growing portfolio of buy-to-lets and holiday rentals. Becca imagined the agent being on the receiving end of Liam's bargaining and couldn't help feeling sorry for him.

She gravitated to the window in the living area, trying to put her finger on why this spotless apartment with its freshly painted walls, shiny bathroom, open-plan living and kitchen area and generous double bedroom with built-in wardrobes wasn't getting her more excited. On paper it was perfect. It was close to the town centre, had a parking slot more than big enough for her Honda Jazz, and miraculously was just within her budget. What more could she want?

And then it came to her. The reason why this apartment would never do.

It didn't have a sea view.

She'd seen nice apartments with sea views online but they were well out of her price range. She'd understood that finding somewhere to live would inevitably involve some degree of compromise but she hadn't understood until now the one factor she'd be unwilling to compromise on. Such a simple thing, taken for granted her whole life. The freedom to sit by the window and gaze out at the ever-changing sea and sky, to watch the waves roll in across the bay and witness the relentless rise and fall of the tide.

On the darkening street outside, a man with a dog paused beneath a streetlamp before continuing on his way. In the building opposite, a light turned on in a sitting room, giving Becca a brief glimpse of a cosily furnished space before the curtains were pulled tight against the gloom. A car door slammed shut and a woman hurried along the pavement to her house.

Other people's lives going on all around. And yet the activity beyond the window made her feel suddenly lonely. She tried to picture herself living in this flat, sitting by herself in the open-plan living space, or alone in the shiny new kitchen cooking for one. Was she ready to make such a leap, sea view or not?

Her thoughts drifted to Jess, back at her parents' house in Rosedale Abbey. A comforting, solid building, made to withstand the wind, the rain and the cold. A place of refuge in the storm, with a fire in the grate and a bustle of activity in the kitchen. More than a building – a home.

'Would you like a few minutes to have another look around?' asked the ever-hopeful agent.

'There's no need,' said Becca. 'I've seen enough.'

★

Everyone had gone home, yet still Raven lingered at his desk. Another late night, alone in the incident room. What did he hope to achieve here? Was it enough simply to put in the hours, his mind turning over the facts of the case like a puzzle, hoping to catch some fresh insight, for a glimpse of a way forward?

He would be better off taking the advice he'd given to Tony – to go home and get some rest. God knew he was tired enough. That would be the smart move, the sensible course of action.

Yet here he was, staring at his computer screen, his mind churning, his thoughts a relentless repetition of the same few facts.

One dead man. Three dead women. A man convicted of two of the murders.

But those facts made no sense. If Terry had murdered Tanya and Jenny, then surely he had also murdered Caitlin. In which case, who had killed Scott? And why?

Raven reached for a six- by four-inch wooden picture frame that stood on his desk. It held a photo recovered from Scott's flat, showing Scott as a baby in his mother's arms. Caitlin looked so young, like the teenager she was. Sixteen years old.

The photo had been taken on a sunny day on the sea front. Caitlin was leaning against the promenade railing, holding Scott face forwards and pointing at the camera. The castle on the headland was just visible in the background. Whoever had taken the picture was standing on the sand, the sea behind them.

Raven's own mother had often taken him to the beach to play as a small boy and he imagined Caitlin doing the same with Scott. Hot sand, blue sky, a bucket in one hand and a spade in the other. Sandcastles, ice cream, sandwiches with grit in the wrapping, the gulls swooping and diving to try and steal them. Growing up by the seaside was a privilege. A constant adventure.

The photo wasn't sitting quite right in its frame, one side bulging against the glass. Raven turned it over, slid the catches that held the back in place, and removed the photograph from the wooden frame.

It was as he'd thought. The photograph had been folded over, cutting off Caitlin's left shoulder.

He unfolded it and studied the new image it presented.

A third person.

A man.

He stood on Caitlin's left, six inches taller than her. Heavily built, his sleeveless vest revealing muscular biceps. His eyes were obscured behind dark glasses but Raven noted the narrow face, the strong jawline, the swept-back hair. Was this Scott's father? The man Dani had described as a "waste of space"?

There was no telling whether it was Scott or Caitlin who had folded the photo in half in order to conceal the mystery man from view. But one thing Raven knew for sure. Some people couldn't simply be folded out of your life.

He pinned the photo to the evidence board and drew a question mark above it.

CHAPTER 19

Liam Shawcross had never attended a business meeting in a gentlemen's club before, but he'd give anything a go once. Twice, if attractive women were on display and the costs were tax-deductible. He paid the exorbitant entrance fee for himself and his business associate and entered the luxurious surroundings of the *Mayfair*, taking a moment to admire the upscale décor. Brass lights, wooden bookcases, polished leather chairs.

Classy. He should come here more often.

But the mahogany and leather fittings didn't hold his attention for long. Thumping music blared from hidden speakers. A young beauty clad in a sparkly bikini and silver platform boots was contorting herself around a vertical pole into positions he wouldn't have thought physically possible.

'Blimey,' said the man he'd brought with him. 'Her legs must be made out of rubber.'

It had been a right job persuading Barry Hardcastle to accompany him to the meeting. The builder could be surprisingly conservative in his tastes. 'Not my sort of place, mate,' Barry had said dismissively when Liam had first floated the idea. 'What if the missus finds out where I've been?'

'No one will know, Barry,' Liam had assured him. 'Why don't you let your hair down for once.'

'Don't have much of that left,' said Barry, running thick fingers across his balding scalp. 'I'm getting too old for that kind of joint.'

But Liam's charm had worked its magic in the end. It always did.

And besides, money was on offer. Easy money. An opportunity to get rich.

'So where's this mate of yours?' asked Barry, peering into the gloom around the edges of the venue.

'He's not a mate as such. More of an old business contact,' said Liam, keen to put a little distance between himself and the man they had come to meet. Just in case the deal went sour.

There was always the possibility that this was a scam. Smoke and mirrors. An opportunity not to make money, but to lose it fast. Liam would know when he had all the facts to hand and could look his potential business partner in the eye.

Around the dance floor, tables were laid out in secluded booths, all occupied, as far as he could see, by male clientèle, their eyes glued to the dancer who was now raising herself effortlessly into an upside-down position. How did she do that? Liam tore his eyes away and searched for the person they had come to meet.

'Liam, over here.' A bald, fat man with a deep tan that made his head look like a chestnut stood up at one of the tables close to the dance floor and waved him over.

Liam cringed to hear his voice being shouted out so loudly. Now everyone in the club would know he was here. He hoped the man would prove to be more discreet in his business dealings. He made his way over to the table, Barry at his heels.

'Dennis, good to see you.' Liam extended a hand and felt his knuckles being crunched in the older man's grip.

Dennis Dewhurst was built like a wrestler, flabby on the outside but all muscle beneath. He wore a well-cut suit and open shirt with a heavy gold chain looped around his neck. A huge gold signet ring adorned the pinky finger of each hand. Their wearer was clearly a believer in the "more is more" principle of style.

Although Liam had described Dennis Dewhurst as a business contact, in reality he was little more than a passing acquaintance, someone he'd once been introduced to back in the day, when he was just getting started on his property empire. Liam had been green then, a wide-eyed youngster hoping to make it big, and Dennis had been a local star, a mover and shaker in the leisure industry. Supposedly the guy had made a fortune from his chain of hotels then sold up and headed for the sun. Who could blame him? The mystery was why he'd come back to Scarborough.

'So who's this with you?' asked Dennis, tipping his large head in Barry's direction.

'Barry Hardcastle.' Barry extended a beefy hand, one iron grip encasing another. The two men eyeballed each other across the table, their bone-grinding handshake seeming to go on for far too long, as they sized each other up.

'Barry's my builder,' explained Liam. 'And a potential investor.' Barry had been tied up recently working for Becca's boss, DCI Raven, but had assured Liam that the work on the detective's place was as good as finished. Liam hoped that was true because he had several jobs in need of Barry's expert attention. He'd brought him along tonight because Dennis had indicated that he wanted to discuss a "golden opportunity" and in Liam's experience "opportunities" – golden or otherwise – never came without needing a lot of work. He was no longer as green as when he'd first met Dennis Dewhurst.

'Always good to have a builder on board,' said Dennis, nodding his approval. He extracted his hand from Barry's grasp and indicated a fourth man who was seated in the booth. 'And this is Dale Brady.'

The stranger was another brute of a man, tall and strong, but younger than Dennis and lean rather than flabby. A boxer, not a wrestler, but a heavyweight nonetheless. The kind of guy you'd expect to see pumping iron at the gym. Liam tried not to stare at the scar that stretched all the way from one corner of his mouth to the bottom of his chin. Men with scars like that usually had a story to tell. But not necessarily one that you wanted to hear. He shook Dale's hand and took a seat opposite.

'What'll you gentlemen have to drink?' asked Dennis.

Both he and Dale were drinking Scotch, so Liam asked for the same, glad that Dennis was picking up the tab. If the drinks prices matched the entrance fee, a round here would cost a small fortune.

'I'll stick with a beer, if you don't mind,' said Barry.

'No worries.' Dennis clicked his fingers at a passing waitress in a skimpy black cocktail dress and passed on their orders. She smiled and strode away on teetering heels, Dennis's gaze lingering on her pert behind.

The woman on the pole finished her routine and took a bow to rapturous applause.

Dennis whistled and cheered along with the rest of them. 'Nice one, Jade!' He turned to his companions. 'She's new here. Got talent.'

Liam wondered if Dennis was familiar with all the dancers in the club. Was this a place he regularly used for business meetings? Or did he come here for entertainment? He clearly knew the place well.

'She's not a bad looker, either,' said Dale, giving the young dancer a leer.

'Aye, you're right about that.' Dennis gave a throaty laugh and Liam recalled that the last time they'd met, the older man had puffed his way ostentatiously through an enormous cigar.

'So, Dennis, what brings you back to Scarborough? Spain too sunny for you?' Liam had been surprised when he'd received a call out of the blue from Dennis saying that he was back in town and suggesting they meet up. He hadn't even realised that Dennis still had his number. He'd been drawn here in part out of curiosity.

The waitress brought their drinks and the four men took a moment to clink glasses. Then Dennis leaned forward, placing his elbows on the table, suddenly all business-like.

'There's a pub come up for sale out Hackness way.'

'Hackness?' Liam took a sip of his Scotch. The amber liquid was smooth and warming and he felt himself beginning to relax. Another attractive woman had taken to the dance floor, but he turned his back to her, keeping his attention focussed on Dennis, keen to hear the meat of the deal. Hackness was a village a few miles west of Scarborough. A small, picturesque place, lying within the boundaries of the North York Moors National Park. Not much to it, really. Just a church, a country house hotel and a scattering of houses, all of them chocolate-box pretty. 'What sort of pub?'

'A real gem of a place.' Dennis's arms moved expansively as he painted a picture of the business's potential. 'Proper traditional. Half-timbered, oak panelling, wooden beams, open fireplace. Garden for when the weather's nice. It's got the lot, I tell you. And Dale here' – he gave the other man a hearty slap on the back – 'has recently come into a bit of money and wants to invest it in something tangible. Don't you Dale, my good feller?'

'Got lucky in the casino,' said Dale, who unlike Dennis seemed sparing with his words.

'Good for you,' said Liam. 'No point leaving it to gather dust in the bank is there? If you've got a bit of money, you want to make it work for you.'

'The thing is,' continued Dennis, his voice now dropping to a conspiratorial hush, 'we haven't quite got the funds to make it work. An opportunity like this needs proper investment to do it right, I'm sure you understand. You've got to put money in if you want to get it back. No point in half measures. So that's where you come in, Liam. As a developer yourself, we thought you might like to go equal shares with us. And you too, Barry, if you're interested.'

'Equal shares, eh?' Liam knew nothing about running a pub but he had always fancied owning one. There was something about the idea of enjoying a drink in your own establishment that appealed to his sense of proprietorship. He could picture it now – a summer's evening, sitting outdoors, a pint in his hand, the last rays of sunshine warming his face. And maybe Dennis was right. Maybe this opportunity was as golden as he said. The man was certainly a living legend in the hospitality business. 'Tell me more about this pub. What's the asking price?'

Dennis pointed at Liam's nearly empty glass. 'Get you another drink?'

'Don't mind if I do.' Liam sensed it was going to be a long night. There was certainly plenty to talk about. He nudged Barry in the ribs. 'Another beer for you too, mate?'

★

At the end of her shift, Jade removed her false eyelashes and changed out of her costume into her regular clothes. She enjoyed dressing up and being the centre of attention, always had done ever since she was a little girl, although she was still getting used to having men's eyes crawling all over her skin in her undies. Pervs, some of them. Especially the older guys. Bunch of creeps. She was glad her own father never came anywhere like this. She'd die if he ever found out what she was doing for a living. The prospect of meeting someone she knew there was terrifying. What if she bumped into one of her old teachers from school? How cringing would that be?

She thought the evening's performance hadn't gone too badly. Dani had been watching and said she'd done well, although she needed to smile more at the clients. It was hard to remember to smile when you were gripping a vertical pole with all your strength and trying not to fall off and land on your head. But Jade had nodded eagerly and said she'd be sure to smile more next time. She didn't want to lose this job, not after she'd worked so hard to get it.

It was tough though. Much harder than she'd expected, and not half as glamorous. The other dancers were okay, but they were all a bit older than her and knew each other already. They were dead sophisticated too, and made Jade feel tongue-tied. One of them had mockingly called her "Jade from the Arcade" and if Dani hadn't stood up for her and given that other girl a right telling off, she might have bottled it then and gone scurrying back to her old job.

She did miss Ava. The two of them used to have a right laugh, scoffing fish and chips together down the seafront in their dinner break. Jade hadn't eaten much at all since getting the new job. She had to watch her figure now that she was a professional dancer. All the other girls were so slim. But tomorrow was Sunday and her day off. She thought she might drop in at the arcade and see how Ava was doing. Maybe even get some fish and chips for old times' sake.

You couldn't be skinny every day of the week, could you?

She grabbed her bag and set off for home. It was a cold night, and she put her hood up, thrust her hands into her pockets and walked quickly, head down. She had a twenty-minute walk to her flat on Prospect Road. There were no buses this late at night and she couldn't afford a taxi. The tips weren't proving to be quite as generous as she'd been led to believe. Not yet, anyway. Maybe once she was more experienced and got to know some of the regular punters she could earn a bit more. Until then she'd be walking home each night. She might get herself a bike once she'd saved up enough money. Cycling would help keep her trim and get her home faster.

She crossed the road to avoid a group of lads who were staggering their raucous way down the street after a night of heavy drinking. One of them shouted something obscene at her.

Fuckwits. At least in the club there was a strict "no

touching" rule, and a couple of bouncers on hand to enforce it if things got rowdy. Out here it was the rules of the street, and after closing time on a Saturday night that meant no rules.

She ignored the catcalls and stepped up her pace, widening the gap between her and the drunks, and turned down a side street out of sight. You couldn't be a woman walking home alone without being alert to danger. That's why she carried the can of pepper spray in her pocket, even though Ava had told her it was illegal. Well, bollocks to that. Whoever made that law had no idea what it was like to be a woman on your own at night. Just let someone try something on with her and the bastard would be blinded before he knew what hit him. Oh yes, she'd whip that can out and spray it all over his ugly mug without a second thought.

The attack was so sudden she didn't even see it coming.

One second she'd been imagining how she'd fight off anyone who dared lay a finger on her. The next she was being dragged into a dark alleyway between a couple of shops, one of them boarded up.

Heavy breathing in her ear. The reeking stink of sweat in her nostrils. One clammy hand clamped over her mouth so hard she couldn't even scream. Her heart was hammering in her chest, the vein in her neck pulsing with fear.

Now she wished she'd stuck to the main road and the safety of the streetlights. Even those drunken lads might have come to her aid if they'd seen what was happening. Her fingers fumbled for the pepper spray but her attacker knocked the can from her hand as soon as she grasped it. It landed on the ground with a loud crack and rolled away uselessly into the gutter. Tears smarted her eyes. She struggled to break free from his grip but he was taller and stronger than her. She didn't stand a chance.

He shoved her roughly against a wall, knocking all the breath out of her. The fingers that covered her mouth pulled back and she opened her mouth to scream. Then silver flashed in his hand and she felt the point of a blade pressing into her neck.

'Don't you make a sound,' he hissed. 'And don't try to struggle. You're going nowhere, darling. Not until I'm done with you. Now keep your mouth shut or I'll slash your throat.'

She did as he said, making no sound except a pathetic whimpering. All her courage had fled, leaving her alone with a monster, only her tears for company. She did nothing to stop him as he went about his business.

His hands were everywhere. Up her skirt and tearing at her tights and knickers. She stared, horrified, into his face.

It was a grinning skull.

CHAPTER 20

'Here you go, love, get this inside you before you head off to work. There's fresh tea in the pot too.'

There was no point Becca protesting, whatever her waistline might think. She took a seat at the kitchen table and accepted the plate of hot food her mum had made for her with thanks. As Sue said, it was no bother cooking for one extra mouth when she was already catering for all the guests staying in the guest house.

Liam was sitting opposite her, his eyes underscored with dark shadows, looking like he was nursing a hangover, but still quite capable of seeing off a full English washed down with mugs of hot tea. It had always annoyed Becca the way her brother took advantage of their mum's generosity by turning up at mealtimes, often with a bag of dirty laundry, even though he had a flat of his own. Now for the first time, she understood.

Liam wasn't lazy. He was lonely.

Perhaps.

He slid his empty mug across the table towards her. 'Pour some tea in there, will you, sis?'

'Pour it yourself,' said Becca, passing him the teapot. 'What happened to you last night, anyway?'

A guilty look immediately fixed itself to Liam's face. 'Nothing. What do you mean?'

Becca reached for the marmalade and began spreading it on her toast. 'I was talking about your hangover. Now you've got me wondering what else you got up to.'

Sue came bustling over to make sure they were tucking in. 'Liam was telling me about an exciting new business opportunity that's come up.'

Liam shovelled a fork load of egg and baked beans into his mouth, looking like he wished Sue would keep his news to herself.

'What business opportunity would this be, then?' asked Becca. Liam always had some money-making scheme up his sleeve. Some of them worked out, some fell by the wayside. Not all of them were strictly legal, as far as Becca could make out.

He slurped his tea noisily. 'Nothing to concern you, Becs.'

'Well, now you've really got me interested.'

'It's a pub that needs a bit of work doing to it,' explained Sue.

Becca scoffed at the idea. 'What does Liam know about running a pub? All he knows is how to drink in them.'

Sue immediately rushed to her son's defence. 'I'm sure he knows a lot. It can't be all that different to running a guest house, really. They just serve beer instead of tea. Isn't that right, Liam?'

'I think there might be more to it than that, Mum,' said Becca. 'Licensing laws, for instance.'

Liam looked as if he was regretting his decision to stop over for breakfast. 'How hard can it be? Anyway, it wouldn't just be me. There's a couple of other guys who are interested. Experienced businessmen. We were discussing the possibility of going into partnership together. A consortium.'

'That sounds like a posh word for a bunch of grown-up

men going out and getting smashed,' said Becca, unable to feel much pity for her brother.

Liam really did look ghastly, though. His eyes were bloodshot and his face pale. She could scarcely imagine how much he'd had to drink.

'They went to some fancy place I hadn't heard of,' said Sue.

'Mum,' cautioned Liam.

But Sue was on a roll and couldn't be stopped. 'What did you say it was called, Liam? The *Mayfair?*'

Becca nearly choked on a mushroom. 'You went to the *Mayfair?*'

'It wasn't my choice,' said Liam sulkily. 'Anyway, it's a very nice club.'

'I'm sure it is,' said Becca. 'All those scantily-clad young women performing for your benefit. I was there on Friday following up a murder inquiry.'

'A murder?' Liam blanched even more, which hardly seemed possible given the washed-out state he was already in. 'At the *Mayfair?*'

Sue was back at the table in a jiffy, her jaw wide open. 'What happened? Who was killed? All I heard about was the body in the harbour.'

Becca poured a second mug of tea for herself and stirred milk into it. 'That's the one. Raven and I went to the club to follow up a lead. Did you know that three women connected with the *Mayfair* were stabbed to death about eight years ago?'

A look of relief passed across Liam's face. 'Eight years ago! I thought you were talking about something recent.'

But now it was Sue's turn to go pale. 'I remember that. They were dancers at some kind of strip club, weren't they?' She turned to address her son. 'Liam, did you go to a strip club? Is that where you were last night?'

He groaned. 'It's not a strip club. Tell her, Becs!'

Becca said nothing for a moment, enjoying her brother's discomfort. But she couldn't be cruel for long. 'It's a pole dancing club, Mum. The women don't entirely strip off. And there's no lap dancing or any physical contact between the women and the clients.'

Sue didn't look the least bit reassured. 'Pole dancing, lap dancing, stripping, it all sounds the same to me. I don't want you going back there, Liam, do you hear me?'

Liam rose to his feet, shooting daggers at Becca, as if this were all her fault. 'I can go where I like! I don't have to put up with this. I'm a grown man.'

'Is that so?' demanded Sue, her hands on her hips.

The door to the kitchen opened and David Shawcross entered, bringing a stack of dirty plates back to be washed. 'Whatever is the matter?' he asked his wife.

'Our Liam's been cavorting with strippers and goodness knows who else,' said Sue.

'Strippers?' echoed David.

'Oh, for goodness' sake,' said Liam, grabbing his leather jacket from the back of the chair. 'I'm out of here.'

'Aren't you going to finish your breakfast?' asked Becca.

'No he isn't.' Sue snatched the half-empty plate away before Liam could change his mind. 'There'll be no more cooked breakfasts for you, young man, until you've apologised for your behaviour.'

'Yeah, well that's not happening.'

Becca watched her brother go, half amused, half pitying him. The row would blow over soon enough, no doubt. Sue wasn't capable of harbouring a grudge, especially against her son, and Liam wouldn't risk losing his source of home-cooked food and his free laundry and ironing service.

But it had certainly been a lively start to the day.

'Well,' she said to no one in particular, and setting to work on a jumbo sausage, 'Who would have thought it?'

★

'Briefing in the big meeting room in five minutes.'

Becca had only just arrived at the station and barely had

time to take her coat off. 'What's it about?' she asked.

But it seemed that Raven was determined to be as unhelpful as ever. 'Get your skates on,' he said, striding away down the corridor. 'You don't want to miss it.'

She lifted an enquiring eyebrow at Tony, but he just shrugged. 'Don't know. Some big new development. Everyone's going.'

'Oh well, I guess we'll find out soon enough.' Becca gathered her notepad and pen and headed off in Raven's wake.

By the time she reached the meeting room, there were only a few spare seats left. Whatever was happening, it was important. She joined Tony and Raven at the back of the room, which was filled with officers from all departments. Once everyone was settled, one of the senior uniformed officers, a chief inspector, rose to greet everyone and to introduce the speaker, Sergeant Catherine Howell, sexual offences liaison officer.

'Thank you all for coming here this morning.' PS Catherine Howell was a tall, broad-shouldered woman with a strong West Yorkshire accent. She looked like she'd be compassionate with victims and merciless with offenders. A woman after Becca's own heart. 'I won't take up too much of your time because I know you're busy, but everyone needs to be aware of the sexual attacks that have been perpetrated in Scarborough in the past week.'

Becca exchanged a glance with Tony but it was clear that this was news to him too.

'The first incident took place four nights ago on Ramshill Road. The victim, Ava Jennings, aged nineteen, fought him off and managed to escape. Last night another woman wasn't so lucky. Jade Brown, eighteen years old and a dancer at the *Mayfair* nightclub, was dragged into an alleyway off Gladstone Road and brutally raped at knifepoint. We believe it was the same attacker because both women reported that the man was wearing a face mask in the style of a skull.'

The speaker pressed a key on her laptop and an image

of a scarily realistic rubber mask appeared on the overhead screen. It was the sort of thing that could be bought online or found in a joke shop for a few quid.

Becca's stomach churned. Jade was the girl who'd been dancing at the time she and Raven had visited the club to talk to Frida and Dani. She pictured the young dancer's supple limbs, her tumbling blonde hair, her lovely smooth skin. The thought of her being subjected to a violent sexual attack was nauseating.

'Obviously the use of a mask by the offender makes identifying him more difficult,' said Catherine. 'We don't even have his hair colour. Thanks to the fact that Jade came forward so quickly, we've been able to send a DNA sample off to the lab, but it will be a few days before we get anything back. In the meantime, it's essential that all officers are aware that we appear to have a serial sex attacker in our midst and to be on the lookout for suspicious behaviour. Especially given the escalation of the seriousness of the attacks and the use of a knife in the most recent incident. Any questions?'

Becca raised a hand. 'Could the perpetrator have followed Jade Brown home from the *Mayfair*?'

'It's certainly a possibility,' said Catherine. 'At this point in the investigation we just don't know.'

'And were both victims blonde?'

Catherine narrowed her eyes. 'Do you have information that may be relevant to the inquiry?'

Becca hesitated. It was hard to ignore the fact that Tanya Ayres, Jenny Jones and Caitlin Newhouse were all blonde and had been stabbed to death with a knife. But a man had been convicted of Tanya and Jenny's murders, and there had been no similar attacks since he'd been put behind bars.

Until now.

'No,' she said eventually. 'It was just a thought.'

'All right,' said Catherine. 'But yes, since you ask, both victims were blonde. I can't say yet whether that's a pattern or a coincidence.'

It was Raven who asked the next question. 'What can you tell us about the type of weapon that was used?'

Catherine turned off the projector as she considered her reply, making the image of the skull mask disappear, much to Becca's relief. 'From the description the victim gave, I'd say it probably had a medium length blade, possibly serrated. I can't really tell you more than that.'

Raven nodded. 'And in your opinion, how far would the attacker have taken the assault if the victim had resisted?'

Catherine paused for a moment, weighing her answer carefully. 'It's impossible to know for certain, of course, but I'd say this man was a determined attacker who wasn't afraid to use violence to get what he wanted. If Jade had put up more of a fight, I wouldn't like to think what he might have done in response. Any further questions?'

No one had any, and the meeting began to disperse. Becca stayed in her seat, the image of the horrible mask imprinted on her mind, and the thought of Jade being raped and threatened with a knife still making her feel sick. Her thoughts then turned to Liam and his visit to the *Mayfair* the previous night. She hoped he would heed Sue's ultimatum and stay well away from that place.

But since when had Liam ever listened to good advice?

CHAPTER 21

Raven's phone vibrated on his desk. The name that flashed onscreen was the last person he was expecting to hear from, but he took the call gladly and held the phone to his ear. 'Raven.'

'Sir?' Jess's voice came on the line, hesitant yet quietly determined. She wouldn't have phoned him this early on a Sunday morning unless she had something to tell him.

'How are you doing?'

'I'm okay.'

He sensed that was only partially true. Nobody could be okay so soon after facing the kind of blow that Jess had received. But Jess was hardy, the kind of person with enough resilience to pick herself up and carry on. 'Becca told me you were staying with your parents.'

'Yes, but I'm thinking of coming back to Scarborough.' There was a pause before she continued. 'I found something. A letter from Scott. I think it might be significant.'

Raven pictured the parcel he'd found wrapped in brown paper with Jess's name written on it. 'Becca told me he left you a book.'

'Yes, but there was a letter with it.' Jess carried on breathlessly, stumbling over her words in her hurry to get them out. 'I'm pretty certain that Scott knew his killer.'

'Tell me what you know.'

He listened as she read out the letter, or parts of it at least. He suspected that she was omitting the more personal remarks. But what he heard confirmed his hunch that the answer to Scott's death lay in the past.

'For the longest time,' read Jess, *'it felt like I was getting nowhere, that it was just an obsession that would lead me to a brick wall. But now, finally, I think I'm close to the truth.'*

Raven envied Scott that feeling of being near to closure. He still felt a million miles away.

'There's just one final piece of the jigsaw I need to confirm.'

Raven was only just beginning to discern the shape of the jigsaw, let alone its individual pieces. And yet Scott had recorded all his notes and ideas on his evidence board. The answer must be in there somewhere. Raven stared at the board again as he listened to Jess speak.

Caitlin Newhouse. Tanya Ayres. Jenny Jones.

One killer, or two?

Jess paused, as if weighing whether or not to read out the next lines. After a moment she resumed. *'Then I'll have all I need to go to the police. When I do that, I'd like DCI Raven to lead the investigation. I know he'll do whatever it takes to get justice for Mum.'*

Well, no pressure there. 'Is that all he wrote?' Raven asked.

'There's one last bit. This is the crucial part. Listen.' He listened carefully as she read aloud Scott's final words. *'But now I have to go and meet someone.'*

The implication of that last line was chilling. Scott had knowingly gone to meet the person he'd suspected of killing his mother. And he'd done it alone, late at night. What had he been thinking?

But Raven already knew the answer to that question. Scott had been willing to do whatever it took to get to the truth. Whatever the risk. Whatever the consequences.

Because not knowing was worse.

'All right, Jess,' he said when she'd finished. 'We're following up Scott's evidence and doing our best to get to the bottom of it. You know I can't tell you any more than that.'

'I know that, sir.'

'But what you've told me is extremely helpful. You did the right thing in calling me.'

The relief in her voice was palpable. 'Thank you, sir.'

'All right. Take care.'

He hung up, feeling invigorated by the call. He was convinced now that to find Scott's killer, he would need to solve the murder of Caitlin Newhouse. And possibly also of Tanya Ayres and Jenny Jones. No easy challenge, but at least he knew the direction he was aiming for.

Meanwhile, two women had recently been attacked in circumstances that bore at least a passing resemblance to the historic cases. His instinct told him that it was part of the mix. A dark blend, that would have to be untangled in order to get at the truth.

All the victims were blonde, attacked in their own homes or on their way home from work. The use of a knife, the sexual nature of the attacks... the only difference was the level of violence employed. Plus the interval of eight years between the spates of the assaults. Had Terry Baines been innocent all along? Or did he have an accomplice?

There was one other name on Scott's evidence board.

'Tony,' said Raven, 'remind me how long Dennis Dewhurst spent out of the country.'

The DC referred to his notes, even though Raven suspected he already had the facts committed to memory. 'A total of seven years, sir. He went abroad the year after Caitlin Newhouse's body was found and returned nearly three months ago.'

'What do we think?' Raven asked. 'Coincidence?' He looked from Tony to Becca, but neither answered his question. They knew it was rhetorical.

'Shall we go and pick him up?' asked Becca. 'Do we

have enough to arrest him?'

'No,' said Raven. 'Everything we have is circumstantial.'

Despite the period that Dewhurst had spent in Spain coinciding with the gap between the spates of assaults, there was a hole in Raven's theory that you could drive a tractor through. It was that Terry Baines's DNA had been found on Tanya and Jenny's bodies. Not to mention the murder weapon found in Terry's possession. Dewhurst's DNA, meanwhile, was nowhere to be found. On the face of it, the man was innocent.

'Still,' he went on, 'Scott did single out Dennis Dewhurst as a person of interest in his mother's murder, and at the very least I want to find out if he has an alibi for the times of these two latest assaults.'

Becca picked up her coat. 'Then what are we waiting for? Let's go and have a chat with him.'

★

Raven parked the BMW on Montpellier Terrace in front of a long row of white houses, five stories from the basement to the roof and separated from the street by elaborate black iron railings. The building had broad bay windows, Roman arches and columns above the front door, and some fancy ornamental detailing on the drainpipes that suggested to Raven that the builders of these imposing townhouses were far removed from the Barry Hardcastles of this world.

'Not too shabby,' he said, mentally comparing the property with his own house on Quay Street and finding himself wondering what kind of kitchen Dennis Dewhurst had.

'Well out of my price range,' said Becca with a sniff.

'I didn't know you were looking for a place to live?'

She gave the building a sullen glance. 'I might be. But I wouldn't choose to live here. It doesn't even have a sea view.'

'I suppose you can't have everything.' Raven's own house lacked a view of the sea even though it was situated just yards from the harbour. It had a sea smell, but that probably wouldn't offer the same kind of appeal to potential buyers. It might even, he conceded, be something of a turn-off.

They approached the entrance to the house by a short flight of stone steps and Raven leaned on the doorbell of the flat number that Tony had given him.

The man who opened the door was fat, bald and ugly, and neither the gold chain around his neck, nor the caramel-coloured tan that he'd brought back with him from Spain was going to change that. That tan wouldn't last long in Scarborough either, unless he topped it up at a salon, or got some more out of a bottle.

'Yeah?' snapped Dewhurst. 'What is it?'

'DCI Raven of Scarborough CID, and this is my colleague DS Becca Shawcross. We'd like to have a word with you, if you've got the time, Mr Dewhurst?'

The man scowled, which did nothing to improve his looks. 'And what if I haven't?'

'Then I suggest you make time. Now.'

He looked as if he wanted to shut the door in their faces, but then thought better of it. 'What's it about?'

'Why don't we explain once you've invited us inside?' Raven suggested.

'You know I don't have to let you in,' said Dewhurst grumpily.

'Had dealings with the police before, have you?' said Becca.

Dewhurst gave her a dirty look but retreated inside the hallway, leaving the door open for them to enter. They followed him through to a ground floor flat.

The apartment was well appointed, with high ceilings, polished wooden floors, and plenty of natural light spilling through the south-facing windows. But the presence of Dennis Dewhurst hadn't added to its charm. The man was living a bachelor life, with minimal furniture, no pictures on the walls, and half of his possessions apparently still stored in big cardboard boxes piled up around the edge of the living room.

'Planning to move house?' enquired Raven.

'Haven't got round to unpacking yet.'

Raven eyed the boxes, wondering if one of them might contain a rubber skull mask.

The same idea seemed to have crossed Becca's mind. She casually opened the nearest box and peered inside.

'Oi,' said Dewhurst. 'That's my personal property. You can't just go rummaging through my stuff.'

Becca offered him a smile. 'Of course not, Mr Dewhurst. I wouldn't dream of it.'

He regarded her suspiciously for a moment as if expecting her to resume her search as soon as his back was turned, then shrugged his heavy shoulders wearily. 'Well, we may as well have a seat.' He led them through to an airy kitchen and took up residence on a chrome stool at the breakfast bar.

Raven cast a knowledgeable glance around the room. Marble countertops, high contrast paintwork, low level cabinets. He was enough of an expert now on kitchen fashion to spot the latest trends at work. It didn't look as if Dewhurst was making much use of the facilities on offer, however. The place was spotlessly clean apart from a collection of dirty coffee cups piled next to the sink.

Raven pulled out a barstool and sat next to Becca. 'Nice place you've got here. I understand you're into property.'

'Is that a question?'

'No, I suppose not,' acknowledged Raven. 'All right then, try this. Where were you last night between the hours of ten o'clock and midnight?'

Dewhurst presented them with a stony face. 'Is this a police question? Is this an interview?'

'Let's call it a chat, shall we?'

'Am I entitled to a solicitor?'

Raven made a show of studying his watch. 'You can call a solicitor if you like, Mr Dewhurst. But it could take ages to find one on a Sunday. We might be waiting all day. We might even decide to invite you down to the station to conduct a formal interview under caution. On the other hand you could simply answer our questions, especially if you've nothing to hide. And then you could get back to doing whatever it was you were planning to do on your Sunday morning.'

Dewhurst glowered at them, considering his options. But they all knew that he didn't really have any. 'Okay then, I'll tell you. I was out at a club last night until late.'

'Does it have a name, this club?' asked Becca.

'The *Mayfair*.'

'You're a regular there?'

'Aye, and what if I am? Not a crime to watch a bit of dancing, is it?'

'Not at all,' said Raven. 'What time did you say you left?'

'Late.'

'That's not technically a time, is it?' said Becca. 'It doesn't really make for a convincing alibi.'

'Alibi for what?'

Raven left that question unanswered. Instead he asked another one. 'Where were you on Wednesday evening?'

'Long time ago, Wednesday,' said Dewhurst.

'Four days,' countered Raven. 'Try to think back.'

Dewhurst scratched the back of his thick neck, setting his gold chain dancing. 'Probably at the club.'

'The *Mayfair*?'

'That's it.'

'You seem to like it there,' said Raven affably. 'But here's my problem. Eight years ago, three women who worked at the *Mayfair* were murdered. Two of them were dancers, and one of them worked behind the bar. Not long afterwards, you disappeared off to Spain. And now you're back and two more woman have been attacked, one at knifepoint. She was a dancer at the club too. What do you make of that?'

Dewhurst's face could have curdled milk. 'I don't make

anything of it, and neither would any solicitor worth his salt. Who do you think you are, coming here, accusing me of... I don't know what. In my own home! You've got a bloody nerve.'

'The thing is, Mr Dewhurst, unless you can come up with a more convincing alibi, you're looking like our prime suspect.'

'Right, that's enough!' shouted Dewhurst. 'If you want to talk to me, you'll have to arrest me, and I'll have my lawyer present, Sunday or not. I know how these things work. You can't just go around throwing out accusations. And if you think you can intimidate me, you've got no idea who you're dealing with. Now get out of my apartment, the pair of you.'

'What did you make of that?' Raven asked Becca once they were back on the street.

'I think that Mr Dennis Dewhurst is a very unpleasant man,' she said. 'I also think we need to check out his alibis more thoroughly. See if anyone else at the club can say precisely when he was there. If he even was.'

'I think you're right,' said Raven. An image of the *Mayfair* presented itself to him, all leather armchairs and polished wood. And there, her long legs crossed in casual elegance, a certain Swedish woman sitting waiting for him. He'd been hoping for a reason to speak to Frida again and now he had one. 'Leave it with me.'

CHAPTER 22

'**S**ir, some new information that may or may not be relevant.'

Raven and Becca were back in the incident room after the interview with Dennis Dewhurst. Raven was planning to drive over to the *Mayfair* later. But he wanted to go there alone. There was no need for Becca to accompany him to the club. She had other jobs she could be getting on with, and it would be more efficient for him to go by himself. Or at least that was the story he was telling himself. It seemed quite convincing to him, although Becca might not be so quickly persuaded.

'What is it, Tony?'

'The cellmate who testified against Terry Baines at his trial, saying he'd confessed to the murders of the two women' – Tony checked his notes – 'a man called George Grime. Well, he was released from prison a few weeks ago.'

'Interesting,' said Raven. 'You think we should talk to him? Find out if he still insists that Terry confessed?'

'Possibly, sir. But the thing is, I've been doing a bit of digging into his background and I found a couple of interesting coincidences.'

'Go on.'

Tony scratched his nose tentatively. He was a diligent copper, but reluctant to go out on a limb when his ideas seemed speculative. And yet his relentless pursuit of the facts had often led Raven in the right direction in the past. 'The first thing that struck me was the dates. Grime served a seven-year sentence and was discharged from prison just before the recent assaults on women.'

Raven was quickly catching on to Tony's thinking. 'You're saying he might be the attacker?'

'I'm just saying that the dates fit. But there's more to it than that. Grime was arrested around the same time as Terry Baines, shortly after the body of Caitlin Newhouse was found. So we can't rule out the possibility that he killed Caitlin. Or even Jenny and Tanya too.'

'And then claimed that Terry confessed to those crimes to divert attention from himself.' Raven turned the idea over in his mind, probing it for flaws. He had to admit – at first sight, he liked the way it looked.

'What was this George Grime in for?' asked Becca.

'A range of sexual offences.'

'Specifically?' queried Raven.

'Quite a variety.' Tony adjusted his glasses and consulted his notes. 'A series of sexual assaults. Plus the possession of grossly offensive images including indecent images of children.'

Raven curled his upper lip. 'He sounds like a thoroughly objectionable human being. Did any of his assaults involve the use of a knife?'

'No. But you know how these things tend to go.'

There was no need for Tony to spell out his meaning. Raven knew well enough that offenders generally started small, working up to more serious and violent acts as their criminal careers progressed. In the most recent spate of attacks, the perpetrator had quickly advanced to an aggravated assault with the use of a knife, possibly as a result of the failure of his first attempt.

'He fits the pattern,' said Becca.

'There's something else,' said Tony. 'George Grime was also a resident at the children's home where Scott and Cameron lived.'

'You've got to be kidding.' Raven didn't believe in coincidences without consequences. Especially not one as huge as that.

'He's a few years older than Scott and Cameron, so they might not have known him. But on the other hand...'

Raven thumped the desk in triumph. 'Scott went to visit someone he knew on the night he was attacked. Someone he believed had killed his mother. This is good work, Tony. You may have found our man.'

Becca sounded a note of caution. 'I read through Scott's personal file from Hiddenbeck Hall. There was nothing to suggest he experienced any kind of trouble there, and no mention of George Grime.'

'Maybe not,' said Raven. 'But that doesn't prove they didn't know each other. Come on, let's go and bring this Grime in for questioning.'

★

As a registered sex offender, George Grime's address hadn't been difficult to find. But the man himself was proving to be more elusive. Raven rang the doorbell for a third time and banged at the front door, but there was no answer from within, and the closed curtains prevented him from peering through the windows.

He cast a frustrated gaze around the low-rise block of flats. 'No sea views here either,' he remarked to Becca. 'So I expect this is well within your price range.'

'I expect so.'

The windswept building on Scarborough's Barrowcliff estate was no Montpellier Terrace. Squat and ugly, it was surrounded by a chain-link fence and its views were of the derelict lot next door. Still, George Grime was lucky to have anywhere to live. If his new neighbours discovered he was a convicted sex offender, his luck might run out very quickly.

'I'll give his probation officer a ring and see what they know about him,' said Becca.

Raven waited as she made the call, speaking to the officer responsible for supervising Grime. It didn't take long for her to establish the facts. 'She told me that Grime registered his address when released from prison and that as far as she knows he hasn't breached any of the terms of his licence.'

'Does she know where he is?'

'He's registered as living here, but obviously she can't vouch for his whereabouts 24/7.'

'No.' Raven glared once more at the locked door and closed curtains. He couldn't rule out the possibility that George Grime was crouching behind the door right now, listening in to the conversation. But wherever he might be, Raven didn't have enough evidence to apply for a warrant for his arrest. 'Let's circulate his details to patrol and get an officer to check on him later. I want to know as soon as he's found. In the meantime, let's go and have another word with Cameron Blake. He may be able to tell us if he remembers Grime from the children's home.'

★

When Cameron opened his door a look of unease spread quickly across his face. He was visibly holding his breath and Raven realised that he was expecting to be told that his friend's killer had been arrested.

'Have you found out who killed Scott?' he murmured. 'Do you know who did it?'

Raven was sorry to have to disappoint him. 'I'm afraid it's still early days in the investigation. But we're following up a number of leads.' The statement was true, but like all police language it concealed more than it revealed. Raven wished he could offer the young man more, but it would be a mistake to build up his hopes too much. He had been let down too many times already.

Cameron's face fell. 'Yeah. Okay. I suppose I should have expected that.'

Raven and Becca hadn't bothered ringing the front door bell at Filey Road this time, but had come straight to the annexe at the bottom of the garden. There was no need to speak to Veronica Gibson again, and Raven had no desire for a second encounter with the crazy cat landlady.

'Can we come inside?' he asked, adopting what he hoped was a soothing tone of voice. He didn't want to spook the young man. 'We just have a few follow-up questions to ask you.'

Cameron nodded silently and turned away.

Raven followed him in and he and Becca took up their previous places around the wooden table. Today, Cameron was wearing paint-splashed overalls over his clothes. An almost overpowering smell of glue, oil paint and turpentine pervaded the enclosed space of the annexe.

'Do you mind if we open a window?' asked Becca. 'Before one of us passes out from the fumes?'

Her comment elicited a shimmer of a smile from Cameron. 'Yeah, no probs. Sorry. It's a bit strong isn't it? I guess I'm used to it.' He went to the nearest window and cracked it open to let in fresh air. It was good to see him smile for a change, revealing a glimpse of the man he might have been if he'd had a more fortunate start in life.

'Can I start by asking if you and Scott were in the habit of communicating by phone?' asked Raven.

'Yes,' said Cameron, surprised by the question. 'Of course.'

'Would you mind telling us your number?'

The request tipped Cameron back into his guarded state, but Raven gave him a reassuring smile. 'It's simply so that we can eliminate it from the list of calls that Scott made. There are still two numbers he made regular calls to that we haven't been able to identify.'

The explanation seemed to have the desired effect. 'Okay, I understand.' Cameron wrote the number on a scrap of paper and handed it over.

It was one of the two unlisted numbers identified by Tony in Scott's phone records. Raven made a mental note to cross it off the evidence board when they got back. That just left one unidentified number that Scott had regularly called and texted in the months before his death.

'Thanks,' said Raven. 'Next, we want to ask if you've ever heard the name, George Grime.'

Cameron's reaction was instant and visceral. His face paled and his hands knotted together protectively across his chest. 'W-why?' he stammered. 'Has he done something bad?'

Becca rested a hand on his arm. 'There's no need to be afraid, Cameron. Just tell us what you know about him.'

It was obvious from the lad's demeanour that he and Grime had crossed paths. And not in a good way. Raven's mind was already painting a picture of the two boys encountering each other at the children's home. Grime would have been a much older boy, in a position of power over a younger lad, especially one with a shy, nervous disposition. Had Grime bullied Cameron? Or worse? Raven couldn't ignore the fact that one of the offences Grime had been convicted of was the possession of indecent images of children.

Cameron had become withdrawn, hunching his shoulders over. He shook his head from side to side. 'I don't want to talk about that man. I already told you I don't want to talk about the children's home.'

'We're not going to force you to talk if you don't want to,' said Raven. 'But anything you can tell us might help with our investigation into Scott's death.'

Cameron glanced nervously from Raven to Becca, perhaps debating whether he could trust them. His lips remained steadfastly closed. Raven wondered how many times the lad's trust had been broken by people in authority. To get Cameron to open up, he would have to earn that trust.

'Listen,' he said. 'I know you don't want to talk about your time at Hiddenbeck Hall' – Cameron flinched even at the very mention of the home's name – 'but anything you can tell us about George Grime could be vital.' He let that sink in for a moment before adding, 'I told you that we were following up a number of lines of inquiry. Well, one of those is the possibility that George murdered Scott, and that he may also have murdered Scott's mother.'

He caught Becca's look of surprise and admonishment, but shook his head to dismiss it. It was against procedures to reveal that kind of information to a witness, but in Cameron's case, playing it by the book would simply make him clam up and say nothing.

Cameron's hand was trembling, his eyes glued to Raven as if he could somehow see through a window into his soul and know whether to put his faith in him.

'You can trust us, Cameron,' Raven urged. 'Help us find out the truth.'

'The truth…' began Cameron tentatively. 'Sometimes the truth should stay in the past.'

'Sometimes,' said Raven. His mind turned to his own murky past and the dark, self-destructive thoughts that lurked there. The self-blame for his mother's death; the hatred of his father; his fear of unlocking the monster within. He had tried to bury those thoughts, had run off to the army to escape them, had spent his entire life running, but they always bubbled back to the surface, more toxic than ever. They would never go away.

Cameron, too, had run from his traumas, hiding himself in this annexe at the bottom of a garden belonging to an eccentric old lady. Veronica Gibson had rescued him from his old life, keeping him from harm and acting as his bastion against a hostile world. But sometimes the enemies were inside your head. You could never out-run that kind of fear.

Raven spoke again, his voice soft. 'We can never really leave the past behind, you know. If we hide from it, it will continue to cast a shadow over the present. Don't let yourself walk in that shadow forever, Cameron. It will only grow taller if you allow it.'

His words hit home. Cameron stared into his face, hungry for the release that might come if he opened up at last. If he finally found someone who wouldn't let him down.

'I was abused,' he murmured, so quietly that Raven had to lean in to catch his words. 'At the hall. Not just me. Some of the other boys too. We didn't tell anyone, though. We were too afraid.'

'Afraid of George?'

'No. He was a victim too.'

Raven frowned, thrown by Cameron's reply. 'Then who?'

A hesitation. Cameron teetered on the brink of revelation.

'You can tell us, Cameron,' Raven assured him. 'There's nothing to fear. You're in safe hands now.'

The boy's lips parted in soundless movement and Raven held his breath in anticipation.

'By the home's manager,' said Cameron eventually, and the look of relief on his face was palpable.

Becca gasped. 'Colin West?'

'He wasn't always the manager,' said Cameron. 'When I was sent to the home he was a carer in charge of the younger boys. But he didn't care about anyone except himself. If he had, he could never have done the things he did. He was a bastard. An evil bastard!' A sob escaped his lips and his hands began to shake.

Becca reached out to comfort him and Cameron allowed himself to be embraced, to be gathered into her arms. She patted him on the back, making soothing sounds, her face turned to Raven's in anguish.

Raven waited for the boy to calm down before speaking again. 'We'll arrange for a specially trained police officer to come and talk to you, Cameron. You can tell them everything that happened to you, and they'll take your statement. They'll be responsible for investigating your case and taking it forward. If you want, you can ask for Veronica or someone else to be present when you speak to the police. Do you understand?'

Cameron nodded through his tears.

'But before we go, I have to ask you more about George Grime. Did Scott know him?'

'Yes.' The tears continued to roll down Cameron's cheeks, but he forced the words out regardless. There was a new determination in his eyes that hadn't been there before. A need to tell his story and be heard. 'George was a bully. He picked on the little kids, especially the new ones. At the time we were terrified of him, but looking back, I can see now that he wasn't so tough. He always picked out the weakest kids, the ones he could push around and who wouldn't fight back.'

He accepted a tissue from Becca, blew his nose and continued. 'By the time Scott came to the home, George had already stopped picking on me. I guess he'd got bored and wanted someone new. He messed with Scott for a bit when he first arrived, but Scott was already fourteen. He was too big for George. Anyway, George left the home and was arrested very soon afterwards. But it was no secret that George had been abused by Colin when he was younger. He was one of Colin's "special boys".'

'Like you?' asked Becca.

'When I first came to the home, I was only six. Colin was kind to me for a while, or at least he pretended to be. He knew that George was bullying me. He said he would help. But instead...' More tears ran down his face and he came to a halt.

'Cameron,' said Becca, 'we're going to investigate these allegations very seriously. We're going to find out exactly what happened and make sure that anyone who broke the law gets the punishment they deserve.'

Cameron shuddered, nodding his head gently. 'You told me that George may have been the man who killed Scott and his mum?'

'That's right,' said Raven.

'Then it may have been my fault that Scott's dead.' Cameron's shoulders shook as he struggled to get the words out.

'How can it be your fault, Cameron? You did nothing wrong.'

The lad swayed his head from side to side. 'But I think I did. When I heard that George was about to be released from prison, I texted Scott about it. It was just after Christmas. I knew that George was one of the men Scott had considered as a suspect in his mother's murder. He didn't really think it was George, because George was only seventeen at the time, and the crimes he committed weren't as serious as murder. But if George really was the killer, and I told Scott about his release, then...' he dissolved into tears once more, unable to continue.

Raven had heard enough. 'Stay with him,' he told Becca. 'Arrange for a specialist officer to come and take a statement from him.'

'What about you?' she asked.

'Me?' Raven got to his feet. 'I'm going to pay a visit to Colin West.'

CHAPTER 23

The drive from Filey Road to Hiddenbeck Hall did nothing to calm Raven down. If anything, it only made his anger blacker. He turned over the accusations that Cameron Blake had levelled at the manager of the children's home. The singling out of vulnerable young boys for abuse. The creation of a regime of fear that had prevented anyone from raising the alarm. If there was a shred of truth in those allegations – and Raven didn't doubt Cameron's sincerity for an instant – he would make sure that Colin West answered for them.

On arrival at the hall he was greeted by a youthful receptionist wearing multicoloured clothing and a bashful smile. 'Hi, I'm Cheryl. How can I help you?'

'You can point me in the direction of Colin West.'

'His office is just over there,' said Cheryl, her ponytail swaying as she pointed down a corridor. 'But I think he might be busy. Do you have an appointment?'

'No,' said Raven. 'It's a surprise visit.'

'Oh,' said Cheryl anxiously. 'I don't think Colin will –'

'Thanks for your help. I'll find my own way,' he told her, setting off in the direction she'd indicated. The manager's office wasn't difficult to find, given that his name was engraved in capital letters on a brass plaque on his office door. Giving the door a loud rap, Raven opened it without waiting for an answer and stepped inside.

Colin West was seated behind his desk, mounds of paperwork organised into neat piles across its polished surface. He looked up crossly at Raven's intrusion, quickly working himself into a state of indignation. 'I don't think I'm expecting anyone just now. Why don't you go and make an appointment with my secretary.'

'That won't be necessary,' said Raven, slamming the door behind him and thrusting his warrant card in West's flabby face.

The manager regarded it sullenly. 'Police, eh? What are you poking around for now? I had a police woman in here just t'other day. I told her everything she wanted to know. I doubt I can tell you owt I didn't already say to her.'

'Oh, I hope you can, Mr West. You see, I'm here about a rather different matter. I've just been speaking to a former resident of this home who has accused you of child sexual abuse.'

'Of what?' There was a brief moment of panic in West's eyes that told Raven all he needed to know. And then the manager of the home began to chuckle heartily, his cheeks wobbling from side to side like slabs of raw ham. He had switched back to his evasive manner, doing his best to compensate for the brief flicker of guilt that had already betrayed him. 'Who was it said that?'

'That's confidential.' There was no way Raven was about to reveal the source of his information to this man.

But West wasn't giving up that easily. 'Come on, you can tell me his name. I remember all the kids who passed through this home. I were like a father to some of 'em.'

'Interesting,' said Raven, 'that you're assuming it's a boy I'm talking about. I didn't say whether the witness was male or female.'

'Boy, girl,' blustered West, 'what difference does it make? It's all a pack of lies! I bet it's just one person's word.

You can't believe everything you hear from some of the kids that live here. Damaged they are, some of 'em. Broken homes, no mums or dads to look after 'em. They'll tell you anything to grab your attention. So, what evidence have you got to back up this accusation?'

When Raven hesitated, West pounced. 'I thought so. Just the word of some sad individual against mine.' He stabbed a chubby finger in Raven's direction. 'I suggest you come back when you have something more concrete to go on, or when you're in a position to reveal your source so that a proper inquiry can be opened through the right channels. You can't just wander in here throwing around that kind of baseless accusation. There are rules to be followed. Do you understand that?'

The longer Raven listened to West's denials, the more his anger grew. 'What I understand perfectly well,' he growled, 'is that you're not fit to look after a herd of cattle, let alone be entrusted with the welfare of vulnerable children.'

West regarded him insolently. 'There you go again, see? No evidence to back up your claims. That's slander, that is. I could sue you for false allegations.'

If Colin West believed that bullying was the way to get what he wanted, he had made a grave miscalculation. Raven advanced to the edge of the desk, placing his palms firmly on top of the manager's paperwork. He was gratified to see the man draw back in alarm. 'Let's try another question, shall we? What do you know about George Grime, one of the boys who was in your care?'

At George's name, West's face soured. 'George Grime, not one of our most fondly remembered residents. The lad was a bully and a pervert, preying on girls at the home, molesting them sexually. No doubt you know that he committed a rape shortly after leaving the home and was sent to prison.'

'I'm aware of that,' said Raven. 'Were you aware that he was released recently after serving his sentence?'

West shrugged. 'I did hear something to that effect.

What's George Grime got to do with me?'

'Because an accusation has been made that you abused him too.'

West narrowed his eyes, then his mouth twitched into a wolfish smile. 'Another of your allegations, eh? And not a shred of evidence to back it up, I expect. This conversation is starting to become very repetitive, DCI Raven. I suggest you bring it to an end. You know the way out.' He waved his hand dismissively in the direction of the door.

Raven lifted his hands from the desk, squeezing them into heavy fists. He was *that* far from putting them into action and beating a confession out of the man sitting on the other side of the desk.

West drew back in his chair, genuine fear registering on his face for the first time.

Raven glared down at him, imagining what that round ruddy face would look like after a couple of well-placed blows. Much the better, by his reckoning. But then he lowered his fists to his sides, uncurling his fingers and breathing out. Physical violence wasn't the answer. It never was.

He would make West pay for his crimes. But he would do it the right way, according to the law.

'I'll be back,' promised Raven. 'And next time I'll have all the evidence I need to arrest you.'

★

Jess packed her bag, folding the few clothes she'd brought with her to Rosedale and laying the book of Poe's poems carefully on top. She'd returned from her walk the previous day still filled with uncertainties and doubts, but having made one very important decision which she had communicated to her family over dinner that evening. She was returning to Scarborough.

Their reactions had been predictable enough.

Her mother had worried that she wasn't ready, that she

needed more time at home to grieve. More time to think about her future. Why not stay a little longer? There was no hurry to get back to work. Without actually saying so, it was clear she was hoping Jess would resign from the police and stay at Rosedale Abbey for good.

Her sister had told her outright not to be daft. That she was better off at home, in a place she could be safe.

Her brother had suggested she might help him run the camping and caravan park. There was always work to be found, although much of it was seasonal.

Her father's response had been more muted, but she could tell that he was worried about her.

But Jess's mind was made up. She had read *The Raven* multiple times sitting by the ruined iron ore kilns, and had gradually come to a fuller understanding of herself and what she wanted from life. She refused to become like the narrator of the poem, peering ever deeper into the darkness, fearful of the future, forever trapped by the raven's curse.

Scott had been the victim of a crime. She refused to become one too.

Would she return to her job as a police detective? It was too early to say. In some ways that would be the easy option. Go back to work and pick up where she had left off. No need to face a difficult decision. But if she was going to change course, now was the time.

She ran through the reasons she'd joined the police force in the first place. Looking back, they didn't seem that compelling. Really all she'd wanted was a job where she could be on her feet and not simply stuck behind a desk. It was hardly a vocation she'd dreamed of since childhood. She wasn't like Scott, who had dedicated his life to obtaining justice for victims of crime.

She wasn't even a particularly good detective. Her own boyfriend had lived a double life filled with secrets and she hadn't begun to guess at them. Her world had been turned upside down twice – first by Scott's death and then by everything she had learned about him subsequently.

She took one last look around her childhood bedroom, her eyes lingering on the books she had read and loved. She held fond memories of this space, having spent her formative years here. But it was no longer hers. She should tell her parents to redecorate it as a proper grown-up guest room. She had moved on and it was time for them to let go.

She understood now that when she'd left home and gone to live in Scarborough they had suffered their own kind of bereavement. Not one for the dead, but for the living. Although she would always be their daughter and would return to see them whenever she could, she was a child no more and had outgrown their care.

They had suffered their own loss, but that mustn't hold her back from living life to the full.

On an impulse she went back to her bag, removed the book of Poe's poems and slotted it into an empty space on the shelf, beside all the other books she would never read again.

She went downstairs. Andrea was in the kitchen, making preparations for the evening meal. A meal her parents would eat alone. Andrea had begged her to stay another night and Jess felt a pang of guilt that she was abandoning them after they'd been so kind. But she had to get back on her own two feet. She had to escape before her resolve faltered.

'You're off then?' said Andrea.

'I want to get back before it gets dark,' said Jess.

Andrea nodded. 'Come here.' They hugged each other tightly. 'You know you can always come home at any time, don't you?'

'I know,' said Jess. But she also knew that this was no longer her home. She kissed her mother on the cheek, then turned, picked up her bag and walked out of the front door.

CHAPTER 24

Raven was still in a foul temper when he arrived back at the station. He'd worked out some of his aggression behind the wheel of the M6, turning his music up loud. Fields of the Nephilim: jagged guitars, a ruthless drumbeat, heavily overlaid with sonorous lyrics.

Dark music for a dark mood.

The encounter with Colin West was something he wouldn't soon forget. The way the man had blustered and bullied, ridiculing the charges against him and trying to weasel the identity of his accuser out of Raven had left a bad taste in his mouth. As if coming that close to a paedophile had contaminated him with the same filth that polluted West's own sick mind.

He went to the bathroom and gave his hands a thorough wash before making his way back up to the incident room.

As expected there was no sign of Dinsdale, but Tony was still hard at work and Becca was back from Cameron's studio, her hands wrapped around a mug of hot tea. 'Hi,' she said. 'How did you get on with Colin West?'

'That man!' said Raven, throwing his coat over the back

of a chair in disgust.

Becca gave him a grim smile. 'I know,' she said. 'He's a creep. A rodent. Although that's probably being unfair to rodents. Rodents would sue me if they heard me compare them to Colin West.'

It was good to be back in her company. 'What happened with Cameron?' he asked her.

She took a sip of her tea. 'I waited with him and Veronica until someone from the historic child abuse team arrived to speak to him. She was very good at her job. Calm, sympathetic. She said just the right things to encourage him to open up. He seems to have decided that he can trust the police at last.'

'Excellent. He deserves some justice after all he's endured.' Raven hoped that Cameron wouldn't live to regret his decision. It was up to the authorities to put right now what should have been done many years ago.

'I don't suppose that Colin West admitted anything?' asked Becca.

'Not a chance,' said Raven.

'So where does that leave us?' asked Tony.

'Good question.' The investigation was moving, but it was in danger of being blown off course, getting tangled up with historic child abuse, attacks on women both now and in the past, not to mention Caitlin's unsolved murder. Raven knew he mustn't forget that he was supposed to be finding out who had killed Scott.

He moved over to the evidence board and studied the section headed "Suspects".

The faces of three men stared back at him. Dennis Dewhurst. George Grime. And a third man, whose identity was unknown, but was probably Scott's father. The folded image that Raven had removed from the photo frame showed a young man with looks that some women might find attractive if they were drawn to the bad boy type. Muscular, with an insolent expression bordering on a sneer, he certainly looked capable of violence.

Plus, he fitted the bill. It was a shocking fact that most

murders of women were carried out by their current or former partners. The person they had trusted most to look after them. Had Caitlin been stabbed to death by the father of her child? And had that man gone on to kill Scott?

Raven's thoughts grew dark as he recalled his own father's drunken bouts of violence and the cuts and bruises that his mum had worn as constant reminders of his behaviour.

'Tony,' he said, 'find out all you can about Scott's father. Name, address, criminal record, anything. According to Caitlin's friend, Dani, he abandoned the family when Scott was still very young. I want to know where he went, where he's lived for the last ten years and where he is now.'

'I'll see what I can do, sir.'

'Any news on George Grime?' he asked Becca.

'Not yet. A patrol car called round at his flat but couldn't get an answer. The officers asked his neighbours when he'd last been seen but they couldn't remember. They described him as a loner. Someone who talks to no one and keeps himself to himself.'

'I bet he does,' grumbled Raven. A convicted sex offender like George Grime would want to keep a low profile. It would only be a matter of time before someone in the community found out who he was and what he'd done, and he would have to move on to somewhere new. Raven felt no sympathy for him. He had brought his suffering on himself. 'Well, he can't stay hidden forever. He's bound to turn up sooner or later.'

He turned his attention to the third man on the board. Dennis Dewhurst. Another of Raven's least favourite people, and another one whose status as a suspect was well deserved. A regular at the *Mayfair* at the time that Tanya, Jenny and Caitlin were killed; away on a criminal sabbatical in Spain for a number of years; then back in Scarborough just in time for Scott's murder. Not to mention the recent attacks on Ava and Jade.

'I'm going to go and check out Dennis Dewhurst's

alibi,' he announced to the room.

'Do you want me to come with you?' asked Becca, swigging the last of her tea and depositing her empty mug next to her computer screen.

'Oh, I think I can handle this one myself.' He grabbed his coat and slipped it on, wrapping it around him like a cloak. 'You've worked hard enough today. Why don't we catch up again tomorrow morning?'

★

Raven left the station with his head still full of suspects. George Grime, Dennis Dewhurst, Scott's dad. Rogues, the lot of them. Not to mention that slimeball, Colin West. If Raven had his way they'd all be behind bars, and maybe if he worked this case to its conclusion, one or more of them might actually end up there.

The world would be better off without them.

He thrust his hands in his coat pockets and set off in the direction of his car.

On the other side of the street, a big white van with some kind of electronic equipment fixed to its roof was parked. A man leaned against the door of the van smoking a cigarette, and as soon as he caught sight of Raven, he tossed the cigarette butt to the ground, stamped it out with the heel of his shoe and gave a sharp rap on the side of the vehicle.

Immediately the back of the van flew open and a small TV news team disgorged, as if they were taking part in some kind of special forces operation.

Raven had no doubt who their target was.

He stepped up his pace, but the crew were heading straight for him, wrestling a tripod-mounted camera and a large metal box of tricks across the road. Before he knew what was happening, a microphone was in his face and an immaculately made-up presenter with a headset mic was smoothing down her jacket and readying herself to interview him.

She stepped lightly into his path and fixed a smile to her face. 'Liz Larkin reporting for BBC Look North. You join us this evening outside the central police station in Scarborough, North Yorkshire to hear from a senior detective about progress on the recent murder of a young man that has taken place here in the town.'

She fixed her attention on Raven. 'Detective Chief Inspector Raven, we understand that a suspect has been interviewed in relation to this horrific crime. Can you tell us any more about that? Has anyone been charged with the murder?'

Raven stared at her in a mix of outrage and astonishment. How did this woman know who he was? And who had tipped her off that he was investigating Scott's death?

'I'm sorry, I can't release any information about the investigation at this time.'

The reporter's smile didn't waver for a nanosecond. Indeed, he seemed to have said exactly what she was expecting to hear, as if she had scripted his lines for him. He tried to move past her but found his way blocked.

'There are reports that the murder may be connected with a series of violent sexual assaults that have taken place on women in the town in recent days,' said the reporter. 'Can you confirm that connection?'

Raven's face fell. How had she managed to make that leap of deduction? Perhaps because of the use of a knife in both instances. Or more likely, by simply putting two and two together and smelling a good story.

'I'm sorry,' he said again. 'We have no information to suggest that these crimes are in any way related.'

But something in his voice must have told her that she was on the right track. Her eyes glowed in anticipation of a newsworthy quote, and she continued as if Raven had confirmed her speculation. 'We also understand that the recent killing and the related attacks on women may be associated with the murder of a local woman some eight years ago that was never solved by police. Can you assure the residents of Scarborough that their streets are safe? Or is there a serial killer at large in the town?'

The suggestion of a serial killer was more than Raven could reasonably be expected to handle. He frowned hard, treating the reporter – Liz Larkin, or whatever her name was – to his fiercest stare. 'I think that's a very irresponsible suggestion to make, don't you? And if you don't mind, I have a murder investigation to be getting on with.' He pushed past the camera crew, flinging out an arm to push the microphone aside and strode off in the direction of his car.

It was only after he had entered the sanctuary of the BMW and his heart rate had begun to return to normal that he realised his outburst had been recorded and was likely to air on local TV.

*

Raven nosed the M6 along St Thomas Street, passing the casino that occupied the site of the old opera house. In Raven's day there had still been an opera house there, but times changed and the new casino seemed to be doing well, judging from the number of people queuing up to lose their money. Or perhaps to win big. Who knew what luck might bring?

His own luck hadn't brought him much to speak of that day. An interview with an uncooperative and unsavoury property developer, a suspicious sex offender who was impossible to track down, and a confrontation with the thoroughly disagreeable manager of a children's home. Not to mention his altercation with the news crew.

Perhaps things would get better now that he had finished work.

He slotted his car into the last vacant space on the street and walked the short distance to the *Mayfair*. A big man in a black suit intercepted him as he stepped up to the door. Raven flashed his warrant card at him and was duly shown inside.

A narrow escape, considering the eyewatering price of the entry fee.

'I can hang your coat up for a tenner,' offered the cloakroom attendant, but Raven declined her offer. 'Thanks, but I think I'll keep it with me.' He entered the main area of the club and stopped.

The last time he'd been here, the lights had been turned up and the cleaners had been hard at work. The room had seemed ordinary, mundane. Now with subdued lighting, music, the clink of glasses, and the background hum of voices, the atmosphere was congenial and inviting. A kind of magic had taken hold of the club. It was a place where you could leave ordinary life behind and enter a world of fantasy and dreams. On the dancefloor a woman in a sparkly leotard was effortlessly lifting and twisting her body around the pole, arching her back and giving her rapt audience sultry stares through heavily made-up eyes.

Raven allowed his vision time to adjust to the dimmed interior. He wanted to observe the clientèle, get a feel for the sort of men who frequented the club. He wanted to judge for himself what the relationship between the dancers and their audience was like.

And to see if Frida was present.

He couldn't spot her, although the club was large and dark enough for any number of tall Scandinavians to be concealed amid its many shadowy corners. He did, however, recognise the face of the woman working behind the bar. He walked over and lifted a hand to attract her attention. 'Evening, Dani.'

'DCI Raven, what's the news about Jade?' Dani's brow was creased with concern.

Raven did his best to reassure her. 'She was taken to hospital to be checked out, but she seems to be all right, physically at least. She's back home with her parents now.'

Dani nodded with relief. 'I'll tell Frida. She'll want to send flowers and a card, I'm sure. Do you know who did it yet?'

'Not yet. Jade gave us all the help she was able to. I'm

sure it won't be long before he's caught.'

'I hope so. Frida's arranged for security to be stepped up at the club, and for all the girls to take a taxi home at the end of their shifts.'

'Sensible,' said Raven, glad to hear it.

Dani had swapped her sports top and leggings for a more glamorous evening outfit, making her appear simultaneously younger and more sophisticated. Carefully applied makeup smoothed the crow's feet from around her eyes, and her dark hair hung loose, falling to below her shoulders. 'What would you like to drink?'

Raven allowed his gaze to drift along the backlit shelves of the bar, taking in the many bottles of whisky, spirits and liquor on display. Glowing colours of glass and liquids, arranged almost like a work of art. He sniffed, inhaling the familiar whiff of alcohol, an aroma that still triggered a warning bell in his head, decades after he'd last smelled his father's breath as he staggered home from the pub, fists ready to greet his wife and son.

'A lime and soda, please.'

Dani raised her dark eyebrows at his choice. 'You're not on duty now, are you? Why not relax a little?'

'I'm always on duty. Even when I'm not being paid for it.'

She poured the drink into a tall glass and added a twist of lime and a cherry. The cost was outrageous – as much as he'd have expected to pay for one of the fancier cocktails listed on the drinks menu.

Not that Raven ever drank cocktails.

'I thought you might be on the dance floor tonight.'

Dani smiled back at him. 'Kind of you to say so, but my dancing days are over. Professionally, at least. Dancing's a young girl's game. These days I watch over the girls and make myself useful helping Frida run the club.'

'Is Frida in this evening?' Raven glanced to the back of the room where the studded red leather door was draped in shadows. If you didn't know it was there, you would never notice it.

'She'll be in later,' said Dani. 'Was it her you came to see?'

'Not exactly.'

'What, then?'

'Do you know a man called Dennis Dewhurst?'

Dani leaned her elbows on the bar and lowered her voice, requiring Raven to lean in close to hear her. 'He's a regular. He's been calling in a few times each week ever since he got back from Spain. We call him Double-Baked Dennis, on account of his implausibly deep tan.'

'What do you make of him?' Raven could already tell that Dani's opinion of the wheeler-dealing property developer wasn't very high.

She gave a half-suppressed titter. 'I'm not supposed to have opinions about our clientèle, DCI Raven. It's bad for business.'

'I guess so. But what if you did? Hypothetically speaking.'

'Hypothetically?' Dani glanced over her shoulder to make sure no one was listening. 'I'd probably say he was a jerk. Too loud, too free with his hands, and if he wasn't so generous with his tips, he'd have been booted out of here a long time ago.'

Raven nodded in appreciation of Dani's directness and found himself in complete agreement with her assessment of the man with the chestnut tan. 'I don't suppose you can remember if he was here last night?'

'Yes, he was in with a bunch of his cronies. Here comes one of them now.' She stood up straight, shifting her attention to an approaching customer and fixing a polished smile to her pink lips. 'What can I get you?' she enquired of the newcomer.

'Just a beer, love, if you don't mind. I'm parched.'

Raven spun at the sound of the loud voice and was startled to see a familiar face.

'Er... Raven!' said the man in equal astonishment. 'What are you doing here?'

'Barry!' The last time Raven had seen his builder, he'd been up to his elbows in wiring, a screwdriver between his teeth and a crack at the back of his trousers revealing the hairiest arse in Scarborough. Now he was transformed, in a jacket and shirt, black shoes polished to a dizzying shine.

Barry's eyes drifted to his attire, seemingly embarrassed at appearing so smart in Raven's presence. 'Dress code,' he explained hurriedly. 'Got to make an effort or they won't let you in.' A pink glow was developing at the top of his collar, slowly spreading up his neck. He tugged at his top button even though it was already undone. 'I didn't expect to bump into you here. Didn't think this was your kind of place.'

'It isn't,' said Raven. 'I'm here for strictly professional reasons.'

'Oh... um... right,' said Barry. 'Me too.'

Raven looked him up and down, trying to picture what kind of business a builder might be doing in a pole dancing club. Especially when he was dressed to the nines and carrying an empty glass of beer in one hand. 'Are you planning to install a new kitchen here after you've finished mine?'

'What? Er, no.' Barry's blush had now covered his entire neck and face and was becoming almost radioactive in its intensity. 'I'm here to discuss an investment opportunity with a few guys.' He laughed nervously. 'Can I buy you a drink?'

Raven indicated his untouched glass of soda. 'Thanks, but I've already got one.'

'Okay.' Barry glanced awkwardly around the club. 'To be honest, this isn't my kind of place at all. Too glitzy, too expensive, too...' His eyes caught the sight of the pole dancer, swivelling her belly, her hands moving erotically over her breasts, and he tailed off, lost for words. 'Don't tell my wife you saw me here,' he said hurriedly.

'I didn't even know you were married.'

'Well, I am. And I'd like to keep it that way.'

Raven touched his finger to the side of his nose. 'No

problem. Your secret is safe with me.'

'Cheers, mate.' Barry breathed a sigh of relief, raising a toast to Raven with his freshly filled glass of beer. His initial embarrassment had faded, his usual brash attitude reaffirming itself. 'Hey,' he said, a goofy grin spreading over his face, 'do you know what "twerk" means?'

Raven looked across the floor to where the dancer was now clinging to the pole with her hands while simultaneously squatting low, thrusting her hips and buttocks at the audience suggestively. 'It means to dance in a sexually provocative manner while shaking your booty.'

'Nah,' said Barry, almost unable to stop himself from laughing. 'It's where Yorkshire folk go every day to earn a living. They go t'work. Get it?'

Raven gave him a friendly pat on the back. 'If you're thinking of starting a new career in stand up, I'd say stick to building instead.'

Barry's face fell. 'Well, I thought it was funny.'

'You'd better be getting back to your business associates,' said Raven. 'I've got work to do.'

'Right,' said Barry. 'I wonder if you know Liam Shawcross. His sister was the one who recommended me to you.'

Raven wasn't sure that Becca had recommended Barry exactly. *Warned* was perhaps a better way to describe it. But she had certainly put the two men in touch with each other. And Raven had heard her talk about Liam on a number of occasions. His curiosity was aroused sufficiently to follow Barry over to a nearby table.

When he reached the VIP booth where he and Becca had sat talking to Dani on his first visit to the club he stopped, his feet suddenly blocks of lead. Sitting at the circular table was a young man who he took to be Liam, but next to him were two other men, one of whom needed no introduction.

Dennis Dewhurst.

Liam rose to his feet eagerly and seized Raven's hand,

shaking it energetically. 'DCI Raven. We meet at last! Becca's told me so much about you.'

'Is that right?' Raven wondered idly what Becca might have told her family about him. That he was a grumpy old sod who was difficult to work with, perhaps. That he drove a ridiculously large car that was impossible to park. And that he was secretive and uncommunicative and never opened up to his colleagues.

But his attention was fixed on Dennis Dewhurst.

Dewhurst narrowed his eyes, regarding him with outright hostility. 'What the fuck's he doing here?' he demanded, glaring furiously at Barry.

'Why shouldn't he be?' asked Barry.

'Because he's a copper, and he's been harassing me, making all kinds of outrageous accusations.' Dewhurst leaned across the table, his shoulders as broad as a bulldozer. 'So why don't you just clear off and leave us in peace, Raven?'

Liam released Raven from his grip, his hand falling awkwardly to his side. 'Hey, Dennis, just cool it. I'm sure there's a good reason DCI Raven's been talking to you.'

'Well, there isn't,' said Dewhurst, his eyes like a snake about to strike, not leaving Raven for a second. 'So piss off, copper. Before there's any trouble.'

Raven squared up to him, refusing to be intimidated by that brute of a man. 'I'll go where I want and speak to whoever I like,' he told him. 'And if I find out that you've broken a single law, no matter how small, I'll be down on you like a ton of bricks.'

'See?' said Dewhurst triumphantly. 'Like I said, harassment.'

'Leave him, Dennis.' The fourth man at the table, seated to Dewhurst's right, laid a hand on his associate's arm to calm him down. 'He's not worth it.'

Raven turned his attention to the stranger. A younger man than Dewhurst, probably about forty, although by the look of it life hadn't treated him kindly. He was dressed in a sharp suit and may have been handsome once, but the scar running from the corner of his mouth all the way down his chin rather spoiled the cut of his jaw.

He gazed through narrow eyes in a quietly threatening manner and Raven sensed the latent violence within him. Dennis Dewhurst might be the type of man to start a fight, but his friend would be the one who finished it. With a knockout punch and a kick in the ribs.

'Do I know you?' Recognition was slowly dawning on Raven. The man was twenty years older than in the photograph he'd seen and he hadn't had that scar then, but Raven never forgot a face.

'I don't think so. The name's Dale. Dale Brady.' He offered his hand but Raven didn't take it.

In the photograph, Dale's blue eyes had been hidden behind dark glasses and his hair had been longer and thicker. But there was no doubt in Raven's mind who he was.

Scott's father.

The man whose image either Scott or Caitlin had sought to obliterate. The man who had vanished from Scarborough shortly after Scott's birth.

Now he was back.

One of the dark-suited bouncers had drifted over to the table. 'Is there a problem here?' A mountain of a man, with arms like tree trunks straining to burst out of his suit. He slapped a heavy restraining hand on Raven's shoulder.

Raven knew he could get rid of the hired muscle with a flash of his warrant card. And he could put Dennis Dewhurst on the floor if the man was stupid enough to pick a fight. The bigger they came the harder they fell, and they didn't come much bigger than Double-Baked Dennis. He might even be able to handle Dale Brady if he had to. But not both Dale and Dennis.

Besides, he had no wish to cause trouble for Frida.

'No problem. I was just about to leave.' Raven shook the bouncer's arm from his shoulder and smoothed his coat down. 'I'll see you another time, Dewhurst. And you too, Brady.'

He stole a quick look at the leather door as the bouncer escorted him from the premises, but it was still closed.

CHAPTER 25

The back row seats of the chapel gave Raven an unobstructed view of all the mourners present.

He'd last been to the crematorium for his father's funeral. Then, it had been just himself and a couple of Alan Raven's drinking pals. Old men, who had coughed and hacked their way through the service before shaking his hand and disappearing off to the pub. Raven had declined their invitation to join them. It was drink that had done for his father, and by the look of them, they wouldn't be long following him.

This time, however, the chapel was packed. Holly Chang and her forensics team filled a whole row of seats. Everyone who could be spared from the police station had turned out, many in their uniforms. Detectives, too, were in abundance. Tony nodded to Raven as he slipped into a seat across the aisle next to Dinsdale. Detective Superintendent Gillian Ellis occupied a more prominent position towards the front, close to the other top brass. According to the order of service, she would be delivering a reading. Piped music played softly in the background.

There was a clatter of bangles, a whiff of patchouli, and

Veronica Gibson swept into the chapel, clothed in swathes of black velvet. Beside her, Cameron Blake looked like a lost child. Dressed in a grey suit and black tie he glanced around nervously, as if afraid of stumbling into one of his persecutors, Colin West or George Grime. Veronica ushered him into an empty row, patting him gently on the back and using her own body to screen him from onlookers.

Fortunately there was no sign of the children's home manager at the funeral. The passing of a former resident was obviously not enough to divert Colin West from his paperwork. Or perhaps he had the sense to keep well away.

Heads turned as Frida and Dani made their entrance and walked down the aisle searching for somewhere to sit. The older woman was the epitome of elegance with her long blonde hair tied up in a chignon above the fur collar of her cashmere coat. Dani wore a black leather coat teamed with high-heeled suede boots. An unconventional look for a funeral perhaps, but there was no doubting the sincerity of her grief.

To Raven's surprise, Dale Brady, Scott's father, crept into the chapel and stood at the back, looking around for a spare seat. His gaze met Raven's and his blue eyes narrowed to slits before he slunk off down the aisle looking neither to left nor right. As he found his way to one of the last remaining seats at the front, it didn't escape Raven's attention that Dani turned her head and fixed him with a look of such loathing that it was a wonder she didn't smite him on the spot. Dale lowered himself into the seat with hunched shoulders, his head bowed.

Last to arrive was Jess in the company of Becca. Both women appeared sombre but composed and determined to carry themselves with dignity. They were guided to reserved seats by the female celebrant who would be conducting the service.

The piped music faded out and everyone rose.

The coffin, in plain oak, was carried in by the same pall bearers that had attended Raven's father's funeral.

Professionally expressionless and gliding like ghosts, they deposited the coffin on the platform at the front of the chapel then melted away to the side as if they really were just phantoms.

The celebrant's words were sensitive and well chosen. She didn't dwell on the circumstances of Scott's death, but focussed instead on all that he had achieved during his short life. Holly took the stand and spoke movingly about his invaluable contribution to the CSI team. Her words may have been characteristically plain and to the point, but Raven found them unexpectedly expressive and moving. Gillian Ellis read out a passage from Corinthians. *For now we see through a glass, darkly; but then face to face: now I know in part; but then shall I know even as also I am known.*

Raven found himself reflecting on the mysteries of life and death. As a police officer he was more than passingly familiar with the latter but would be the first to admit that he still knew nothing about what lay beyond.

Paradise. Oblivion. Eternal damnation. It was anyone's guess, and though Raven had been brought up by his mother to believe in the first, his experiences of life had moulded him in ways that led him to strongly suspect one of the less savoury options.

Jess made perhaps the most emotional contribution to the proceedings. Her words were few, but in them she painted a vivid picture of a man whose life had been cut tragically short. A kind and gentle man who had adored his mother, loved nature and the outdoors and who had longed to do good in the world. Raven wiped a tear from the corner of his eye and wasn't the only one in the chapel to do so.

The hymn singing wasn't the usual wash-out that it so often was on such occasions. The ranks of Scarborough's police force appeared to contain quite a few competent baritones, not least of all Tony Bairstow who more than held his own during *Amazing Grace*. Raven adjusted his opinion of the usually quiet DC.

At the end of the service, Raven remained seated as the

other mourners slowly filed out of the chapel. He watched them go, scrutinising their faces one by one before finally rising and stepping outside to join them.

Four months earlier, on that blustery day in October when he had bidden farewell and good riddance to his father, a stiff north-easterly had chilled him to the bone. Winter had been on the ascendant, its white fingers steadily tightening their hold over the landscape. Today, the seasons were changing once more, the first hints of spring arriving to banish memories of cold days and long nights. Sunlight gilded the bare arms of the trees, and birds filled the sky with song. Daffodils were rising from hard earth, their buds turned already to find the sun even though it would be some weeks before they burst into yellow radiance. This was Yorkshire after all, not the soft belly of the south where Raven had hidden himself these past thirty years.

The mourners had clustered into groups, an awkward distance between the police officers and the other members of the congregation that no one seemed to know how to bridge.

Raven caught a scent of perfume, something exotic and musky with a hint of vanilla. He felt a hand on his arm and turned to find himself looking directly into the eyes of Frida Baines. Disconcerting, the way she matched him in height. Disconcerting too, the directness of her gaze, and her close proximity. So close he could feel her moist breath against his skin.

'Good of you to come, Chief Inspector.' Her words, so perfectly formed, diamond hard in their articulation. Warm and soft as petals. It was a voice he could lose himself in. Could drown in.

'It's the least I could do.'

She glanced over at a huddle of uniformed police officers. 'It's an impressive turnout.'

'Yes.' He felt an urge to explain it to her. To make her understand. 'The police force was Scott's family. We stand together.'

Stand or fall.

That was the nub of it. From the bobbies on the beat to the techies in their labs and the call responders at their desks, the institution was only as strong as the bonds that tied its members together. Like a cloth woven from a single thread, the thin blue fabric that upheld the law depended on the interweaving of its warp and weft.

But he couldn't put any of that into words. 'Scott was one of our own,' he concluded.

Frida nodded, her hair catching the sun and holding it like liquid gold.

He wondered if she felt the same about the dancers at the club. Her girls. He'd been impressed by the way she'd stepped in so quickly after the attack on Jade, arranging for them to be taken home by taxi. To do whatever it took to keep them safe.

'I spoke to Dani last night,' he told her. 'She was asking about Jade.'

'Yes, Dani told me you'd been to the club. I'm sorry I missed you.'

He fell silent, recalling his unexpected encounter with Dennis Dewhurst and Dale Brady. The sight of them together had unsettled him. Wolves running in packs. No good could come from those two in cahoots, he was sure of it. And what had Barry been doing in their company? Raven would be having a difficult conversation with his builder when next he saw him.

'I've told Jade to take as much time off as she needs,' said Frida.

Her words brought him out of his reverie, to the matter of the latest victim of the skull-masked rapist. 'You've spoken to her, then. How is she?'

'Badly shaken. Her confidence has suffered a massive blow. But I think she'll come back once she's had time to recuperate. Dancing's what she's always wanted to do.'

'I hope she does,' said Raven. Pole dancing wasn't a career he'd have wanted for his own daughter, but he knew that standing in the way of someone's ambitions was a fool's errand. If Jade wanted to be a dancer, then he wished her all the best.

'Do you have to go straight back to work after the funeral?' asked Frida. 'I've arranged a small wake at a pub in town. I hope you'll join us there.'

'A wake?' Raven's habit was always to shun such occasions. He was no good at small talk. The ritualised greetings. The forced politeness. The determination to avoid causing offence. He couldn't do it.

He just didn't fit.

It had been easy for him to decline the invitation to his father's wake. The prospect of an hour in the company of two ancient alcoholics wasn't an enticing one.

This time he was tempted.

Frida smiled her encouragement. 'Do say you'll come. I'm sure that Scott would have wanted you there.'

It would be easy to say yes. To do what was expected of him. To tell her what she hoped to hear. But in the end his natural reticence to join in with any kind of formal socialising won out and he found himself declining with regret, saying that he had too much work to do.

Her smile wavered for a moment but she quickly recovered herself. 'I quite understand, Chief Inspector. You're a busy man. But perhaps you'd have time to join me for supper this evening at the club? Just you and me.'

'Just the two of us?' This time Raven didn't need to think. 'There's nothing I'd like more.'

Her smile felt as warm as the sun on his skin. 'Then I'll see you tonight.'

*

Raven returned to the station to find he wasn't the only one who had decided to give the wake a miss. Tony had also gone straight back to work, assuaging Raven's sense of guilt at turning down Frida's invitation to the wake.

He was glad however to find that Becca had accompanied Jess to the after-funeral drinks. He trusted her to be his eyes and ears should anything of note occur there. Dinsdale, too, had joined the wake, the prospect of free sausage rolls and beer no doubt an irresistible lure for the older detective.

Tony approached Raven's desk, a sheet of paper clutched in his hand.

'Good singing there, Tony,' Raven told him.

'Thank you, sir. I've been looking into Scott's dad like you asked me to.'

'Dale Brady. He was at the funeral today.' Raven was glad that Brady had sensibly kept his distance. Judging by the fact that he'd arrived alone and sat by himself, Scott's dad could count few friends among the mourners at his son's funeral. If any. 'Did you see him?'

'Aye, I did.' Tony's tone of voice made it clear he hadn't been impressed with what he'd seen.

'I bumped into him last night at the *Mayfair*,' said Raven.

Tony nodded at the news. 'I knew he was back in town.'

'So what's his story?'

'Not a happy one.' Tony referred to his notes. 'Born in Scarborough, now aged thirty-nine. He left school at sixteen and drifted around a lot, never settling in one place for any length of time. Judging from his tax and employment records, he's mostly done casual work, sometimes in Scarborough, sometimes in Whitby or further along the coast. He has a conviction for common assault.'

That fact came as no surprise to Raven. Brady had the look of a fighter all over. 'Did he go to prison for that?'

'No, just a community order. The magistrate didn't consider it serious enough for a custodial sentence.'

'So what brings Dale back to Scarborough?'

'I don't know, sir. Seasonal work? A job prospect? A change of scene?'

Raven considered what Barry had told him the previous evening. 'When I met him he was with a group of men discussing an "investment opportunity"' – Raven used his fingers to add air quotes to the term – 'whatever that might mean.'

Tony responded with a puzzled look. 'I wouldn't have thought Dale Brady was the sort of person with money in the bank. Do you know what kind of investment?'

'I didn't get a chance to ask,' said Raven, choosing not to mention the neatly avoided bar brawl that had almost taken place, 'but I can tell you that it involves my builder, as well as Liam Shawcross and Dennis Dewhurst.'

Raven had lingered at home that morning, waiting for Barry to show his face and to be grilled about what on earth he was doing hanging out with the likes of Dennis Dewhurst and Dale Brady. But there'd been no sign of him. No message, no phone call. Nothing. Like Raven's kitchen cabinets, he was nowhere to be found.

Tony looked pained at the mention of Liam, Dennis and Dale. 'Oh dear, sir. That doesn't sound good. That doesn't sound good at all.'

*

Raven was just heading out of the office when he bumped into Gillian. Judging by the expression on her face, she wasn't best pleased to see him.

'Tom, my office, if you don't mind.'

Raven followed her in and took up residence in front of her desk, wondering what he'd done this time. The investigation was on track, with several suspects already identified and a number of different avenues under investigation. If he'd been asked for an assessment of progress so far, he'd have said it was going pretty well.

And then he remembered. The car-crash interview with the TV reporter.

'Tom, perhaps you can explain this to me.' Gillian tilted the screen of her phone on its side and hit the play button on the video. Immediately a familiar scene began to unfold in front of Raven's eyes.

It was different to the way he remembered it. The reporter, Liz Larkin, seemed less aggressive and more trustworthy than he'd perceived her to be the previous night. As for Raven, he came across as, well, altogether more hostile and uncooperative than he'd intended. You might even have described him as shifty and evasive if you didn't know better.

And that bit when he shoved aside the guy with the microphone, well, he could see how that kind of behaviour might easily be misinterpreted as aggressive.

Gillian's eyes blazed with fury. 'What the hell was that supposed to be, Tom?'

'It... um...' Just when Raven needed them, his wits seemed to have fled him entirely.

'I'll tell you what it was,' snapped Gillian. 'It was a PR disaster!'

'It didn't play well, did it?' he conceded. 'Maybe I ought to have...' But what exactly ought he to have done?

Not behaved like an arsehole, would have been a good start.

'If you weren't in the middle of such an important investigation, I'd have to seriously consider suspending you from duty,' said Gillian. 'Perhaps I ought to suspend you anyway, for precisely that reason.'

'I hope you're not going to, ma'am,' said Raven. 'We're making excellent progress, we–'

Gillian finished the sentence for him. '–have not yet made an arrest.' She eyeballed him as if she could force him into either revealing the name of the murderer or else handing in his resignation.

But Raven could do neither of those things.

'I expected better from a senior detective, Tom, especially one with your experience.'

He grimaced, hoping that his record in the Met wasn't going to be dragged up and paraded in front of him yet again.

'What I'm going to do,' said Gillian, 'is send you on a media awareness course as soon as this investigation is over. I think that's just what you need.'

A media awareness course. It sounded like the exact same bullshit that his boss in the Met had insisted would be good for furthering his career development. But it was a whole lot better than a suspension.

'Yes, ma'am,' he said. 'Thank you. I'm sure I'd get a lot out of that.'

CHAPTER 26

Jess hadn't had a moment to herself. Ever since leaving the chapel and arriving at the wake she'd been surrounded by people offering their condolences. She'd had no time to think back over the funeral service and begin to come to terms with the finality of her loss. Perhaps that was a good thing. If she'd been left to herself, to mull over the fact that she'd just witnessed a ceremony in which the man she loved had been turned into ashes, she might have drowned in anguish.

She'd been touched by how many of her colleagues had turned out for the funeral. She hadn't expected to see such a large crowd of them. The sight of familiar faces – Raven's, Tony's, Holly's, even Dinsdale's and the Detective Superintendent's – had been a comfort to her. Of course, she was most grateful to Becca, who had been a total rock, driving her to the crematorium and then on to the wake.

Most of the police officers had gone back to work, but Holly and the other CSIs had stayed and looked like they were here for the day. They were standing in a group, reminiscing about cases they'd worked on together.

Anecdotes that would go down in CSI lore, like the time Scott had discovered bones at the back of a child's wardrobe. They had turned out to be rabbit bones.

Some of their other stories were more grisly, suitable only for the ears of those for whom death and human remains were the stuff of the nine-to-five.

Jess turned away. She wasn't ready for gallows humour. The pain of her grief was still too raw. When the coffin had disappeared behind the curtain she'd thought her heart would break in two. 'Goodbye,' she'd whispered, wishing she could have made her farewell when Scott was still alive. What good was it to say goodbye to someone who had already gone?

She spotted Cameron Blake, Scott's friend from the children's home, and drifted over to say hello. She'd met him a couple of times before and had taken a shine to him. Cameron was another bruised survivor of the care system, even more damaged and less confident than Scott, but she sensed his innate goodness.

Jess didn't know the older woman who was sitting at the table next to him, nursing a gin and tonic. She introduced herself as Veronica, then caught Jess off guard when she threw her arms around her, enveloping her in a cloud of exotic scents.

'My dear, what a frightful ordeal for you to go through, and at such a young age!'

'Thank you.' Veronica's perfume was suffocating, as was her embrace, and Jess extracted herself as tactfully as she could.

Cameron, who'd always been shy with her, took her hand, not quite meeting her eye. He looked as bereft as Jess felt. She sensed a bond between them, forged from loss, and wished the two of them could sit quietly for a few moments together. But then a tall blonde woman with strikingly sculpted cheekbones came over and held out her hand.

'Hello, I'm Frida Baines. I own the nightclub where Scott's mother worked. I knew Scott from when he was a small boy. I'm so sorry for your loss.'

Jess mumbled her thanks. Despite Frida's kind words, she found the presence of the newcomer rather intimidating. Perhaps it was the woman's height, or the unwavering stare of her startlingly blue eyes.

Jess found it impossible to hold her gaze and was the first to look away.

'Forgive me,' said Frida, resting a cool hand on her arm, 'I hope you don't mind me saying this, but I couldn't help thinking, just now, how you look so much like her. It's quite uncanny.' She was looking at Jess as if seeing a ghost.

'I'm sorry,' said Jess, forcing herself to lift her eyes once more to take in those ice blue diamonds, 'like who?'

'Caitlin. Scott's mother. Have you ever seen a photograph of her?'

'I have, yes.' Jess summoned up an image of the photo that marked the opening page of *The Raven*. The pretty blonde woman with that carefree smile and lightly tanned skin, the silver pendant dangling around her neck and blazing in the sun like fire.

Scott himself had told Jess how much she reminded him of his mum. He had once broken off their relationship because they looked so alike, expressing the fear that what had happened to Caitlin might also happen to Jess. That there was a curse that followed him around.

Jess had told him he was being silly. But now an icy shiver ran the length of her spine. She didn't believe in curses, but Scott had suffered the same fate as his mother, and the chances of that happening at random seemed vanishingly small.

Once more the same nagging doubts bubbled up inside her. How well had she really known him? He had never once confided in her that he was investigating Caitlin's murder, never once showed her the evidence board in his flat. What else had he concealed from her? The letter he had written to her – yet never sent – came so close to revealing the truth, but stopped short, leaving the circumstances of his death clouded in mystery.

A dark-haired woman in a black leather coat walked over to join them. She was carrying two glasses of wine and handed one to Frida.

'This is Jess, Scott's girlfriend,' explained Frida to the newcomer in that intense yet also slightly stilted way she had of speaking.

'Hi,' said the new arrival. 'I'm Dani. I work at Frida's club.'

'Nice to meet you,' said Jess.

'I was Caitlin's best friend from school,' said Dani. 'I knew Scott all his life. What happened to him is just horrible.'

'Yes.' Jess wondered why Scott had never mentioned either of these people to her. They'd known him far longer than she had. All his life. She was beginning to feel like a fraud. Like someone who'd only just briefly met Scott.

Almost as if she hadn't known him at all.

A disturbance at the bar caused everyone to turn their heads. A man with wavy hair and an ugly scar running down his chin was arguing with the barman. Jess had noticed him in the chapel and wondered who he was. She was certain she'd never seen him before and yet there was something disquietingly familiar about him.

There seemed to be some problem with his drink. It wasn't what he'd asked for. The barman stood his ground. Voices were raised.

'I'll sort this out,' said Dani, depositing her glass on Cameron and Veronica's table and striding over to the bar in her high-heeled boots.

'Take care, Dani,' warned Frida. 'He's dangerous.'

'Who is that man?' asked Jess.

'Scott's father,' Frida whispered in her ear. 'Dale Brady.'

'His father?' Once again Jess felt the ground lurch beneath her. Scott had never once mentioned his father. She felt like she was drifting away from shore, the anchor that held her lost on the sea bed. She placed a hand on the table to steady herself.

'What the hell do you think you're doing here?' Dani was facing the man with the scar, squaring up to him, her hands on her hips. Her outrage was plain to see.

'Why shouldn't I be here?' demanded Dale. 'Scott was my son. My only son. I've got every right to be here.'

'You were no father to Scott!' shouted Dani. 'The way you treated Caitlin was a disgrace.'

Jess flinched at the sharp words, wondering what Dale had done to deserve such a rebuke. Whatever it was, it was bad enough for Scott to have edited him out of his life entirely, not even mentioning his existence to Jess.

'You bitch!' Dale took a step towards Dani, his hand raised.

Dani ducked back and Becca was on the scene in a flash. 'Police!'

Jess watched anxiously from the sidelines. She didn't know Dale but he looked like a rough character, unafraid to use his fists. Frida had warned Dani that he was dangerous, and Jess had sensed the fear in her voice. What was this man capable of?

She hung back, feeling scared but relieved that Becca was taking charge of the situation.

Another woman stepped in to join Becca at the bar. Holly Chang. Scarcely five feet tall yet entirely fearless. 'Come on,' she said to Dale, 'you'd best be off now. Hop it before you find yourself in a police cell.'

The other CSIs had gathered round in a protective ring, although Dinsdale was nowhere to be seen.

Dale looked from Becca to Holly, his face sour. 'Fucking 'ell. What's this? Bleeding *Cagney and Lacey?* I didn't do owt!'

'Then I suggest you leave now before you give us a reason to arrest you,' said Becca.

Dale shot her a look of utter loathing, then stomped off, the disputed pint of beer left standing on the bar. The room breathed a collective sigh of relief and Dani returned to collect her drink from the table.

'Are you all right?' Frida asked her.

Dani nodded, looking shaken but undaunted by what had happened.

The murmur of conversation was creeping back into the room after Dale's violent outburst. Jess melted into the crowd, disappointed with herself that it was Becca who had stepped into action and not her. Her neck began to burn, a feeling of shame taking hold. She was clearly unfit to continue as a police officer. She would speak to Raven the following day and hand in her resignation. It would be better all round.

Dani drifted across to her, a spare glass of wine in her hand. 'Here, you look like you could use a drink.'

'Thanks.' Jess accepted it with two shaking hands and took a large gulp of the wine to steady herself. All the confidence had been knocked out of her by the sudden confrontation. 'You were very brave back there.'

'It was nothing.' Dani took a sip of her own drink. 'I'd been wanting to tell Dale what I thought of him for a long time. He's a nasty piece of work all round.'

'I can hardly believe he's Scott's dad.' Jess wondered how that brute of a man could have fathered someone as kind and gentle as Scott. Thankfully, despite a faint resemblance, Scott had taken more after his mother. 'What on earth did Caitlin see in him?'

Dani gave her a sardonic smile. 'Some women pick the wrong men. Caitlin was like that unfortunately. But at least she had the sense to dump him before he could really mess up her life. And without Dale there would never have been Scott.'

'I suppose not. I wish he'd told me more about his life. He never mentioned his dad. Or you and Frida.' Now that Jess had found someone to confide in, she found that she was hungry to hear all she could about Scott.

'Perhaps he was ashamed,' said Dani. 'Not everyone wants to admit to having a pole dancer as a substitute aunt.'

Jess raised her brows. The flood of information was

going so fast she could hardly keep up. 'A pole dancer? Wow, there really is a lot Scott never told me. But I'm sure he never felt ashamed of you.' She hesitated, unsure how her next suggestion might be received. But she was curious now. Desperately curious to fill in the gaps. 'Are you doing anything tomorrow?'

'No,' said Dani. 'Why?'

'Perhaps we could meet up, get to know each other a bit better. You could tell me what you remember about Scott. If you don't mind, that is.'

Dani smiled. 'I don't mind at all. I'd love to tell you all I know. Caitlin was my best friend and Scott was like a son to me. I'm so glad that he found you. You must have made a great couple.'

'Thanks,' said Jess.

'It's a date then. Is three o'clock good for you? Shall we meet in Peasholm Park?'

Jess nodded eagerly. 'Yes. I'd like that very much.'

CHAPTER 27

The hotel was a boutique four-star establishment facing Scarborough's largest and most famous hotel, the Grand, where Raven's mother had worked as a chambermaid. The building formed part of an imposing six-storey Victorian terrace on St Nicholas Cliff and was more than a little reminiscent of Dennis Dewhurst's place on Montpellier Terrace. Raven hoped for a more productive meeting than his tetchy encounter with Dewhurst the previous day. He left his car beside the well-tailored green in the centre of the square and hauled his leg up the short flight of steps leading to the porticoed entrance.

The hotel was a nice one, not the kind of dive Raven had imagined a friend of Terry Baines might run. Baines was proving to be an enigma, impossible to pin down. Every time Raven thought he had the measure of the man, another curve ball came his way, throwing him back into uncertainty.

At the reception desk, Raven requested an audience with the manager and was shown into the front bar to wait. Resting his leg for a minute, he let his eyes wander around the room, taking in the furnishings and ambience. The décor was plush yet relaxed. Wood panelling on the lower half of the walls, framed prints above. Leather sofas, a corniced ceiling. The interior of the *Mayfair* may have been layered with an instant veneer of period grandeur, but this place had the real thing.

Had Terry Baines really brought Caitlin here for a drink, with the intention of taking her upstairs afterwards? And had he really been left sitting here, perhaps in this very chair, as she was stabbed to death by some mysterious and unknown killer in a nearby street?

Or was it all, as Dinsdale claimed, a fantasy? A web of lies spun by a first-rate phony.

'What can I do for you?' A dark-haired man in a three-piece suit appeared from the reception area and shook Raven's hand with a firm grip. 'Simon Grant. I'm in charge here.' Smiling and confident, he seemed not the least bit worried to find a police detective on his premises.

'DCI Raven. I'd like to speak to you about Terry Baines.'

'Terry?' Grant gave Raven a measuring stare. 'Goodness me. It's a long time since anyone mentioned that name to me. You'd better come through to my office.'

Raven followed him through a door marked "private" and Grant gestured towards a small L-shaped sofa positioned around a coffee table. Glossy hotel brochures were arranged in a fan shape over its polished surface.

'Shall I ring for tea or coffee?' Grant seemed eager to please. No doubt a consequence of working in the hospitality business.

'No need,' said Raven, accepting the offer of a seat. 'I won't take up much of your time.'

'Take as much as you need.' Grant sat down and crossed his legs, turning his head to face Raven.

'I'm investigating the murder of Caitlin Newhouse.'

'Caitlin.' Grant nodded. 'I remember it well. But that must have been over seven years ago. I thought her case was long since closed.'

'Cases are never officially closed until they're solved. They just grow cold.' There was no statute of limitations in the UK, except for petty crimes tried exclusively in magistrates' courts. Caitlin's case had grown as cold as any Raven had known, with all the evidence lost and the man presumed guilty locked up securely behind bars. Until now that was, with Scott turning up dead and Raven stumbling into play like a bull released into a china shop.

A bull with no qualms about breaking every piece of porcelain on display.

'I see. And has this case warmed up?'

'You could say that. Tell me, were you ever interviewed by the police around the time of her death?'

'Yes, I was.'

'Do you remember the name of the police officer who spoke to you?'

'Well, yes, it was the senior officer in charge of the investigation.' Grant frowned as he searched his memory for the name. 'Peel, or something like that.'

'DCI Gareth Peel?' prompted Raven.

Grant clicked his fingers. 'That's him. I thought it was odd that such a senior officer would come and speak to me directly, but I put it down to the fact that I was a key witness.' He smiled self-deprecatingly. 'So much for my delusions – the case was never even brought to trial.'

'Tell me what you told DCI Peel if you would. I realise this was eight years ago, but please try to recall as much detail as you can.'

'Certainly.' Grant leaned back in the sofa, steepling his fingers in concentration. 'It was all about Terry. Peel wanted to know if Terry had visited the hotel that day, and if so at what time. I told him that Terry had come to the hotel that evening. It wasn't the kind of thing I was likely to forget, because Terry arrived in the company of a very attractive young woman who wasn't his wife.' He chuckled. 'I'm sorry to say, that wasn't the first time Terry had done such a thing.' A frown crossed his brow and his face clouded over. 'Of course, at the time I didn't know who the woman was. It was only the next day that I saw on the news that she'd been murdered.'

'How well did you know Terry?'

'Pretty well. I make a point of getting to know most of the hotel and club owners in Scarborough. It's not such a big town. I'd always got on well with him. I've met Frida once or twice too. Nice woman. She didn't deserve to be treated that way.'

'What way exactly?'

'Cheated on. But that was Terry for you. Couldn't help himself. I think Frida knew that already. But still...'

The tale Grant was telling Raven was the same one he'd heard repeated over and over. Terry Baines, the man who couldn't help himself from sleeping with any woman who smiled his way. The man that women couldn't help smiling at. Was he a roguish charmer or a calculating sexual predator?

'So Terry came in with Caitlin,' Raven prompted. 'Do you recall what time that was?'

'Well, I was on duty covering for my barman who went off sick, so it was about ten o'clock. I'm sorry, I can't remember the time more precisely, but it was one of the questions DCI Peel asked me at the time. I'm sure my answer will be in the statement I gave him.'

'I'm sure it will,' said Raven. Except for the minor inconvenience that Grant's statement had gone missing. Had never even been submitted as evidence, as far as Raven could tell. Had disappeared along with all the forensic evidence relating to Caitlin's murder. 'So what happened next with Terry and Caitlin? How would you describe the relationship between them? Did you get the impression they were having an affair?'

Grant chuckled again. 'I got the impression Terry *wanted* them to have an affair. He had a room booked for the night. Perhaps he was hoping a few drinks would loosen her up. They had a drink together in the bar and I think the plan was to go upstairs afterwards... but something changed. Caitlin must have had misgivings.

After she'd finished her drink she got up and left.'

'Alone?'

'That's right. Terry stayed behind.'

Raven leaned in. 'Are you sure about that, Mr Grant? Are you absolutely certain that Terry stayed in the hotel?'

Grant nodded. 'A hundred percent. He came and sat with me at the bar, drowning his sorrows. He wasn't used to attractive women turning him down. I let him have a whisky on the house as consolation. We must have sat together for, oh, a good hour after she left.'

'So what time did Terry go?'

'Midnight,' said Grant without hesitation. 'The bar stays open late for guests, and Terry was technically a guest as he had a room booked. I remember him making a joke about turning into a pumpkin if he stayed any longer. He'd had a fair few by then, but he could hold his drink could Terry.'

'Caitlin Newhouse's body was found just after eleven,' said Raven, thinking aloud.

'That's right,' agreed Grant. 'Peel asked me several times about the time Terry left, to find out if I was willing to admit any uncertainty. I told him what I've just told you – that Terry was here until midnight. Peel kept saying, "Are you sure about that?" and "Could Terry have left earlier?" But I told him there was absolutely no doubt about it. Terry was here at the time Caitlin was murdered. I expect that's why the charge against him was dropped.'

Raven leaned back, contemplating the implications of what he'd just heard. He didn't like the way this was going one little bit.

'Just one more question,' he said. 'As someone who knew Terry well enough to sit and have a drink with him, do you think he could have killed those two other women? Tanya Ayres and Jenny Jones?'

Grant leaned forwards in a gesture of confidentiality. 'I'll tell you this. When Terry was convicted, I didn't believe it for one moment. And I still don't. Don't get me wrong, Terry was no angel. He had his faults. If Frida was my wife, I wouldn't dream of cheating on her. But murder? Terry just isn't the type, whatever people say.'

Raven rose to his feet. 'Thank you for your time, Mr Grant. You've been most helpful.'

CHAPTER 28

'**D**I Dinsdale, a word.' Raven didn't wait for Dinsdale to agree to his request, but marched straight into his office, leaving the door wide open for the other man to follow.

As he'd anticipated, Dinsdale slouched reluctantly after him, loitering in the doorway like a naughty schoolboy about to be given a thorough dressing down. 'What's this about, Raven? I haven't got time for games.'

'Shut the door,' commanded Raven, too furious to placate Dinsdale with an answer to his question immediately.

If Raven really was a bull in a china shop, the dinner plates were well and truly beginning to fall from their shelves and shatter on the floor. By the time he was done, there would be nothing left intact.

Only the truth, the most fragile item of all.

He perched on the edge of his desk but didn't invite Dinsdale to sit. 'I've just been to see Simon Grant, manager of the hotel where Terry Baines claimed to have gone with Caitlin Newhouse on the night she was killed.'

'And?' Dinsdale shifted his weight from one lumbering

foot to the other.

'He reiterated the alibi he provided for Terry Baines eight years ago. Said that after Caitlin left, he and Terry remained in the hotel bar together until midnight.'

Dinsdale gave a dismissive wave of his hand. 'Some people will tell you anything you want to hear.'

'Simon Grant came across as a very credible witness. His memory was pin sharp. He recalled the times and details of the evening's events quite vividly.'

'So maybe Terry didn't kill Caitlin,' said Dinsdale truculently. 'He wasn't tried for her murder anyway. What are you getting at, Raven?'

'Why was the charge that Terry Baines murdered Caitlin Newhouse dropped before going to court?' It was a big question and Raven let it fill the room.

'I already told you why,' whined Dinsdale. 'Lack of evidence.'

'But that's not true, is it? There was an abundance of evidence. Caitlin's phone, the murder weapon, fingerprints, DNA and samples of blood recovered from the scene of the crime. But it all disappeared into thin air, along with Simon Grant's witness statement which Peel himself took.'

Dinsdale was visibly squirming under Raven's unflinching stare and hostile questioning. 'I don't know what happened to the evidence and I don't know anything about this Simon Grant. Peel never mentioned him to me.'

'Did he not?'

'No.'

Raven got to his feet and moved closer to Dinsdale, who took a step back. 'Do I look like a fool to you, Derek?'

'No. Why do you ask?'

'Because either you're taking me for a fool or else that's what Gareth Peel thought of you.'

Dinsdale's lips made a thin line. It seemed he wouldn't be easily goaded into saying anything that might paint his former boss in a bad light. Why was that? Loyalty? Or guilt?

'Start talking, Dinsdale. What is it you're hiding from

me?'

'Nothing.'

'Let me help jog your memory.' Raven retreated a step, clasped his hands together and summoned the relevant facts from his memory of the case file. 'The timeline looks like this. First to be killed was Tanya Ayres. Her body was found in her flat by a friendly neighbour. Peel immediately went to the *Mayfair* and his eyes alighted on Terry Baines, owner of the club and widely known to be a playboy. No need to look any further for her killer. The only problem with Peel's theory was a complete lack of evidence. With me so far?'

Dinsdale pursed his mouth. 'Baines's car was seen outside Tanya's flat. He was known to be having an affair with her.'

'Which was why Peel bothered to look no further for suspects,' countered Raven. 'One year later and a second dancer goes missing. This time around, no one even thought to open a missing persons inquiry. After all, Jenny was just a pole dancer, wasn't she? It wasn't as if she really mattered. It wasn't like she was someone's daughter.'

'I wasn't responsible for making those decisions,' bleated Dinsdale. 'It was nothing to do with me.'

Raven's eyes bored into his. 'It wasn't until Caitlin's body was found lying in the street that Peel swung into action. This time he went full tilt, arresting Terry and almost immediately finding the evidence he needed. The murder weapon used to kill Jenny, still conveniently covered in her blood. How convenient. Now he could put Terry away for good.' Raven paused for breath. 'Except there was one small inconsistency in his thesis. Terry's alibi. As soon as Peel found out about it, he didn't send a junior officer, but went and interviewed Simon Grant himself. What Grant told him confirmed his worst fear – that Terry couldn't have murdered Caitlin after all. And if he was innocent of that murder, what jury would ever believe that he'd killed the other two women?'

Dinsdale's face had turned several shades paler. 'I

didn't know. I didn't. Honest.'

'And so,' concluded Raven, 'Peel did what any pig-headed, rule-breaking, self-righteous and unprincipled SIO running his last big case before retirement would have done – he destroyed the evidence that didn't fit, obliging the CPS to drop the charge against Terry for Caitlin's murder, and proceeded with the two murder charges he thought he could make stick. Even though he must have known that he was sending an innocent man to jail!'

Raven finished his speech, breathless, and waited for Dinsdale's response.

When it came it was spineless. 'This was all a long time ago, Raven. I wasn't the SIO. I didn't have any say in how the investigation was conducted. Peel had decades of experience as a detective. He had a nose for hunting down criminals and a reputation for putting together a watertight case. You said yourself that he kept his interview with the hotel manager to himself. How could I have known about that?'

Raven was clinging to the last ounce of his patience by a thread. 'But you were there all along! You sat in on the interviews with Terry. You were a detective inspector, second in charge to DCI Gareth Peel. You must have seen the way he operated, overheard what he said. Did you suspect nothing?'

Dinsdale fell silent. He seemed suddenly to have taken a great interest in the appearance of his shoes. Eventually he looked up. 'I suspected,' he mumbled. The words were little more than a murmur.

'Suspected what?'

'That Peel had planted evidence.'

Raven leaned back against his desk. This was even worse than he'd feared. He'd known that evidence had gone missing, that the crucial witness statement had never been filed. But actual planting of evidence? 'He did *what!?*'

Dinsdale wouldn't look at him. Instead he glanced sidelong at the wall. 'I can't know for sure. But the murder weapon used to kill Jenny – the knife that was covered in her blood – I think Peel put it in Terry's bedroom.'

Raven shook his head, lost for words. 'You suspected that and you did nothing?'

'What could I do?' pleaded Dinsdale. 'I had no proof. It was just a hunch. I was there when we were searching Terry and Frida's place. One minute there was no knife. The next moment, Peel had found it. It seemed like a miracle. It was the breakthrough we'd all been praying for.'

'Get out!' roared Raven. 'Get out of my office before I throw you out!'

★

DCI Gareth Peel had done very nicely for himself, retiring to a large detached house on Holbeck Hill. The grass at the front of the property was mown in perfect stripes, the flower beds neatly edged, the hedges trimmed with mathematical precision. All signs, in Raven's opinion, of a person with far too much time on their hands.

Not to mention someone who liked to be in control.

He rang the bell. A two-tone chime sounded inside the house. A minute later the door was opened by a man in his late sixties wearing a mustard-yellow, chunky-knit cardigan buttoned over a bulging belly. His drooping jowls gave him a hangdog expression. He regarded Raven with rheumy eyes.

Raven produced his warrant card. 'DCI Raven from Scarborough CID.'

'You're new,' snapped Peel as if addressing a raw recruit fresh out of police college. 'Where have you come from?'

'I was with the Met,' said Raven grudgingly.

Peel harrumphed as if he didn't think that was any kind of recommendation. 'A Londoner!'

Raven was growing tired of being told that working in the capital was nothing special and that Yorkshire police knew just as well as their big city counterparts. 'May I come in, please?'

'I'll decide that,' said Peel. 'Tell me what this is about.'

'We can conduct this interview on your doorstep if you like,' said Raven, looking over his shoulder. Across the road a net curtain twitched in a neighbouring property. 'Or you can invite me inside. It makes no difference to me.'

Peel harrumphed again in irritation. 'Very well, come inside. We might as well make ourselves comfortable.'

Raven followed him into the house.

'Who is it, dear?' A woman's voice called from the kitchen where strains of Radio Four could be heard in the background.

'No one important,' called Peel. 'Just an old work matter. We'll talk in here.' He ushered Raven into a side room at the back of the house that overlooked an even larger expanse of striped lawn and ornamental shrubbery. It was a study or snug, cosily furnished with bookshelves, a wingback chair piled high with loose sheets of paper, and a mahogany desk occupied by an old-fashioned desktop computer. Peel took up residence behind the desk as if positioning it as a barrier between himself and Raven. 'Sit over there,' he commanded, indicating the wingback chair in the corner.

'I'd rather stand.' If Peel was determined to keep giving him orders, Raven would rather stay on his feet than sit, aching leg or not.

'Suit yourself. Now tell me what this is about.'

Peel's manner was imperious. A man used to giving instructions and watching his minions scurry about to obey. No wonder Dinsdale had been so ineffectual at standing up to him.

'I'm here to talk to you about Terry Baines.'

'Baines.' The name rolled off Peel's tongue as if the very taste of it was disagreeable. He placed his hands on the desk as if he wished he could propel it and Raven out of his office. 'What about him?'

'I assume you're aware that a body was recovered from the harbour last week.'

Peel nodded. 'Of course. I follow the news.' Raven

winced, wondering if Peel had seen his performance on local TV, but the man gave no sign of recognition. 'It was a man's body. What does that have to do with Terry Baines? Baines stabbed two women to death, and he's safely behind bars.'

'The murdered man's name was Scott Newhouse.' Raven waited for the significance of that name to sink in.

'Caitlin's son.' The lines on Peel's forehead deepened into a frown. 'How unfortunate.'

'Unfortunate?'

The retired DCI shrugged with indifference. 'First the mother, now the son. Bad luck runs in some families.'

Raven felt his anger growing. 'I don't believe in luck. Good or bad. I believe in consequences. I believe that Scott Newhouse died because he'd been investigating his mother's murder and got too close to the truth. And the reason he was carrying out his own investigation was because *you*' – he levelled a finger at Peel – 'failed to do your job.'

Peel's face darkened and a vein in his neck bulged. 'How *dare* you come barging in here and accuse me of negligence! You were busy swanning about London back then. You know nothing about what went on during that investigation.'

'On the contrary,' said Raven, 'I know that you destroyed the statement of a witness who provided a firm alibi for Terry at the time of Caitlin's death. I know that you removed physical evidence recovered from the crime scene, forcing the CPS to drop one count of murder from the charges against Terry. And I know that you fabricated evidence by planting the murder weapon used to kill Jenny Jones in Terry's possession.'

'That is *enough!*' Peel banged his fist on the desk. 'You can't prove any of those allegations.'

'Can't I? Do you want to risk that?'

Peel scrutinised Raven's face as if he could tell whether Raven could indeed prove what he was saying. 'Listen.' He dropped his voice, continuing in a hoarse whisper. 'Even if what you claim is true – and it isn't! – even if Terry Baines didn't kill Caitlin Newhouse, there is no doubt that he was responsible for the deaths of Tanya Ayres and Jenny Jones. That is what the prosecution alleged and that is what the jury decided. Terry Baines needed to be put away and I made sure that happened.'

'By fabricating evidence?' Raven couldn't believe what he was hearing.

Peel leaned back in his chair, clearly frustrated by Raven's response. 'I would have thought that a DCI from the Met would have understood the difference between intelligence and evidence. I *knew* Baines killed those women. I had all the intelligence I needed to prove it. I just made certain that the evidence matched it.'

Peel's statement was as good as a confession. Or it would have been, if this interview was being conducted under caution and was being taped. But Raven knew that the man would never say a single word that might incriminate himself. He would play the system, the same system he had treated with contempt to get the result he wanted.

Before he knew what he was doing, Raven was striding across the room, closing the distance between himself and the older man.

Peel cowered back in his chair, scared by the look he saw in Raven's eyes. Suddenly that big desk didn't seem to offer much protection.

'What you did was break every rule in the book. Not only did you send a man to face trial for crimes you must have known he didn't commit, but you allowed the real killer to go unpunished and to take another life. Not only that but he's out there still, attacking women as they walk home at night. Two assaults this week alone!'

Peel paled, shrinking back under the weight of Raven's accusations. Afraid of what he might do next.

'Scott Newhouse,' said Raven, 'an upright young man and a promising crime scene investigator, is dead because of you! And I'm going to make sure that you face the consequences of your actions!'

'You don't have a shred of evidence,' protested Peel, still putting up a fight. 'If you had, you would have presented it to me today.'

'Is that right?' said Raven. With every word that Peel uttered, Raven could feel his temper rising. He leaned across the desk and grabbed the retired DCI by his collar, lifting him from his seat. 'Well, I hope you can sleep at night, because I'm going to find proof. And when I do, I'm going to put you away.'

'Now you're committing common assault,' said Peel, gasping for breath, his eyes white with fear. 'I'll have you arrested for this. You mark my word. No one will believe a word you say.'

Raven knew he was in danger of crossing a line. One that risked ending his career. One that would let Peel off the hook. If Peel made an official complaint against him, he might be suspended from duty and taken off Scott's case.

He had allowed his anger to get the better of him.

Peel was the villain here. Peel was the corrupt detective who had taken shortcuts to get what he wanted, regardless of the consequences. Raven was supposed to be the good guy. He had to do it by the book.

He released Peel from his grasp.

The older man rose to his feet, his legs shaking. 'Get out of my house!'

Raven gave him one last look of contempt. 'With pleasure. But I suggest you get in touch with your lawyer, because this isn't over by a long way.'

CHAPTER 29

Raven was still fuming when he arrived at the *Mayfair* that evening. But now the anger was directed at himself.

In his mind's eye he pictured himself leapfrogging over Peel's mahogany desk and delivering a well-aimed punch into that smug face. Beating it black and blue.

Of course, his leapfrogging days were long gone. And physical violence would have brought the opposite of what he intended, causing the case against Peel to crumble and shining the spotlight on his own integrity.

And it would have ended any hope he still clung to of bringing Scott's killer to justice.

He needed to keep his wits about him if he hoped to achieve that. And he needed to keep the beast within on a tight leash.

This time, when the doorman raised a meaty hand to block his path, he paid the unreasonable entry fee, and even allowed the attendant to take his coat. After all, he could hardly kid himself that he was here for work.

Yet if it wasn't work, what was it? He shied away from the question, unwilling to call it what it surely was.

A date.

Frida had said "supper", and he was happy to go along with that story, whatever supper at a gentleman's club might turn out to entail.

She met him at the bar. She had changed out of her funeral attire into a cobalt blue dress that perfectly complemented her golden hair and pale skin. The neckline was plunging, revealing a deep cleavage, and stopped above her knees, displaying long, slim legs. Her shoes were strappy and sexy, the heels lifting her blue eyes to meet his. Subtle makeup brought her face to life.

Meanwhile, he was still in the same suit and tie he'd worn to the funeral. A black tie seemed unduly formal for a nightclub, so he undid his top button, slid the tie from around his collar and folded it into his trouser pocket.

The club was only half full, but then it was a Monday. How much demand for pole dancing could there be on a weekday evening in Scarborough in the slow season? A blonde dancer was draped languidly around the pole making slow, graceful movements with her lithe body. Raven guessed this was just the warm-up routine before the more acrobatic manoeuvres later.

'You look like you've had a hard day,' said Frida, scrutinising his face with her clear eyes.

'Feeling better already.' The sumptuous surrounds, subtle lighting and general air of sensuous pleasure were already having a positive effect on his mood. Not to mention Frida's presence. It was like stepping into a hot bath after a hard day's physical labour. Gareth Peel and his nefarious police methods were fading into the background like a bad dream that dissolves upon waking.

'I've had sushi delivered,' she said. 'I hope that's all right.'

'Wonderful.' Raven was no stranger to fish, although with his kitchen still not functional, the kind he was used to came deep-fried with chips in a cardboard box. He toyed with the idea of telling her that he was descended from a long line of fishermen, but the thought of inviting memories of Alan Raven into the conversation held little appeal.

'Shall I order a bottle of champagne on ice from the bar?' asked Frida.

'You drink what you like, but I'd prefer sparkling mineral water.'

She didn't question his choice, but clicked her fingers at the bar attendant and asked for the drinks to be delivered to her office. 'It's quieter there,' she told him. 'We can be together, just the two of us.'

'Sounds good to me.'

He followed her through the studded door and into the room where they'd first met. Here, the lighting was turned down low and orchestral music played softly from hidden speakers – something rich and melodic with occasional snippets that he thought he recognised. It made a stark contrast to the pounding dance beat within the main club. The coffee table was already spread with a colourful assortment of sushi dishes. One of the bar staff brought the champagne and water, then discreetly withdrew. Frida invited him to sit.

Raven took a place on the sofa he'd last occupied with Becca. This time Frida didn't sit opposite but joined him, kicking off her shoes and tucking one leg under the other. Up close, he could smell her perfume. Fragrant and heady. Almost intoxicating in its intensity.

Or was it her proximity that did that to him?

'You never told me your first name,' she said.

'No.'

She arched her eyebrow inquisitively.

Raven rarely revealed his first name, guarding it against strangers, shunning its use whenever he could. What was he afraid of? Of exposing some sensitive part of himself? Of making himself vulnerable? Of opening himself up to the possibility of loss and heartache?

'It's Tom.'

'Tom.' The name rang like a bell on her tongue and he liked the way it sounded. 'It suits you.' She indicated the spread of food. 'Well, help yourself, Tom.'

Raven suddenly realised he was starving. He'd had hardly anything to eat since breakfast – just a limp sandwich from the staff canteen shovelled down in a hurry at his desk. It seemed a little rude to get stuck in like an ape invited to a tea party, but Frida didn't appear to mind his hearty appetite. The sushi was delicious and he tried everything on offer.

Frida topped up their drinks and they clinked glasses.

He asked her to tell him about life in Sweden. Her childhood sounded idyllic compared to his – swimming in lakes, hiking in forests. He wasn't sure he liked the idea of eating pickled herring at midsummer but she made him laugh with her description of people dancing around the maypole pretending to be frogs. *Små grodorna*, she called it, and sang him a song that involved a lot of croaking.

The Swedish art of death cleansing intrigued him – clearing out all your clutter before you die so that your family don't have to deal with it after you're gone. He made a promise to himself to do that so that Hannah wouldn't have to sort out the detritus he would otherwise leave behind. Although, he admitted, there was very little clutter in his life already.

'What about you?' she asked. 'What was it like growing up in Scarborough?'

He immediately shut down. He didn't want to spoil the mood by telling her about his past. His alcoholic and frequently violent father. His loving but downtrodden mother. The wasted teenage years hanging out with the likes of Darren Jubb and Donna Craven, committing petty theft from Woolworth's in order to impress them.

The past was where the demons lived, and Raven wasn't letting them out now. Not here, when so much was going his way for once.

'Not a lot to tell,' he said, shrugging it off.

'Never mind.'

She was sitting sideways on the sofa, facing him, one arm draped across the sofa's back, her fingertips trailing on his shoulder. She lifted her face to his, her eyes glowing warm in the low light of the table lamp. Her lips parted gently in anticipation of a kiss. All he had to do was reach out and take her in his arms.

He was divorced, a free man. No more Lisa. No need to feel guilt about how he spent his time or who he spent it with. Frida too was divorced, her ex-husband in prison.

For a crime he almost certainly didn't commit.

The thought of Terry Baines behind bars killed any ideas of romance in Raven's head. What was he doing here, taking advantage of the man's ex-wife, while all the time harbouring grave doubts about a miscarriage of justice?

He heard himself saying, 'I don't think Terry killed those women.'

The effect on Frida was like pouring a jug of cold water over her. Her eyes blinked wide open. 'What?'

'I think he's innocent. I'm going to try and clear his name.'

She withdrew her arm, sitting up straight. A gap opened between them, the distance stretching out like clear water. 'What on earth are you talking about? The verdict was unanimous. The case was crystal clear.'

He wondered how much he could tell her. Not much at this stage, even though she of all people deserved to hear it. 'I don't yet have all the proof I need, but I have reason to believe that evidence was planted in order to falsely incriminate Terry, and that someone else murdered Tanya, Jenny and Caitlin. And Scott too.'

There he was, talking like a policeman again. He just couldn't help himself.

'But who?' asked Frida.

'I don't know. But I'm getting close.'

She held his eyes in hers for one last time. 'Is this why you came here tonight? To tell me this?'

'No, I came to see you. I thought—'

But she had withdrawn from him, cut him off. 'I don't know what you thought, Tom.'

Raven didn't know what he'd thought either. What was

he doing here, involving himself with someone so closely connected to the investigation?

'Perhaps you'd better leave.'

'Yes.' He rose from his seat and she didn't look at him again. He slid from her room, letting the leather door swing shut behind him.

★

The night had turned cold and Raven's breath made pale clouds in the freezing air. He turned up his collar and set off for the side street where he'd left his car, cursing his stupidity as he went.

He'd done it again. Sabotaged his own chances of happiness through sheer bloody-mindedness. He'd had a connection with Frida, one as strong as electricity. He could have let the night play out. A little romance, a shared intimacy, a brief respite from the cold, cruel world. What harm would it have done?

There'd been no need to say anything to her about Terry tonight. Frida was done with her ex-husband, whether he was a killer or not. She'd testified in court about his violent outbursts. She'd moved on, a long time ago.

Raven could have been with her now.

Instead he'd pressed the self-destruct button and boom! She'd withdrawn her affection in an instant. He doubted he would ever win it back.

Bugger and damnation, he was an idiot.

An ear-piercing scream cut through his self-pity and immediately he was on full alert.

The cry was a woman's. Panicked. In terror. It came again, but less distinct, as if muffled by a hand.

Raven set off, running instinctively in the direction of the sound, ignoring the stabbing pain that immediately set his right leg on fire.

Pounding the pavement, one foot before another, just him and the need to give help.

He spun round a corner into a lane choked thick with parked cars and wheelie bins. In the dim lighting he could just make out a pair of figures up ahead, locked in a desperate struggle. They fell to the ground.

Raven put on one last spurt and launched himself at the man who was kneeling astride his victim. The woman was pinned to the ground and he caught a glimpse of her terrified face.

Raven seized her assailant by the shoulders, hauled him to his feet and slammed him face first against a wall.

The impact was brutal and knocked the wind out of both of them.

Raven panted, grappling to regain control. But the man was an eel, twisting and slipping in his grasp. He broke free, striking out with his fists, turning to face Raven head on. His face was that of a grinning skeleton.

Skull-Face reached inside his jacket and drew out a knife. A bastard of a blade, long and curved, its edge ice-white in the gloom. 'You want some of this?'

The knife was quick in his hands. It cut at Raven, catching him on the cheek, drawing blood from the wound.

Raven responded with a kick to the man's shin. This was no time for playing fair.

Strike hard. Strike dirty.

That was the rule he'd learnt from his very first boss back in London, an old-time sergeant who'd seen it all. 'There's a time to play by the rules, Raven,' he remembered being told that first time out in uniform, back when he was a mere Constable Raven, just the two of them on foot patrol at the wrong end of town on a Friday night. 'And a time to make your own rules.'

Now was that time.

The man's knee crumpled and Raven fell on him, forcing his head to the cold ground, digging his knee into his back. The knife clattered to the ground at his side.

'Shitting 'ell!' bellowed Skull-Face, but Raven had him now and wasn't letting go.

He'd made one almighty cock-up this evening, he wasn't making a second.

He yanked the man's arms behind him and snapped a pair of cuffs around his wrists.

Beside him, the woman was crouched, ready to make a dash for it if she had to. 'Are you the police?' Her voice shook with the shock of her ordeal.

'I am,' said Raven and saw her relax a little. But she was still as jittery as a hot potato, and he was glad to see it. *Better safe than sorry.* 'Dial 999,' he told her. 'Give them our location and say that you've been attacked. Tell them DCI Raven could use some backup.'

'Now,' he said, turning his attention to Skull-Face. 'Time to find out who you are at last.' He ripped off the mask, not caring if he took a handful of the man's hair with it.

The face he uncovered was gaunt, the eyes haunted, filled with desperation.

It was a face Raven knew well.

'You're the scum of the earth,' Raven told him. Then he made a formal arrest.

CHAPTER 30

In the cold light of day, the man that Raven had apprehended appeared more pathetic than evil. He was certainly no danger to anyone now. George Grime sat hunched in his chair, his eyes sunk deep in their sockets, his cheeks like darkened hollows, his sallow skin stretched tight across his jaw. He looked to be on the brink of exhaustion and Raven guessed that he hadn't slept a wink in his cell all night.

Raven wasn't faring much better himself. After being taken to the emergency department of the hospital, he'd had to wait four hours for his knife wound to be treated before being sent home with stitches and a doctor's instruction to take painkillers if things got too much. As for sleep, he'd managed to snatch a couple of hours before the gulls had arrived to torment him with their unearthly screams. After that it had been impossible. He'd reached for the Nurofen and crawled out of bed.

Now he rubbed one finger across the tapes on his cheek, feeling the hard ridges of the stitches beneath. He hoped he wouldn't end up with a scar like Dale Brady's, but if he did it would be a small price to pay for saving a young woman from a vicious sexual assault and putting her attacker behind bars.

'Let's go over this again, George. I want to be sure of the facts.'

Grime had been uncooperative at first, answering every question with the standard "no comment" reply that his solicitor had instructed him to give. But it hadn't taken long for him to grow bored of that, and for Raven to provoke a more forthcoming response. 'All right, I admit it,' he'd told Raven at last. 'I attacked them girls. I liked them. I wanted them. I knew it were wrong, but I just couldn't help it.'

Once that was out of the way, Grime had proven to be far more helpful and the interview had moved along nicely.

'So,' said Raven, 'to recap what we've discussed, you were released from prison on January the thirtieth after serving seven years for a variety of sexual offences.'

'Yeah, I was.' George kept his gaze averted, directing his reply to a coffee cup stain on the table.

Shame, Raven guessed. Even a loathsome individual like George Grime must feel it when forced to face up to what he'd done.

Sitting next to him, the duty solicitor wore a faint look of revulsion on his face. Whether this was because of the nature of his client's offences or because the young man had ignored his advice and was cooperating with the police, Raven couldn't say.

'After your release, you returned to Scarborough and registered your address at the local police station as required by the terms of the Sexual Offences Act. Tell me what you did next.'

Grime shrugged. 'Tried to find work. But no one was having me.'

Raven nodded his understanding. Finding employment was one of the greatest challenges facing an ex-offender. How many employers would want to take on a recruit with a criminal record and an employment gap of seven years? Grime must have found it especially difficult, considering that he had no qualifications, no job experience and was a convicted rapist.

But perhaps he should have thought about that before he committed his crimes.

'So what did you do for money?'

'Didn't have much.'

Raven could well believe it. From his malnourished appearance, Grime looked to have hardly eaten since his release the previous month. He would be better off back in prison with someone to look after him. For someone as broken as George Grime, perhaps it was too much to expect him to ever stand on his own two feet.

Raven slid a clear plastic evidence bag across the table. The latex skull mask was clearly visible inside. Even under the flat lighting of the interview room, the mask was hideous. At night, on the face of a brutal assailant, it must have been terrifying to Grime's victims. 'But you found enough money to buy yourself this mask.'

'Aye. I did.'

'And why did you want a mask like that, George?'

'So that no one would know who I was when I went out at night.'

'So that you could commit your crimes without being identified?' pressed Raven.

'Yeah.' Grime spoke matter-of-factly as if his behaviour was perfectly normal, the kind of thing that anyone might do.

The solicitor shuddered at the sight of the rubber mask. Whether he was picturing the effect of Grime's sexual assaults on his female victims, or simply lamenting the fact that there would be few pickings to be had from representing his client now that he had admitted his guilt was anyone's guess.

Raven had been joined for the interview by Sergeant Catherine Howell, the sexual offences liaison officer who had delivered the briefing about the assaults on Ava Jennings and Jade Brown, the dancer from the club. She leaned forwards now, her expression stern. 'And you admit to the rape of Jade Brown on Saturday night, and the attempted rape of Ava Jennings and Stacey Connell.'

Stacey was Grime's most recent victim, the woman that Raven had saved in the nick of time the previous night.

Grime hesitated before responding, but eventually he nodded his head. 'Yes. I do.'

Raven wondered if it was a relief for him to finally own up to his crimes. Perhaps the knowledge of what he had done and what he might do next had been a burden to him. Now he had confessed, he had handed over the responsibility for dealing with his actions to someone else. After spending virtually his entire life in an institution of some kind or other – first the children's home, then the prison – it was possible that he lacked the capability to make decisions for himself.

That didn't absolve him from his behaviour, however. He, and he alone had chosen to attack those three women, and Raven felt no pity for him.

PS Howell leaned back in her chair, satisfied by Grime's admission. She had got what she'd hoped for. A full confession, giving her a straightforward case to take to court and secure a conviction. This time, Grime would go to prison for a long time. The use of a knife, the psychological damage inflicted by the wearing of a mask, the premeditated nature of the assaults and his previous conviction for the same offences would weigh heavily on his sentencing. The only mitigating factor would be his guilty plea.

Unlike PS Howell, however, Raven had concerns that went beyond the immediate attacks. 'George, I'd like to ask you now about the testimony you gave at the trial of Terry Baines.'

'Terry?' The young man seemed disconcerted by the change in direction of the interview. 'What's that got to do with anything?'

'You and Terry Baines shared a prison cell briefly while awaiting trial. At Terry's trial, you told the court he admitted to you that he had murdered two women.'

'I did.' Once again Grime was unable to meet Raven's eye, keeping his gaze glued to the tabletop. In his ill-fitting sweatshirt, his thin hands drifting aimlessly across the table, he seemed a shrunken figure, almost like a victim himself.

'And was that a true statement?'

'Uh-huh.' Spoken without conviction.

'Or was it a lie?'

Grime's fingers wandered like spiders in front of him, his eyes blinking in agitation.

Beside him, his solicitor said nothing.

'Will I get into trouble if I say I lied?' asked Grime.

'I think you're already in enough trouble, George, don't you?' said Raven.

Grime nodded, a defeated man with nothing more to lose by finally telling the truth. 'All right, then. It were a lie. I made it up.'

The admission didn't surprise Raven one jot. 'And why did you do that, George?'

'It were like this,' he began, taking a deep breath before addressing the coffee stain. 'Terry Baines were a right smug bastard. He kept telling me about the nightclub he owned, how he had all these beautiful women working for him. He said that some of them would do anything he asked. It was like he owned them, or summat. I didn't like him.'

Raven listened, faintly amused at the notion that even a scumball like George Grime had judged Terry Baines and found his morals wanting.

Grime wiped his nose with the back of his hand before continuing. 'Anyway, I knew what he was in for. Killing two of them girls at his club. He told me he didn't do it. He said the police had it in for him. But I could tell from the way he looked at me that he thought I was scum.'

'So you invented your claim because of a personal grudge, to ensure that Terry was convicted?'

'I wanted to make sure he didn't get let off. So I told the prison officer he'd admitted to killing them dancers.

But I didn't really think what I said would make much difference either way. I mean, no one ever listens to someone like me. Mainly, I just fancied a day out in court. I knew I were going to be sent away for a long time, so I thought, one last day away from a prison cell.' At last he looked up. 'I didn't do nowt wrong, anyway. He did kill them, didn't he?'

Raven left the question unanswered. What would be the point in telling George that on top of all his other offences, he'd inadvertently helped send an innocent man to prison?

For there was no doubt in Raven's mind now. Terry Baines had not killed Caitlin, and he hadn't murdered Jenny or Tanya either. The killer was still out there.

Unless he was right here in front of him.

'Is that really why you lied to the court, George?' asked Raven. 'Because you'd taken a dislike to Terry Baines? Or did you do it to divert attention away from the real murderer?'

'Dunno what you mean,' said Grime.

'Don't you?' Raven let Grime stew for a minute. 'If Terry didn't kill those women, then who did?'

At last the solicitor roused himself from his stupor. 'DCI Raven, my client is not obliged to answer that kind of speculative question.'

Raven leaned in, close enough to smell the stink of sweat on Grime's body. 'Did you ever go to Terry's club, George?'

'The *Mayfair*? How could I afford to get into a place like that? Do you know how much they charge for entry?'

Raven did. But what interested him more was that George Grime did too. 'Perhaps you went there with a friend,' he suggested. 'To watch the girls.'

Grime looked nervous. Raven could see him thinking desperately, calculating how much he could afford to say. 'I might have done. Once. With a friend.'

'Or did you go alone? Did you like what you saw there, George? Those girls, dancing, with hardly anything on?'

Grime said nothing, but Raven could see the truth clearly enough in his furtive eyes. Grime had visited the club, and he had watched the dancers as they wrapped themselves around the pole.

And he had wanted them.

'Who did you see dancing there, George? Tanya Ayres? Jenny Jones?'

A look of fright flitted across Grimes's face. 'I dunno. They were just girls. I didn't know their names.'

'They were blonde though, weren't they?' said Raven softly. 'Just like Ava, Jade and Stacey. You like blondes, don't you, George?'

'I dunno.' His hands were fidgeting on the table like trapped birds.

'They must have seemed very glamorous to you,' Raven continued. 'Almost perfect. Like goddesses. Unattainable. There was only one way you could have them.'

'No, it weren't like that,' Grime protested. 'I watched them but I didn't follow them home or nowt.'

'Didn't you?'

'No. I already confessed to what I done. You're not going to stitch me up for what I didn't do.'

'And what about Scott Newhouse?'

The question came from nowhere, blindsiding Grime. 'The lad from the children's home?'

'You remember him?'

'Aye.'

'When did you last see him?'

Grime shook his head, unwilling to answer.

'Did you meet him at the harbour, George? Did you kill him?'

'I don't know what you're talking about. I didn't kill anyone!'

Raven decided to move on. Grime wouldn't easily be persuaded to admit to being a serial killer. Not without being presented with some solid evidence at any rate. And Raven didn't want him to clam up now. There was something else he needed to know before he could bring the interview to a close.

'I'd like to go back further now, George, if you don't mind, and talk about your previous prison sentence.'

Immediately the head was hung once more. 'What about it?' asked Grime nervously. 'I served my time, didn't I? You can't lock me up again for that.'

'Can you remind us what you were convicted of?'

Grime spoke sullenly as if even now he might try to deny his crimes. 'They said I molested a girl at the Hall, and that I raped a woman.'

'And did you?'

'Well, yes, I suppose so.'

Raven curled his lips in distaste. 'You were also found guilty of the possession of grossly offensive images, including indecent images of children.'

At that, Grime looked up sharply, moved to defend himself at last. 'That's what they said, but it weren't true, not really. It were a photo of a girl I knew from the home, one she sent me herself. Not a picture of some little kiddies. I'm not like that, I'm not a paedo.'

'She was under eighteen?' asked Catherine Powell.

'Seventeen,' confirmed Grime. 'The same age as me.'

Raven nodded. There was only one more thing he needed to confirm. 'George, when you were a resident at Hiddenbeck Hall, did you ever experience any kind of abuse?'

Grime's head began to move, first to the left, then to the right. His fingers crawled together, tying themselves into knots. A soft keening emerged from his lips, or perhaps from his nose. A lament, an outpouring of pure anguish.

'George?' Raven's voice was soft.

'You won't believe me, whatever I say.'

'Try me.'

The wailing ceased, but the head stayed low. 'It were a long time ago. You can't do nowt about it now anyway.'

'Perhaps not,' admitted Raven, 'but it's never too late to talk about what happened. Perhaps it will help you. And it will help us prosecute the man who did it.'

Grime looked up, a tiny glimmer in his eyes. A yearning to be heard, a hope that had smouldered for years, almost entirely snuffed out, but never quite extinguished. He shuddered, and then began to speak. 'It were Colin West who did it, the manager of Hiddenbeck. He were kind to me at first, when I were sent to the Hall. He were one of the carers back then. He told me I were a "special boy"...'

★

Raven arrived at Hiddenbeck Hall along with Becca and the detective from the historic child abuse team who had interviewed Cameron Blake. A squad car with two uniformed officers had accompanied them, ready to make an arrest. Raven now had two independent accusations of sexual abuse against Colin West and was itching to bring him in.

'He's got a lot to answer for,' he said as he drew the car to a halt. 'Not only what he did to the boys in his care. He's probably also the reason George Grime turned out the way he did. In a sense, he must share some of the blame for George's crimes too.'

'Maybe,' said Becca. 'But we can't know for sure. George Grime might just have been born that way.'

'Perhaps.' There was no time for a philosophical debate.

They entered the hall and proceeded directly to the manager's office. There was no need to wait for Cheryl to guide them this time. Raven banged his fist against the door, making it quake in its frame. Then he turned the handle and pushed it open.

The door swung wide and Raven entered the office, expecting to find the round-faced manager sitting behind his neatly stacked piles of paperwork. But his chair was empty.

'Where is he?' asked Becca.

Raven advanced further into the room. Something was

amiss. 'Stay back,' he cautioned the others.

West's normally tidy desk was a riot of paper. Reports spilled their contents over each other and onto the floor. The computer keyboard was askew, the mouse dangling by its cable over the side.

Raven took another step and saw an arm stretched out across the floor. 'Mr West? Are you all right?'

There was no reply. Rounding the desk cautiously, Raven was met by the sight of the manager's dead eyes, staring glassy and unseeing at the ceiling. Blood seeped from a jagged opening in his chest, pooling over the threadbare carpet, staining the beige a deep crimson.

And rising from the centre of West's torso, impaling him like a stake through a vampire's heart, was the wooden handle of a chisel, the long steel blade of the tool buried deep between his ribs.

CHAPTER 31

The atmosphere in the incident room was grim. Cameron Blake had been picked up by a patrol car dispatched to the annexe on Filey Road and he had immediately confessed to the killing of Colin West and been arrested.

A tearful Veronica Gibson had accompanied him to the station where he was now in custody, pending questioning. But that was a task Raven wanted no part of. Another detective had been assigned to the case, and Cameron's interview and subsequent handling would be conducted without Raven's involvement.

He felt sick as he considered the turn of events. Colin West would never stand trial for his crimes, and the boys he had abused would be denied the chance to obtain justice through the courts. They would, he admitted, have the raw satisfaction of knowing that their tormentor had met a violent end at the hands of one of his victims, but it was a poor consolation. They would never experience the satisfaction of testifying against him and knowing that their words had helped to put him behind bars.

As for Cameron? He had endured too much already.

Now the ghost of Colin West would reach out and make him suffer once again. There were mitigating circumstances, and a charge of murder might be dropped in favour of manslaughter by reason of diminished responsibility. But the consequences would be serious. Raven wondered how much more punishment the lad could take.

He turned to address the members of his team. Becca, Tony, Dinsdale. A much-reduced line-up, with Jess still on compassionate leave, but it was all he had. He had half a mind to dismiss Dinsdale from the room and do without him. But perhaps the man still had a role to play. What did they say about your enemies? Better to keep them where you could watch their every move.

'So where does this leave us?' Raven asked, fixing each one of them with an inquisitive look, inviting them to comment.

Becca was first to kick off the discussion. 'Are you absolutely sure that Terry Baines didn't kill anyone?'

The question went right to the heart of the matter, and Raven appreciated her incisiveness. 'A hundred percent,' he confirmed. 'Terry has always maintained his innocence, both at his trial and subsequently. Simon Grant has given him a watertight alibi for the time of Caitlin's death. And now George Grime has admitted that he lied about Terry's confession. As for the murder weapon used to kill Jenny being found in Terry's possession, that evidence has been brought into serious question. It is my belief that the evidence was in fact planted by the SIO running the case.'

Raven turned to Dinsdale to see if he might offer some kind of protest at the accusation, but it seemed that even his loyalty to his former boss had been stretched beyond breaking point.

'That still needs to be proved,' said Tony. 'It's a very serious allegation.'

'It is,' agreed Raven. 'And if proven there will be consequences.' His gaze lingered on Dinsdale before moving on.

'So,' said Becca, 'if Terry didn't commit those murders, who did?'

'Let's work through the possibilities,' said Raven. He dragged a fresh whiteboard from the side of the room and began to write names on it. 'George Grime. We know that Grime is a serial sex offender who targeted young women, and we know that he used a knife. The murders of Tanya, Jenny and Caitlin took place before he was arrested, and Scott's murder happened after he was released from prison, so he has no alibi for any of them.'

'How old would he have been at the time of Caitlin's murder?' asked Becca.

'Eighteen.'

'Do you think he was capable of murder at that age?'

Sadly, Raven did. In his experience, age was no barrier to depravity. 'I don't see why not. He'd already raped a woman at knifepoint and shown no remorse. He's a very dangerous and disturbed individual. Thanks to Colin West, he was taught from an early age that the way to get what you want is to take it.'

'What was his connection with Scott?' asked Dinsdale.

Raven was pleased to see the detective making a contribution. 'Scott knew Grime from Hiddenbeck Hall. And Cameron informed Scott that Grime had been released from prison. So it's quite conceivable that Scott arranged to meet Grime at the harbour. Knowing about Grime's history of sexual violence, Scott might have challenged him, accusing him of his mother's murder.'

'And we know that Grime was in the habit of carrying a knife,' said Becca.

'Exactly.' Raven underlined Grime's name on the board. He was definitely a strong candidate.

'What about Dennis Dewhurst?' said Tony. 'He was one of Scott's top suspects.'

'Right.' Raven wrote the name on the board. 'Dewhurst was living in Scarborough at the time of the first three murders, and we know that he was a regular at the club. He must have known all the victims very well.'

'What was his motive?' asked Becca.

'Sexual?' speculated Raven. 'The club has strict rules on what its dancers are permitted to do. What if Dewhurst wanted more? And what if they refused to give him what he wanted?'

'It's possible,' Becca conceded.

'After Caitlin's death, Dewhurst made himself scarce,' said Tony. 'It wasn't enough for him to move away from Scarborough, he decided to flee the country.'

'And he returned shortly before Scott's death,' concluded Raven. 'The timings are definitely very suspicious.'

'What about this Dale Brady character?' asked Dinsdale. 'Scott's father.'

Raven turned back to the board and added the third name to his list. He summoned up an image of Dale's hard muscles and chiselled good looks, marred only by the scar on his chin. Brady might have the clear blue eyes of a movie star, but when Raven had looked into those dead orbs, he'd seen the hallmarks of a psychopath staring back.

There was no doubt in his mind that Dale Brady had a killer's instinct, but was there blood on his hands?

'Dale's movements over the past ten years have been erratic,' said Tony. 'He's been moving in and around the Scarborough region, never staying anywhere for long. But his registered address at the time of the three historic murders was here in town, and we know he's back again now.'

'He also has an obvious connection with both Scott and Caitlin,' added Becca.

'And I've run into him at the *Mayfair*,' said Raven. 'He's thick as thieves with Dennis Dewhurst.'

'Could there be more than one killer at work?' queried Dinsdale. 'Perhaps Terry Baines really did kill Tanya and Jenny after all. Someone else might have murdered Caitlin and Scott.'

Raven gave him a sceptical look. It seemed that Dinsdale was still clinging to the hope that Peel's explanation had been true all along, even though his methods had been wrong. Was that possible? It was always good to entertain doubt and not be blind to alternatives. That was the reason Peel's investigation had gone so badly off course.

'We can't rule it out,' he conceded, 'but it does seem very unlikely.'

Or maybe someone else had killed all three women, and Scott's death was entirely unrelated. But Raven's preference was for a simpler explanation. A single narrative that would explain all four murders. But he knew that it was wise to remain pragmatic – if he could find evidence that one of these men had murdered Scott, that alone would be enough to secure a conviction.

'What do you want us do next, sir?' asked Tony.

Raven mulled the question over. His hunch that Scott's murder was all about his mother's death had led them to this point. Together, he and his team had interviewed witnesses, sifted facts and gathered a list of suspects. But they were still a long way from a definitive answer to the question of who had killed Scott.

And there was also the possibility that Raven was wrong, that Dinsdale was right, and that the killer's motive was something else entirely.

He wished he could remove the veil that covered his eyes, blinding him to the truth. Just as he longed to tear out the stitches on his face to reveal unblemished skin beneath. He scratched at the tapes in annoyance.

What was he still missing?

CHAPTER 32

Jess waited beneath the oriental arches at the entrance to Peasholm Park, the Edwardian-era pleasure gardens situated close to Scarborough's North Bay. On the opposite side of the road was the entrance to the open-air theatre. She'd planned to go and listen to a band there in the summer with Scott. Just one more thing they'd never get to do together.

A group of young mums with pushchairs exited the park, followed by an elderly couple walking a dog wearing a tartan coat, and a jogger clad in black Lycra and plugged into wireless earbuds.

The world going about its business as usual.

Jess knew that she would return to normal eventually, whatever normal might look like without Scott. Now that she was back in Scarborough and the funeral was over, the darkness was slowly lifting. Especially now that Edgar Allen Poe was where he belonged – on Jess's bookshelf in Rosedale Abbey.

She hadn't yet phoned Raven to hand in her resignation, but perhaps there would be time to do that after seeing Dani. She checked the time, wondering if Dani had forgotten their arrangement. Three o'clock and already the shadows were lengthening as the afternoon grew old.

Then suddenly she appeared, sauntering round the corner. 'Hi, how are you!' Dani greeted Jess with an open-armed embrace as if they were old friends. She was wearing tight black jeans, high-end trainers, and a leather jacket with faux fur trim, open at the neck.

'I'm good,' said Jess. 'Or at least I'm on the road to recovery.'

Dani looked her up and down. 'It'll take time. Don't rush it.'

'That's what everyone keeps telling me.'

Dani smiled. 'That's because they're right.'

'I know.'

'Shall we go in?' Dani stepped through the gate that led into the park and set off along the path that circled the boating lake. Jess fell into step beside her.

It was good to be back in Scarborough. It felt like home ground. A place that she and Scott had shared. As long as she was here, Jess knew that she would always feel connected to him.

'So,' said Dani, 'what are you going to do next, now that the funeral's over?'

'I don't know,' admitted Jess. 'I feel so confused. The truth is, I still miss Scott terribly. I don't know if I'll ever get over losing him.'

'Perhaps you won't,' said Dani. 'Perhaps it's better if you always keep a memory of him close to your heart.'

Jess nodded, comforted by the idea. 'Yes, I like that.'

A pair of swans glided by, their feet making tiny ripples on the water. A mated pair, together for life. Jess turned away, refusing to let more thoughts of loss and longing crowd in. She knew that if she dropped her guard for a moment she would be in floods of tears yet again.

'I miss him too,' said Dani. 'Caitlin and I used to bring him here when he was little. He loved going out on the paddle boats. And when we'd worked up an appetite with all that paddling, we'd go and get an ice-cream. Afterwards, Scott would ask to walk all the way around the lake again.'

Jess smiled. 'That sounds just like him.'

Her parents had brought her here with Jacob and Nicola for occasional days out in the summer when they were little. She remembered watching the mock naval battles that were sometimes staged on the lake with scale model ships. She too had loved the red-and-green dragon boats that were available for hire. It was perfectly possible that she and Scott had been on the water at the same time without knowing it.

In her memories, the weather had always been hot and sunny. Today the sky was clear, but the sun was weak, still low above the horizon as winter reluctantly gave way to spring. Already it was dipping back beneath the trees, its warmth all spent. There were no paddle boats on the lake. Today was a day for brisk walking, not for stopping to eat ice-cream or listening to the music that played from the bandstand on a hot summer's afternoon.

'Shall we go this way?' asked Dani. She turned off the main path and started to cross the arched footbridge that led to the island in the middle of the lake.

Jess followed. She didn't really mind where they went. It was all the same to her. She'd have preferred to be here with Scott, but being in the company of a woman who'd known him all his life was the next best thing. She wanted to hear more from Dani about what Scott had been like as a child – what TV shows he'd watched, what his favourite flavour of ice-cream was, what books he'd enjoyed.

All the questions she'd never quite got round to asking him.

'I wish Scott had told me about you and Frida,' she said. 'He never even mentioned that his father was still alive.'

Dani scoffed. 'Scott never knew his father. Dale abandoned him and Caitlin when Scott was still a toddler. He was better off not knowing him.'

On the other side of the bridge, a steep path led up the side of the island to the pagoda at the top. Soon they found themselves in a Japanese-style garden with an ornamental pond. Evergreen shrubs and dwarf trees balanced the paved surfaces of the garden in perfect harmony. There were no other visitors so early in the season, and the walled garden was enclosed in a deep hush, like a place out of time.

'Have you thought about where you might scatter Scott's ashes?' asked Dani.

'Me?' The idea hadn't even occurred to Jess.

'I can't think of anyone better to decide,' said Dani. 'You were the closest he had to a living relative.'

Jess swallowed, not knowing what to say. The responsibility seemed too great for her to bear. To decide Scott's final resting place, the place he would spend the rest of eternity. How would she even make that choice? She thought of the walks they had taken together, of the day they had climbed up Blakey Topping, the sacred hill surrounded by cairns and standing stones, where Scott had scattered his mother's ashes.

'Perhaps we should decide together,' she suggested to Dani. 'You, me and Frida. The people who knew him best.'

Dani smiled. 'That's a lovely idea.'

Jess turned her face to the sun, enjoying the last of its warmth. The seasons were turning, the days slowly lengthening and drawing new life from the earth. A world without Scott, but one in which he would be remembered with love.

'Shall we go and take a look at the pagoda?' suggested Dani. 'Scott always loved to see it when he was a boy.'

'Sure,' said Jess. 'I'd like that.'

★

Raven stared out of the upper-storey window of the incident room, watching clouds drift slowly across the sky, casting brief shadows before moving on to let the sunlight return. High clouds, low sun, in ever-changing flux. Almost like a pattern, as if the universe was trying to send him a message.

There was something niggling him, a loose thread that had been tugging at his thoughts ever since he and Dinsdale had paid a visit to Terry Baines in prison.

Terry wasn't always a tender man, Frida had told him. *He found it hard to control his temper.* At his trial, she'd told the court he could be violent.

But when Raven had put this to Terry, he had categorically denied it. *Frida's a good liar. She's had a lot of practice.*

Raven had dismissed Terry's claim out of hand. But was there something in it after all?

During the prison visit, Terry had remained perfectly calm, fending off the many accusations that had been made against him – many of which Raven now believed to be false – but never once becoming agitated.

It was Raven who had lost his rag and left the interview furious with both Terry and Dinsdale.

But why would Frida lie about something like that? The only logical conclusion was that she had been glad to see the back of her husband. Was that because she had an ulterior motive for wanting him convicted of the murders? And if so, what might that be?

His train of thought was interrupted by Tony. He sounded excited, as if he'd made a breakthrough. 'Sir, we've been granted permission to track the phone that was used to send a text message to Scott on the night he was murdered. That message was most likely sent by the person he met at the harbour.'

'Excellent.' The request for permission had been submitted through the appropriate channels at the weekend. Two working days – that was a quick turnaround in Raven's experience. The gods of technology must be smiling on him for once. 'How soon until we get the results?'

'Already got them, sir.' Tony was grinning like a Cheshire cat.

'Okay,' said Raven. 'Put me out of my misery. What do they show?'

Tony produced a set of printouts showing a list of coordinates and spread them over the desk. Page after page, all neatly dated and timestamped. Meaningless to Raven, but Tony seemed to know what they meant. He pored over them as if deciphering runes. 'These are the cell tower records,' he explained. 'Looking at them, it appears that the phone has often been in use in the vicinity of the *Mayfair*.'

'So the killer is no stranger to the nightclub.'

Raven ran through the list of suspects. Dennis Dewhurst and Dale Brady were known regulars at the club, while George Grime had followed one of the dancers home and had attacked his third victim just outside the club. 'That doesn't seem to rule anyone out.'

'Maybe not,' said Tony. 'But look at the timestamps.' He ran a finger down one of the columns. 'On most days, the phone has been in use there during daytime hours.'

'Daytime?' The new information confirmed Raven's worst fear.

Frida, he thought, with a stab of anguish. But why would she have carried out the murders?

It didn't take long for him to work it out.

Jealousy.

Despite her denial, had her husband's infidelities secretly enraged her? The idea that Terry was having affairs right under her nose would have been enough to make any woman furious. But instead of taking out her rage on Terry himself, she had turned her attention to the women he seduced. Tanya. Jenny. Caitlin.

According to Simon Grant's testimony, Terry hadn't actually slept with Caitlin. She'd changed her mind at the last moment and had left the hotel without having sex. But Frida wouldn't have known that.

Raven pictured her following Terry and Caitlin to the

hotel, waiting outside and then following Caitlin as she left, attacking her in a side street and leaving her dead.

A frenzied attack. Vicious. Multiple stab wounds. All the hallmarks of a crime of passion.

'Sir?'

Raven realised that Tony was still talking to him. He'd been lost in his own thoughts, not paying attention. 'Yes, what is it?'

'The cell tower triangulation data suggests that the phone in question is currently in Peasholm Park.'

'Dani!' blurted out Becca.

'What?' Raven had been so fixated on Frida that for a moment he was confused.

Becca was almost breathless with excitement. 'Yesterday at the wake, I overheard Jess and Dani talking together. They arranged to meet at the park today.'

Dani. Could she be the killer?

Raven struggled to re-focus his thoughts. Dani and the other dancers had been like sisters. She was Caitlin's best friend, like an aunt to Scott. Why would she possibly have wanted them dead?

And then it hit him. 'Dani told us that Terry had a kind of magnetism about him. Even though she did her best to portray him as a playboy, all along she was secretly attracted to him.'

Becca picked up the idea and ran with it. 'But Terry had a thing about blonde-haired women. Frida, Tanya, Jenny and Caitlin. They were all blondes.'

'And Dani has dark hair.'

They looked at each other. Was it really as simple as that?

'Dani wanted Terry,' said Becca, 'but all the time he kept having affairs with other women instead. It must have driven her insane with jealousy. Especially when she thought he'd slept with Caitlin. Her best friend.'

'But what about Scott?' asked Raven. 'What did he discover that made it necessary for Dani to silence him? Tony, was there anything in Scott's files or on his computer that indicated he suspected Dani?'

'No, sir. Nothing.'

'Then what made him realise?' asked Raven. 'After all these years, what suddenly tipped him off?'

Becca shrugged. 'No idea.'

'Well,' grumbled Dinsdale, 'are we all just going to stand here debating it? Or are we going to do something?'

Raven stared at him in astonishment. For once, Dinsdale was spot on. They needed to act.

'Sir,' Tony reminded him, 'Jess is with Dani right now.'

Raven grabbed his coat and ran, Becca at his side, Dinsdale shuffling along at the rear.

'I'll try calling her,' shouted Tony.

'And send some backup!' yelled Raven. Then he was out of the door and heading for the car.

CHAPTER 33

The pagoda was built in the Japanese style. Made from wood painted in bright hues of red and yellow, and with red tiles on its wide overhanging roofs, it rose up at the far end of the walled garden. Low wooden railings ran around the edge of a raised veranda, preventing anyone from straying too close to the artificial waterfall that plunged from the top of the island down to the boating lake below.

Jess leaned on the railing, looking out at the view beyond. The bandstand on its own little island in the lake. The boats in the shapes of dragons and swans, moored together at a jetty. The strings of lanterns that would illuminate the lake during warm summer nights.

The lake lay in shadow now as the sun retreated to higher ground, but the garden at the top of the island was still brushed by light.

Perhaps this was the right place for Scott's ashes to be scattered after all. A place that had brought him happiness as a child, and that Jess would be able to visit as often as she liked.

She turned to make the suggestion and caught the flash

of sun on a silver pendant dangling from a necklace around Dani's neck

Jess gasped. She knew that necklace. She'd studied the photograph of the woman wearing it a hundred times. Caitlin.

A silver pendant on a black leather cord. The face of the pendant showed a raven looking over its shoulder against a circular background. Such a striking design. She couldn't be mistaken.

'What's the matter?' asked Dani, straightening up and fixing Jess with an intense gaze. Her eyebrows drew together, deepening the faint creases that crossed her forehead. There was an edge to her voice that Jess didn't like.

'That necklace. Where did you get it?'

Dani's jaw grew tight. 'Why?'

'Because I've seen it before. Or one exactly like it.'

'Oh, really?' Dani brushed the comment away and gave a half-smile. 'It's pretty isn't it? Do you like it?'

But Jess didn't care whether it was pretty or not. An unnerving notion had entered her head, one she couldn't easily shake off. A train of thought that had taken firm root and was growing stronger the more evasive Dani became.

She didn't like the way that train was heading.

There was something in the letter Scott had written that she'd never quite understood. *Sometimes the people we trust are the ones who hurt us most.* She'd imagined he was talking about his time in the children's home. Perhaps someone in a position of authority had been unkind to him. But now she was beginning to think that the hurt he was referring to went much deeper.

Oh Scott, why did you have to be so cryptic? Why couldn't you have simply told me what you were doing and who you were going to meet?

'It's getting dark. Shall we go and buy a coffee now?' asked Dani casually, turning away and heading for the steps that led back down to the garden.

But coffee was the last thing on Jess's mind. She

remained where she was. 'I saw that necklace in a photograph of Caitlin. She was wearing it around her neck.'

Dani turned slowly back to face her. A shrewd look had entered her eyes. A calculating look. The look of a liar. 'Yes,' she said. 'It was Caitlin's once. In fact, I gave it to her.'

Jess shivered, though it wasn't the chill in the air that made her skin creep. 'So how come you have it now?'

Dani's lips drew into a thin line. 'Why shouldn't I? I was her best friend, wasn't I?'

'Were you?'

How could someone who claimed to be Caitlin's friend have done what Dani did? For Jess was certain now that her suspicion was correct. She felt it in her gut, even though it still made no sense.

Dani was dangerous. She had murdered Caitlin and taken the necklace from around her neck.

And she had killed Scott too.

Jess's phone rang, the sound loud in the silent garden. She checked the screen. It was Tony.

'Don't answer it.' Dani took a step closer and Jess automatically moved back, her heart pounding like a jackhammer. Acid bile rose in her throat as her mind drew pictures of what Dani had done. She shook her head to rid herself of the horrible thoughts.

The phone continued to ring, but Jess didn't answer. The edge to Dani's voice had made her suddenly very afraid.

If only there were other people around. If only she hadn't followed Dani onto an island in the middle of a lake. The phone ceased its ringing, diverting automatically to voicemail.

'How did you get hold of that photograph?' asked Dani, the menace in her voice now undisguised.

'It was in a book of poems Scott gave me.'

'Edgar Allen Poe,' said Dani, a look of understanding crossing her face. 'I hated those poems. So bloody morbid.

Always going on about death. Caitlin loved them. I sometimes think she wanted to die.'

Dani slid a hand inside her leather jacket and drew out a short stubby object, black against her pale fingers. Her thumb slid a switch, and a retractable blade shot out of the knife handle, its teeth glinting gold in the last rays of the dying sun.

Jess's guts coiled inside her like a nest of serpents.

'It'll be dark soon and it'll be over,' said Dani. She took another step closer.

Jess retreated again, putting as much distance as she could between herself and the other woman. She could buy herself time that way, but what good would it do? She could scream for help, but who would hear her?

She would have to face this alone.

She was strong and fit and a keen runner. If she made a dash for it she had a fighting chance of getting away.

But Dani was young and supple too. A dancer.

She danced now, weaving the blade before her, cutting sharp lines in the air.

Closer. Ever closer. She lurched forward, striking hard.

Jess snatched her head back, gasping as the knife sliced past her, missing her by inches. She stumbled, one ankle twisting as she backed away. She gave a cry of pain.

A thin smile spread across Dani's face. And she moved in for the kill.

*

This time Dinsdale voiced no complaints about Raven's driving. The distance from the police station to Peasholm Park was short and Raven took it at record speed, the engine of the BMW howling like a mad dog. Four minutes flat and they were there. He pulled the M6 onto the pavement in front of the entrance arch and left it there, much to the consternation of passers-by.

Backup would be with them within minutes and then this area would be swarming with uniformed police. But

Raven didn't know if it would be soon enough.

Jess was with Dani right now.

He jumped out, joining Becca beneath the oriental gate, while Dinsdale hauled himself out of the car laboriously.

Raven had no time to wait for him. 'They could be anywhere,' he shouted. 'Spread out.'

The park spanned an area of some thirty acres, including an island in the middle of a lake inhabited by geese, swans and ducks. Raven recalled a run-in with an angry goose at some point during his childhood. He hoped there would be no savage birds around today.

'I'll take the southern side of the lake,' said Becca.

'Derek, you go the other way round,' yelled Raven. 'I'll take the bridge onto the island. If they're not there, I'll catch up with you on the far side and we'll start searching the ravine.'

The ravine ran inland for almost half a mile, following the stream that fed the lake. It was densely planted with rare and unusual species of trees and flowers. Beyond it lay the twisting labyrinth of footpaths that criss-crossed the Manor Road Cemetery. If Jess and Dani had gone that way, they would be difficult to find.

'Got it.' Becca was already off, jogging along the path that led along the lakeside in the direction of the bandstand.

Raven followed her as quickly as he could. The sun was already hidden behind the island, the lake and gardens sunk in a pre-dusk gloom. The park was almost empty now. He searched the distant lakeside for the shape of two women, but there were none to be seen.

As soon as he reached the brightly-painted Japanese bridge that spanned the water, he hurried across it to the small island. On the other side he looked up. A gravel path led up.

It was a steep one by the look of it. With a heavy sigh, he started up it, one foot in front of the other, the familiar ache in his thigh reminding him he'd been a hero once.

A hero, or a bloody fool.
Sometimes it was hard to tell the difference.

★

Keep her talking. It was all Jess could think of now. Her ankle was sprained, maybe even broken, and every time she put her weight on it, pain shot up her leg as if it were a lightning conductor.

She couldn't run. She couldn't fight. So she had to try to talk her way out of this, or at least delay Dani until… until what? Jess didn't know, but she knew she didn't want to die.

'You don't have to do this, Dani. You can let me go.'

'I don't think so,' said Dani. 'You seem to know too much.' She continued to advance. Light-footed, taking her time. She knew there was no need to rush. Jess was going nowhere.

'I don't know anything,' said Jess. 'Scott didn't tell me what he'd found out or what he was planning to do next. I didn't even know he was investigating his mum's death.'

She had backed all the way to the far side of the pagoda now. If her ankle hadn't turned, she could have made a dash for it, sprinting along the other side of the veranda, back through the walled garden and down the path to safety.

But there was no chance she could make it now.

The sun had all but vanished, cold creeping in as the light faded. The sky had turned to red, infused with blood as if in anticipation of the savagery that was about to come.

Behind her churned the waterfall, frothy water plunging down to rocks below. Dani had driven her all the way to the edge of the platform and she was pressed against the railing, the wooden beam jabbing her painfully in the back.

There was nowhere left to go, and no way Jess could grab the knife from her assailant's hand. Dani held the blade too close to her chest. Like a pro. She knew what she was doing all right. She'd done it before, when she'd killed Scott. And Caitlin too.

Keep her talking.

'How did Scott guess the truth?' Jess asked.

'I never wanted to kill him,' said Dani, her voice cracking with emotion. 'Scott was the last person in the world I wanted to hurt. But he gave me no choice.'

'The necklace,' said Jess. 'He saw you wearing Caitlin's necklace, just like I did.' She slid along the railing, Dani just feet away from her. Following. Not taking her eyes away from hers for a single second. The knife steady in her grip. 'But I still don't understand why you killed Caitlin. She was your friend.'

Dani's face pulled tight, the corners of her mouth turning down as she forced back tears. 'She betrayed me! After everything I'd done for her!'

'How?'

'She slept with Terry.'

'Who?' Jess scrunched her brow in confusion. Scott had never mentioned anyone called Terry. Then again, he had never talked about Dani or Frida either. There were so many things he hadn't told her.

'It doesn't matter,' said Dani. 'None of that matters anymore.'

The sun slid further, disappearing below the tops of trees, sinking the garden into complete shadow. A breathless calm had descended, the world holding its breath, and Jess knew that her time was almost up.

She watched as Dani came on, a grim set to her mouth, the knife almost invisible in the darkness. She waved it once, twice, then darted forwards and slashed.

*

Becca ran around the edge of the lake past the shuttered ice-cream kiosk, the empty putting green and the closed-up jetty leading to the paddle boats. Wooden benches stood empty before the silent bandstand and the path itself was deserted, all visitors to the park now gone. Dusk was closing in, the air growing chill.

Dark water lapped quietly against the lake bank and ripples gently dimpled the water's surface. There wasn't a soul in sight.

Becca paused for breath, convinced she'd gone the wrong way. Perhaps Jess and Dani were on the other side of the lake or had ventured across to the island. If so, Dinsdale or Raven would surely find them.

She was debating whether to carry on or double back when a flash of movement caught her eye. There, on the island that loomed over the lake. Just above the waterfall where the Japanese pagoda jutted out between the trees. A figure crossing the veranda.

Two figures.

Becca stared into the distance.

Two women, one blonde, one with dark hair. Jess and Dani.

She watched as they moved slowly along the wooden platform at the base of the pagoda. Slow motion, viewed from a distance. It seemed unreal, as if Becca was watching the event play out on a screen. Safe, disconnected from reality.

Then Jess cried out and Becca began to run.

★

There was only one way out. Jess brought her good leg high, kicking out at the knife in Dani's hand.

'Ow!' Dani's arm took the blow full on, making her stagger back along the balcony, but she didn't drop the weapon.

But that had never been Jess's plan. With the few precious seconds her action had bought, she scrambled over the railing, putting the heavy wooden beam between herself and Dani. On the other side, the air was thick with the noise of the waterfall and wet with mist and spray.

Dani rubbed her knife arm, eyes narrowing at Jess.

'You think you can get away from me? There's nowhere to go.'

Jess turned away from her, clinging to the railing with one hand, leaning out over the wet rocks below. Water surged, white in the fading light. Cresting at the very top, then plunging over the brink. The sight of it held her spellbound.

It was crazy to think she could escape that way. She drew back in terror, holding on to the wooden beam for all she was worth. Anchoring herself to the only thing that held her. But what choice did she have?

The roar of the water filled her mind, crowding out all other thoughts. It was too late to change course now.

Her world contracted to a single binary choice. The waterfall. Or the knife.

As Dani came on, Jess leapt.

CHAPTER 34

Raven could hear them now. Sharp sirens, splitting the cold air. Blue lights flickering in the gathering dusk. Backup was arriving. And not a moment too soon.

But there was no time to stop and wait for help to come.

He drove himself relentlessly up the winding path cut into the hillside. Onwards and upwards until he came to the top and burst into the Japanese garden through a circular opening in its enclosing wall. His breathing was ragged, his thigh like flaming torchwood, scorching him with pain.

He stopped inside the walled garden and took a moment to gain his bearings, casting his gaze around in search of danger. The ground was hard and mostly laid to paving, with a small pond at its heart and plantings all around. At the far end stood a pagoda, dark against the crimson sky, raised on a stone base with a staircase leading up to a low balcony. A figure came towards him, stalking around the wooden platform, only the white glow of a phone to give her away.

Dani.

Raven stepped forward and called out. 'Where's Jess?'

She looked up and dimmed the phone. 'She's not here. I haven't seen her.'

Raven took another step across the flagstones. 'I know you murdered Scott. We traced the text you sent to him on the night he died. And I know that you came here to meet Jess. What have you done with her?'

She stopped at the top of the steps. Waiting. Saying nothing. Then she slipped the phone into her pocket and her hand returned clutching something long and dark.

Too dim to see, but Raven knew what it was.

Backup was coming, but how long would it take? If Jess was injured, Raven needed to reach her now. He pictured her crumpled body bleeding beside the pagoda, her life slowly leaching into the ground.

He advanced relentlessly, as far as the bottom of the steps. 'It's over, Dani. The squad cars are here already. Can't you hear their sirens?'

She gave no indication she'd heard him. Just waited, knowing she had the advantage of high ground. Bad leg or good, only a fool would try to rush an armed opponent up a flight of stairs.

A fool, or a hero.

Raven put a foot on the lowest step. 'Dani, drop your knife. You can't get away. All the exits are sealed.'

Her face remained defiant, eyes unwavering, lips drawn in a firm line. 'Then I have nothing to lose.'

He took another step, shrinking the distance between them, lessening the difference in height. Raising the danger.

She shifted on light feet, the blade a dark stripe in her hand. It drifted slowly, as if the knife were in control and Dani its puppet.

'Drop the knife, Dani,' Raven repeated. 'Or do you want more blood on your hands? You've already taken the lives of too many people you loved. Caitlin, your best friend. Scott, the son you never had. Jenny and Tanya – you told me they were like your sisters.'

The blade faltered, doubts creeping in. But then it righted itself, fingers clutching tightly at its hilt. 'Do you think I don't know that?' whispered Dani.

Her tattooed hand snaked out and Raven ducked back, the knife whispering past his face by inches.

He dropped back a step, then lunged forwards, making a grab for her arm.

She dodged him easily, the knife stealing past, slashing furiously. Missing him by a whisker.

He stumbled back down the stairs, struggling to regain his balance. A clumsy manoeuvre, arms windmilling, leather soles slipping over stone. A gasp escaped his mouth. He was outclassed and outgunned by a younger, fitter opponent.

Yes, he told himself, he was *that* guy. The one who'd brought nothing to a knife fight.

Nothing except his wits.

Don't give her time to think.

He dashed up again, feinting right then diving left, launching himself up the final step in a great rush of bravura, seeking to overwhelm her in a flurry of movement. All or nothing. Win or lose. Do or die.

Best not to think about that.

The blade swept down to meet him, drawing a line of red across his wrist. He slid his hand along its saw-toothed edge, wincing as it bit through skin, turning his fingers into blood-red stakes.

His fingers curled around her wrist. Nails clawed her arm, biting into flesh. She screeched and released her grip, the knife flying free through the air.

It hit the ground with a clatter of steel and lay still at last.

Dani's arm sagged, her whole body seeming to deflate.

Raven's hand was burning, but at least that made a change from his leg. With his good hand, he teased out a pair of cuffs and fumbled them over Dani's wrists. He was on a level with her now, and the advantage was his. Stronger arms, longer reach. She wilted as he cuffed her, dropping to both knees. And now the tears came.

'I never wanted to do it,' she wailed. 'I had no choice. It was out of my control.'

Raven seized her shoulder, forcing her to look up. 'Where is she?' he demanded. 'What have you done with Jess?'

But the light had gone out of Dani's eyes. She bowed her head again, shaking it sadly. 'She's gone.'

*

The rock rushed up to meet her. A smooth boulder cast from synthetic stone and washed by rushing water.

Jess braced herself for impact, readying herself to grab a hold. Six feet, she reckoned the drop. If she missed her target or failed to hold firm, the next drop would be further.

She slammed against the rock, hands and feet jarring in a blinding smack of pain. She'd never felt a jolt so hard. An agony that knocked all thoughts from her brain.

Her hands slithered uselessly across wet stone, its glassy surface slipping quickly out of reach.

She felt the water take her.

It gathered her in its arms, embracing her like a lover. Strong and tender. Fierce and insistent. It would never let her go. Never give her up.

Her hands stretched out, but the water had her, and now she was under it, only the fingers of one hand casting out for help.

The waterfall at Peasholm Park was no Niagara Falls, plunging vertically to oblivion. Instead it sloped steeply like white water rapids. It tossed Jess from side to side, bending her body like a rag doll's, taunting her with glimpses of white rock just a handhold away.

But those rocks were no longer safe havens. They buffeted her as she fell, pounding and battering. Scraping skin. Drawing blood.

She cried out, but that was a mistake. Now water filled

her throat and all hope of air was gone.

She dropped again, another six feet, the water churning all around. She'd been white water rafting once, on the River Tees, but now her body was the raft, her arms the paddles, and her exposed head her safety helmet. The water dragged her on, her body twisting, her legs like weights, her arms still reeling from the impact with the rock.

She had to breathe, but her face was immersed in icy liquid. Her mouth opened wide and water rushed in, so cold it tasted of fire. She had no choice but to gulp it down and now her lungs were full of burning ice.

A rock bashed against her side and she plunged yet again. She spun like a barrel, not knowing which way was up. Her eyes were open, but all she could see was black water and white foam, the same in every direction she rolled.

She was bursting for air and took another gulp. But the only breath that came was liquid, and she swallowed it down, her lungs slowly filling up with death.

Blood hammered in her head, and water in her ears.

Her lungs were forged from fire.

The current threw her as she fell, down another drop, from side to side and upside down. Then suddenly she was free.

A calm descended, a hush like the grave. Down she drifted, deeper and deeper. As she sank she caught one final glimpse of sky, stretching midnight blue above her. And then it was gone.

Her eyelids closed for one last time. And then she sank, her arms floating limply, weightless in the depths.

CHAPTER 35

Raven hated hospitals, but visiting them was becoming a habit. 'It's really not much more than a scratch,' he'd told the doctor who attended to him this time. But he'd been treated to a stern look and given stitches and more painkillers all the same.

In truth his hand hurt like a bastard and he wondered if he'd ever be able to snap a pair of cuffs on a villain again. Or hold a mug of coffee. Or drive his car. In the end he'd had no choice but to summon a taxi to take him back to the station.

But first he'd gone to see Jess.

She was in a private room, Becca sitting at her bedside. Her eyes were closed, the machine beside her the only source of sound in the room. The blinking numbers across its screen seemed to weigh her life like a judge debating whether she would survive or perish.

'How is she?' he asked.

Becca gave a subdued smile. 'Touch and go for a while. She nearly drowned. But the doctors say she's stable now. She should make a full recovery.'

'Thanks to you, I hear.'

Becca shrugged as if life-saving was a duty she performed every day. 'I pulled her out just in time.'

'How did you manage to reach her?' Raven had been told only the sketchiest of details by a young constable who had insisted on joining him in the ambulance despite Raven's protests that he needed no assistance. Jess had fallen – or jumped – down the waterfall behind the pagoda, and had almost drowned in the lake. Somehow Becca had managed to rescue her. He shuddered, wondering how cold the lake would be in February, and how long anyone could survive in those temperatures.

'I considered diving in and swimming out to her,' said Becca. 'But then I had a smarter idea. I took a boat and rowed out to the island.'

'I wouldn't have thought of that,' admitted Raven. 'I'd probably have just dived in. Probably drowned myself.'

'Probably.' A grin flitted across Becca's face before it returned to its sombre expression. 'By the time I got there, Jess was floating face-down in the water. I thought she'd drowned. I pulled her out and she wasn't breathing. But I did CPR until the paramedics came.'

'She's lucky that someone so calm and composed was there to rescue her. Not to mention someone trained in life-saving procedures.'

Becca shrugged again. 'I only did what anyone would have done.'

But they both knew that wasn't true.

When Raven got back to the station, he was met in the corridor by Gillian. She regarded his bandaged hand with a brief look of sympathy. 'Tom, any news of Jess?'

'She'll be all right, I think, ma'am. Becca pulled her out of the lake just in time. The doctors say she'll be fine.'

'Thank God. And how about you, Tom?'

He dropped his bandaged hand to his side, conscious of carrying it around as if it was some kind of bloody trophy. He'd had his fill of medals in the army and didn't want one now. 'I'll be fine,' he told her. 'Keen to get back to work.'

Gillian met his eyes with a doubtful look. 'I think it would be wiser to take some time off, Tom. Let Derek handle the interview with Dani. He seems eager to make up for any past failings.'

It was hard to picture an eager Dinsdale, unless he was eager for his supper or his summer holiday, but Raven held his tongue. He wasn't going to argue with Gillian now. He had no appetite for interviewing Dani, and the prospect of a rest was an appealing one for sure. Let Dinsdale do the hard work for once.

'What about Terry Baines?' he asked.

'We'll have to wait for Dani to finish giving her evidence, but the indications are that she intends to plead guilty to all charges. If that happens, the Court of Appeal will review his conviction. The most likely outcome will be that he's released.'

Raven nodded. It was what he'd expected to hear, and he ought to feel pleased. He'd arrested the guilty party and righted a miscarriage of justice. And yet...

'Go home, Tom. Get some rest.'

'All right, then, I will.' He turned and left the station, but knew he couldn't go back to his house just yet. First he had one last visit to make.

The *Mayfair* was already open by the time he reached it. This time he'd walked to the club, his limp not too bad, considering. The cold night air had helped to clear his head a little. He still felt fuzzy from whatever the doctor had given him, but he guessed that would clear before morning. His hand would heal too, and the wound on his cheek. Then he would be back to normal, just the old wound in his leg and whatever damage the passage of time had wreaked on the rest of his body.

He caught a glimpse of himself in a mirror in the entrance hall, and almost backed away, so awful was the sight that greeted him. Bedraggled hair, a tear in the sleeve of his jacket, mud smeared over the collar of his shirt. But he knew he had to get this over with. If he bottled it now, he might never return.

He straightened his tie and smoothed his hair roughly back into place. He could probably use a haircut, to be honest. Perhaps he'd get one tomorrow.

Then he steeled himself and walked into the club, keeping his head down and marching straight for the door at the back. It opened to his touch and he walked on through to the inner door of Frida's office. He knocked. Once. Twice. Three times.

'Come in.'

Her voice was like a balm to his injuries. Warm. Soothing. Consoling. He pushed open the door.

'Tom. Is everything all right?' Her voice registered surprise, and then her eyes took in his dishevelled appearance. 'Your hand! What's happened?'

'It's nothing.'

She looked doubtful. Worried. 'I've been trying to get hold of Dani. Do you know what's happened to her?'

He entered the office and stood there like a halfwit, words curled up clumsily on his tongue. He knew that once he'd said them, all hell would break loose. But he had to get them out there. Inside, they were killing him.

'Dani's been arrested. She murdered Scott. And Caitlin too.'

Frida's eyes went wide. 'What?'

'She also killed Tanya and Jenny.'

'No.' Frida shook her head as if that could somehow change the truth. 'But–'

'Terry's an innocent man. He was framed.'

She took a moment to digest what he'd told her, letting it all sink in. But it didn't take her long to weigh it in her mind. He could see her come to a decision. 'Frida–' he began.

'Don't say it, Tom. You know what I have to do.' She came a step closer and pressed a slim finger to his lips. 'I have to stand by Terry.'

'Of course you do.' He'd known it all along, even before coming here tonight. Yet still he'd allowed himself to hope. But just a little. Not so much that her answer would come like a punch to the stomach.

He winced at her words, but didn't crumple.

'I have to ask you one thing,' he said.

'What?'

'Why did you lie at his trial? Why did you tell the court he was violent towards you?'

Her expression stiffened at his questions, her defences kicking in, full-bore. 'We do what we have to, Tom. When Terry was arrested, I had no choice. I had to harden my heart. You see, if I hadn't cut him out of my life completely, I might have died.'

'And now you'll go back to him? As if nothing has changed?'

'I did hope you'd understand.' She softened her face one last time, making herself vulnerable. 'It's lonely being a woman in this business, Tom. For a little while, I hoped...' She trailed off, no longer able to meet his eye. 'I need Terry and he needs me. We're two halves of the same coin. It really isn't any more complicated than that.'

CHAPTER 36

Dinsdale stood on the doorstep, his raincoat flapping in the light breeze that had sprung up overnight. He held out an upturned palm. Spotting with rain and more to come later, according to the morning's forecast.

He ran his gaze over the house. A handsome property, larger than his own, and with more lawn to mow. But Peel had plenty of time on his hands.

Once Dinsdale had retired he would have time too. Time to do a little of whatever he fancied. A morning spent pottering about the garden, an afternoon of golf, then back home for tea in front of the TV. He allowed himself to dream as he waited for an answer.

As soon as the door opened, he could tell that he was no longer welcome here. Peel had always had a temper like a pressure cooker. Retirement didn't look as if it had cooled him down. If anything, it seemed to have turned the heat up higher.

He jutted an angry chin out through the doorway. 'Derek. What brings you to see me?'

Dinsdale glanced around. 'Gareth, can I come inside?'

But Peel seemed in no hurry to let him in. 'Is this about what I think it is?'

'Probably. Yes.' Dinsdale was no mind reader, but in the wake of Raven's visit, there was scarcely any other reason he would want to pay a call on his old boss.

Former boss. It would be helpful to bear that distinction in mind today. Dinsdale no longer owed Peel any debt of loyalty, whatever the retired DCI might think. Not that he owed any to Raven either. That idea would have been preposterous.

But he owed something to himself. To his own self-respect.

'We can talk here if you like, Gareth,' said Dinsdale. 'I have no intention of causing a scene.'

Peel drew himself up to his full height, puffing out his chest like a peacock. A peacock with grey feathers. 'I'm sure you wouldn't be stupid enough to do that, would you, Derek?'

Dinsdale shifted his weight, anxious even though he'd rehearsed what he was going to say before leaving home that morning. He thrust his hands into his pockets, needing some kind of action to bolster him. 'It's like this, Gareth. A woman has confessed to the murders of Tanya Ayres, Jenny Jones and Caitlin Newhouse.'

Peel's eyes blazed in outrage. 'A *woman*? And you believed her?' His voice was laden with scorn.

'Yes,' said Dinsdale. 'The evidence is compelling. She's already been charged. And that means there'll be a review of Terry Baines's conviction, and quite probably an inquiry into the evidence presented at his trial.'

Peel narrowed his eyes, his nose flaring. 'I don't know what you're suggesting, Derek. There was nothing–'

Dinsdale cut him off. It was embarrassing to hear a man you'd once looked up to humiliating himself in this way. The dignified response now would be for Peel to admit what he'd done. All this blustering was fooling no one. 'We both know that the inquiry will be inconclusive, Gareth. No one can prove beyond reasonable doubt that you destroyed evidence or planted the murder weapon' – Peel looked as if his eyes might pop out at the suggestion – 'but I hope you'll consider handing yourself in at the station. Doing the decent thing. No doubt you'll want to issue a public apology and resign from your position as chairman of the Round Table. I don't think that a respectable charity like that will want to be tainted with any continued association with you.'

'You must be out of your skull!' bellowed Peel. His face was beetroot red, the veins in his temples almost fit to burst.

High blood pressure had been one of the reasons for Peel's early retirement, and Dinsdale grew alarmed at the prospect of him keeling over and dying right in front of him. He didn't want that on his conscience on top of everything else.

'I can assure you,' declared Peel, 'that I will absolutely not be issuing an apology or turning myself over to the authorities, as I have done nothing wrong!'

Dinsdale felt his shoulders sag, even though he'd known this would be the outcome. Still, he'd done his best. He'd tried to make Peel see reason. He'd given him every opportunity to go out with dignity. 'Then I'm sorry, Gareth, but you leave me with no other option.'

★

Barry Hardcastle cast a weary gaze across the ruins of the building and sucked at his teeth, disheartened by the sight that confronted him. He'd suspected that an opportunity too good to be true was, well, too good to be true. But he'd still allowed himself to hope.

Big mistake.

The pub might have been nice once, but now it was a ruin. Totally blitzed. It looked as if a fire had taken hold at some point, gutting the building entirely. Stone walls blackened. Windows, doors, roof all gone and long since boarded up. It was hard even to make out the original size and shape of the structure. Now ivy was creeping its way over the tumbling walls, pulling what remained apart, one stone at a time. Wouldn't be long before there was nothing left to see at all. Just a heap of rubble. It made him sad just to look at it.

How anyone could have described this as a golden opportunity... well, it was nothing short of criminal, to Barry's way of thinking.

He was glad he hadn't brought Liam with him to take a look. The lad liked to think of himself as a canny businessman, but he was still wet behind the ears. A sight like this... well, it might be enough to reduce him to tears. It would be better if Barry broke the news to him gently.

As for that pair of crooks, Dennis Dewhurst and Dale Brady, Barry hoped he would never clap eyes on them again. He hadn't liked them from the start and was dreading what he'd say to Raven next time he saw him.

One thing was certain – this was the very last time he would let Liam's silver tongue persuade him into contemplating any kind of investment.

'Bugger it,' he said with a long sigh. He picked up a stone and hurled it at the fenced-off remains of the pub. 'I must have been a right barmpot to almost let myself be talked into this.'

★

The news was its usual gloomy self. Pestilence, war, famine and death. The four horsemen going about their business as always. Becca was about to ask Sue to switch it off, when a reporter came on with a local item.

'Turn it up,' she told her mum, 'this could be important.'

The reporter, a young woman with neat blonde hair and ruby lips, gazed earnestly into the camera, the backdrop a residential street that looked familiar.

'Now where is that?' wondered Sue aloud. 'Oh, I know, it's over Holbeck Hill, just off the Filey Road.'

'Shush, Mum,' whispered Becca. 'Let's hear what she's saying.'

The reporter's expression was serious, her voice ringing clear and urgent as if she were delivering the day's top headline, not merely a local item. 'On this leafy street, outside the home of retired senior detective, Gareth Peel, a storm is quietly growing. Calls have been made for a fresh inquiry to be mounted into police corruption, following the failed investigation into the murder of Caitlin Newhouse, the young mother stabbed to death in a vicious attack here in Scarborough some eight years ago.'

A photo of Caitlin's face appeared on screen.

'Newhouse,' echoed Sue thoughtfully. 'Wasn't that the murder you were involved with?'

'Shh!' said Becca.

The camera returned to the news reporter. 'DCI Peel, responsible for that investigation, has been accused of tampering with evidence in a deliberate bid to disrupt the police inquiry. Meanwhile, calls are growing for the release of Terry Baines, the man convicted of murdering two other women, Tanya Ayres and Jenny Jones. Supporters of the convicted man claim that evidence used against him was fraudulent and that he is a victim of police injustice. His lawyer says that he will be seeking substantial damages and that a private prosecution may be brought against DCI Peel.'

Becca could hardly contain the look of satisfaction that spread across her face as the camera cut to a sequence showing Peel being waylaid by the interviewer as he strode along the street, wearing a look of loathing and shooting furious side glances at the camera. 'No comment,' he blustered as he scurried up to his front door and retreated inside.

'Looks like Peel's been dropped in the deep end,' she told Sue. 'I wonder how the reporters got hold of the story.'

She pondered the question, turning it over in her mind. The leak must have come from within the police and only a few people knew what had happened. Gillian, of course. And Raven and Tony. Oh, and Dinsdale too. But surely Dinsdale would never have pulled a stunt like that. Would he?

Sue switched the TV off. 'So what are you up to today?'

'Up to?' Becca started guiltily. 'Why do you say I'm up to something?'

Sue put down the plate she was drying and studied her daughter. 'It's just a turn of phrase, dear. But now you've got me wondering. Is there something you need to tell me?'

Becca swallowed guiltily. She'd been meaning to put this moment off for as long as she could. But it seemed like that was no longer an option. 'Sit down, Mum,' she began. 'I've got some news to give to you.'

★

The music was just as loud as before, the dancer equally lithe and agile, but somehow the magic had drained away. Now the club felt tawdry and Liam saw it for what it was. An overpriced venue selling a fake dream to gullible punters hungry to believe.

He was no longer so gullible.

And his dream had been well and truly punctured.

He crossed the floor of the nightclub, heading for the VIP seats in front of the dance floor. Dennis Dewhurst was in his usual place, arms stretched expansively as he watched the latest dancer at work. Beside him sat Dale Brady, gazing morosely into his drink.

Liam saw them with fresh eyes now. A pair of ageing men, well past their prime, kidding themselves that the sexy girl performing for their pleasure would have given them a second glance without the easy cash in their wallets.

He stood in front of the table, blocking their view.

'Liam!' Dennis gestured enthusiastically, patting the empty seat beside him. 'Come and join us. Where's Barry tonight?'

Liam remained on his feet, his lips drawn tight. 'Barry's

not going to be joining us this evening. And I'm not staying either.'

Thick lines furrowed Dennis's forehead. 'Why's that then? Is there a problem? Come and sit down. Let's talk about it over a drink.' He snapped his fingers at a passing waitress. 'More Scotch over here. Look sharp!'

'I don't want a drink,' Liam told him. 'And I don't want to hear any more about this so-called pub venture.'

Dennis and Dale exchanged a dark look. 'What have you heard, Liam?' asked Dennis. 'Has someone been talking to you? Is it that Raven? What's he told you?'

'This is nothing to do with Raven,' said Liam. 'Barry's been to take a look at the pub to see how much work would be needed to get it running. It's a wreck. Completely burned down to the ground. It doesn't just need a bit of renovation, but a total rebuild. I think you've been misleading us.'

'Not at all,' said Dennis, a smile flickering back across his lips. 'It just needs the right amount of cash, that's all. I said that from the beginning. Isn't that right, Dale?'

But Dale, it seemed, had been under a different impression. He turned a glowering look on Dennis. 'Burned down? That's the first I've heard of that, Dennis. Perhaps you'd better tell me more.'

Dennis clicked his fingers again for more drinks. 'Gentlemen, let's discuss this like civilised people. These are details, they can be worked out.'

But Dale had heard enough. He seized his business partner by his collar. 'Try this detail, Dennis. Sounds like you tried to swindle me out of my cash. That's about the size of it, isn't it, Liam?'

'Er, yes.' Liam watched with growing alarm as the two men faced off. This was going to end badly and he wished he was out of here already.

A bouncer appeared next to him. 'Trouble?'

'I think there might be,' said Liam.

He wasn't wrong. With a roar of rage, Dennis rose to his feet, turning the table over onto its side. Glasses and bottles crashed to the floor in a shower of glass. The table rolled in an arc, almost sweeping Liam off his feet. Meanwhile Dennis was throwing a huge fist in the face of the oncoming bouncer.

Liam ducked and found himself up against Dale Brady. There was a look of murder in the man's eyes. 'Hey, Dale,' he spluttered. 'No hard feelings, eh? Reckon I may have saved you from a nasty tumble.'

Dale laid a strong hand on his shoulder and tightened his fingers into a vice-like grip. 'Don't worry about it, mate,' he assured Liam. 'My beef's with Dennis. Watch out, here he comes.'

Liam turned just in time to see Dennis's enormous bulk closing in on him. There were no smiles now, no talk of ironing out details. 'You ruined everything!' said Dennis. He raised his fist and threw a punch in Liam's face with all the force of a piledriver.

Liam dodged aside and the blow connected with Dale. There was a crunch like bone breaking.

Dale gave an ear-splitting howl and rushed to the offensive, pummelling Dennis with a barrage of blows.

Liam crept to one side, seeking to make his escape. But the first bouncer had been joined by a second. The big man in black came up to him and seized him by the collar, hauling him to his feet.

'Hey,' said Liam, all smiles of reassurance, 'nothing to do with me. I was just leaving.'

'Oh, you were, were you?' asked the bouncer.

'Yes.'

Liam tried to move off, but he didn't get far. The bouncer held him in a firm grip then shoved him back into the booth. 'Troublemaker.'

'Honestly, I'm not,' protested Liam, but the bouncer was done with talking. He snarled and aimed a jab at Liam's head. It was followed with a punch to the stomach. Liam folded double and tried to crawl away on the floor.

But it wasn't long before he found himself within range of Dennis's feet. 'All your fault!' bellowed the big man. He launched a well-placed kick in Liam's direction.

By the time the police arrived a few minutes later, Liam was more than grateful to be arrested and taken away to the safety of a cell.

'Would you like to make a phone call?" asked the custody sergeant, once first aid had been administered.

'No,' said Liam, holding an ice pack over one eye. 'And whatever you do, don't tell my sister I'm here.'

★

'And so he was arrested for affray and held in the cells overnight,' said Becca.

'No!' gasped Ellie, clutching her drink.

'Released without charge, of course. But I think he learned a lesson.'

They were back in the bar again, wine glasses in hand. Becca had a lot to talk about, and Ellie was just the right person for the task.

Becca had been fully briefed on the previous night's events by the custody sergeant. Liam himself had been rather less forthcoming, and was currently holed up in his flat, his phone switched to voicemail. He hadn't even called in at the guest house for breakfast.

The sergeant had assured her that Liam hadn't been seriously hurt in the punch up. 'A bloody nose and a black eye. Nothing that won't heal in a week or so.'

Becca almost felt sorry for him.

'Anyway,' she continued after she'd filled Ellie in with all the details, 'I told Mum that I was looking for a place to live.'

'How did she take it?'

To Becca's surprise, Sue had been entirely understanding. Almost enthusiastic. Becca would have preferred her to have displayed a little resistance to the idea. Wasn't that what mothers were supposed to do?

'She was supportive. Said it would do me good to spread my wings. The trouble is I still haven't found anywhere I want to live. I'm thinking of giving up on my search. Everywhere with a sea view is just too expensive, and in any case I've gone right off the idea of living alone.'

Ellie sipped her wine. 'I know what you mean. Especially when you're so close to your family.'

Becca cocked her head to one side. 'But you and your dad have always been really close, haven't you? How did you feel when you first got a place of your own?'

'It took some getting used to. Dad and I always got on really well, especially after mum left, but now we have an even better relationship living separately. Now when we see each other, we're on equal terms, like two adults. I'm not dependent on him anymore. I don't have to follow his rules and he doesn't feel so responsible for me all the time.' Ellie took another glug of wine. 'But sometimes I do feel lonely, especially at night. I look out of my window at the empty beach and all that sea and sky, and I wish I had someone to share it with.'

'Right.' Becca tried to picture her friend staring out into the dark, the lights in her North Bay apartment turned down low. In winter especially, with the short days and the dark nights, she could imagine it feeling quite isolated, sea view or no sea view.

Ellie brightened suddenly. 'I've got an awesome idea. Why don't you come and live with me?'

'With you?' Becca felt her mouth fall open in surprise.

'Why not? I know that I can be a bit untidy, but I wouldn't be so bad to live with, would I?'

'You wouldn't be bad at all.'

The idea that Ellie might want a flatmate had never occurred to her. She always seemed so independent and capable, Becca had never even thought of asking if she would want to share. But Ellie had a luxury two-bedroom apartment with two ensuite bathrooms and a huge kitchen diner. There would be loads of space for two.

'Well, that's all sorted, then,' said Ellie. 'Deal done.'

'But–' said Becca. There was so much to think about. A new home. A new way of life. But then she shrugged. It would be just what she needed to finally forget about Sam.

Ellie raised her glass. 'We'll work out the details later. Come on, drink up. The night is young!'

*

Jess woke up, disorientated to find that she was still in hospital and not in her own bed. Her brain was slow and foggy after the near-drowning, although the doctors had run all their tests and told her she would make a full recovery after another day or two.

She was lucky. She might have died, or suffered long-term brain damage from asphyxiation. But Becca's quick thinking had saved her.

She pushed herself up into a sitting position, recalling everything that had happened.

That moment when she'd noticed the raven necklace. The realisation that Dani had killed Scott. The knife. The waterfall. The darkness.

But all that was behind her now, and it was time to look ahead.

She'd been thinking about her future since she'd first woken up in her hospital bed to find Becca beside her. Thinking about what it meant to be a police officer.

It wasn't all about being a hero, or the best detective. Mostly it was about showing up, day after day and doing the job, however difficult it might seem. That's what Becca had done, when she had stolen a boat and rowed out to the island to rescue her. That's what Tony did, every time he ran a search or looked up a fact in the police database. It was what Raven did, although admittedly he did bring a certain glamour to the role.

Doing the job. That's what Jess needed to do.

And she wasn't such a bad detective after all. She'd managed to solve the case in the end, working out that Dani had killed Scott. As a result she'd almost ended up dead herself, but she wasn't going to allow something like that to put her off.

She thought of Scott and his relentless pursuit of Caitlin's killer. He'd got there in the end too, and had bravely gone to meet his suspect. Alone.

If Scott could do that, then so could she. And if she worked as part of a team, with Raven, Becca, Tony and even Dinsdale to watch her back, she could do it well and help put people like Dani where they deserved to be – behind bars.

It hadn't been an easy decision to make. But she knew it was the right one. By sticking to her job she could continue to honour the memory of Scott.

'We did it,' she whispered, a satisfied smile lifting her lips. 'You and me together. We found Caitlin's killer and brought her to justice.'

*

Barry had been avoiding him. At least that's how it felt to Raven.

Ever since their embarrassing encounter at the *Mayfair*, there had been no sign of the builder. It was true that tools had mysteriously moved about the house while Raven was out, and the last of the electrical work appeared to be all finished.

But of the man himself, nothing.

Raven couldn't say he was too surprised. Their meeting at the club would have been awkward even if it hadn't been for the fact that Dennis Dewhurst and Dale Brady had subsequently been arrested by the police and charged with assault. On top of that, Raven had learned from Becca that the business partnership the men had been discussing had fallen apart in mutual recrimination.

It was only to be expected that a proud man like Barry would be ashamed to show his face in Raven's still-unfinished kitchen.

Still, Raven hoped that their relationship wouldn't end this way. He was already missing Barry's words of wisdom in the mornings, his philosophical musings at the end of each day on time's erratic and unpredictable passage, his pithy reflections on the ups and downs of life.

Plus, he still needed to get those damn kitchen cabinets installed.

Raven cleaned his teeth in his swish new bathroom, managing to negotiate the toothbrush with his left hand. His right hand was healing, but was still bandaged and the stitches weren't due to come out for a few days yet. He carefully combed his hair and attempted to put a knot in his tie before abandoning the task.

He was ready for another day at work and who knew what that might bring. Since Dani's arrest and confession, Raven was back on good terms with Gillian, even though she was insisting on carrying out her threat to send him on a media awareness course, whatever that might comprise.

He'd even managed to set aside some of his misgivings about Dinsdale. The DI had denied leaking information about Gareth Peel's involvement in falsifying and destroying evidence to the media, but Raven had his suspicions. Taking risks and showing courage weren't characteristics he had come to associate with Dinsdale, but even a man with no moral conviction might be goaded into action if pushed too far.

As for Jess, she had made a good recovery after her ordeal, and Raven was glad to have her back at work. The team was back up and running, even though Scott would never be a part of it again.

As Raven placed his hand on the banister of the stairs he felt a sudden tremor, and soon the whole house began to shake alarmingly. Thoughts of an earthquake filled his mind, and he pictured his house toppling to the ground in a heap of dust. But then he recognised the sounds of a large vehicle approaching on the road outside. The chugging of an engine, the swoosh and screech of its brakes as it juddered to a halt.

He opened the front door and stuck his head out to see what was happening.

A huge lorry filled the narrow road. Far too big for

Quay Street, its wing mirrors almost clipping the sides of the houses. The engine died in a cough of diesel fumes and the driver's door opened a crack. A man slithered out. Catching sight of Raven, he came to greet him.

'Delivery for Raven, Tom.'

'That's me,' said Raven.

'Where do you want it?'

Raven returned the question with a perplexed look. 'Want what?'

The driver studied his consignment notes. 'Kitchen units times ten.'

Raven stared at the enormous doors of the goods vehicle. His kitchen units, at last. But what was he going to do with them?

A shout saved him from his conundrum. 'Raven!'

'Barry! You're just in time.'

The builder sidled up to Raven's front door, turning his belly sideways to fit through the gap between wall and delivery vehicle. Reggie followed in his wake, slipping easily through the narrow space.

Barry looked very pleased with himself, no indications of awkwardness or embarrassment. Perhaps it had only been Raven who had felt those things. 'In time. On budget, or thereabouts. As ever. You can always depend on Barry, isn't that right, Reg?'

Reg looked doubtful, but kept his opinion to himself.

Barry slapped the side of the lorry with his palm. 'Leave this with me, Raven. I promised to get the job done, and I always keep my word. By the time you get home this evening, your new kitchen will be fully installed.'

'This evening?' quizzed Raven in surprise. The timescale seemed unrealistically optimistic even by Barry's standards.

Barry scratched the back of his head. 'Well, let's say by the end of the week, shall we? What day is it today? Thursday?' He paused, squinting at his watch, which showed no dates on it as far as Raven could make out. 'Let's say end of next week at the absolute latest.'

DAYS LIKE SHADOWS PASS
(TOM RAVEN #5)

Myth. Mystery. Murder.

DCI Tom Raven's hopes for a few quiet days with his daughter, Hannah, are shattered when a shocking murder plunges him into a macabre mystery in the nearby coastal town of Whitby.

In the hallowed grounds of the ruined abbey, a man lies lifeless: drained of blood and marked by the symbol of a dragon.

As rumours of a vampire-like killer echo through Whitby's cobbled streets and his own daughter becomes entwined in the town's dark legends, Raven is forced to play a twisted game of life and death, navigating a deadly maze of myth, mystery and murder.

Set on the North Yorkshire coast, the Tom Raven series is perfect for fans of LJ Ross, JD Kirk, Simon McCleave, and British crime fiction.

THANK YOU FOR READING

We hope you enjoyed this book. If you did, then we would be very grateful if you would please take a moment to leave a review online. Thank you.

TOM RAVEN SERIES

Tom Raven® is a registered trademark of Landmark Internet Ltd.
The Landscape of Death (Tom Raven #1)
Beneath Cold Earth (Tom Raven #2)
The Dying of the Year (Tom Raven #3)
Deep into that Darkness (Tom Raven #4)

BRIDGET HART SERIES

Bridget Hart® is a registered trademark of Landmark Internet Ltd.
Aspire to Die (Bridget Hart #1)
Killing by Numbers (Bridget Hart #2)
Do No Evil (Bridget Hart #3)
In Love and Murder (Bridget Hart #4)
A Darkly Shining Star (Bridget Hart #5)
Preface to Murder (Bridget Hart #6)
Toll for the Dead (Bridget Hart #7)

PSYCHOLOGICAL THRILLERS

The Red Room

ABOUT THE AUTHOR

M S Morris is the pseudonym for the writing partnership of Margarita and Steve Morris. They are married and live in Oxfordshire. They have two grown-up children.

Find out more at msmorrisbooks.com where you can join our mailing list, or follow us on Facebook at facebook.com/msmorrisbooks.

Made in United States
Troutdale, OR
09/28/2023

13261379R00176